"Do we stand here all night, or may I come in, Ms. Scott?"

Cody's patience was in short supply, even for attractive, mysterious women with world-class ankles. He was exhausted, and he couldn't sleep with a typewriter pounding away in the apartment above.

"I'm not receiving, Mr. Macheris."

"I'm not giving, Ms. Scott." Cody was amused, in spite of his irritation. She had style, he'd give her that. Even in rumpled pyjamas, she came across like a duchess.

"Then may I inquire...?"

"You may do anything you please, Ms. Scott, as long as you do it quietly. That's q-u-i-e—"

"I can spell, Mr. Macheris." Val could spell, all right. What she *couldn't* do was type. "If I've disturbed you, I apologize."

Cody found himself at a loss for an exit line. She'd disturbed him, all right. She'd been disturbing him for weeks, ever since he'd passed her at the airport. He'd be willing to bet that Ms. Scott was not the sort of woman who usually gave a man a come-on, but all the same, there'd been something in the look she'd sent him. Something almost...

Dear Reader:

Romance offers us all so much. It makes us "walk on sunshine." It gives us hope. It takes us out of our own lives, encouraging us to reach out to others. Janet Dailey is fond of saying that romance is a state of mind, that it could happen anywhere. Yet nowhere does romance seem to be as good as when it happens *here*.

Starting in February 1986, Silhouette Special Edition is featuring the AMERICAN TRIBUTE—a tribute to America, where romance has never been so wonderful. For six consecutive months, one out of every six Special Editions will be an episode in the AMERICAN TRIBUTE, a portrait of the lives of six women, all from Oklahoma. Look for the first book, *Love's Haunting Refrain* by Ada Steward, as well as stories by other favorites—Jeanne Stephens, Gena Dalton, Elaine Camp and Renee Roszel. You'll know the AMERICAN TRIBUTE by its patriotic stripe under the Silhouette Special Edition border.

AMERICAN TRIBUTE—six women, six stories, starting in February.

AMERICAN TRIBUTE—one of the reasons Silhouette Special Edition is just that—Special.

The Editors at Silhouette Books

DIXIE BROWNING
The Security Man

Silhouette Special Edition

Published by Silhouette Books New York

America's Publisher of Contemporary Romance

SILHOUETTE BOOKS
300 East 42nd St., New York, N.Y.   10017

Copyright © 1986 by Dixie Browning

ISBN: 0-373-09314-4

First Silhouette Books printing June 1986

America's Publisher of Contemporary Romance

Printed in the U.S.A.

DIXIE BROWNING

is a native of North Carolina. When she isn't traveling to research her books, she divides her time between her home in Winston-Salem and her cottage at Buxton on Hatteras Island.

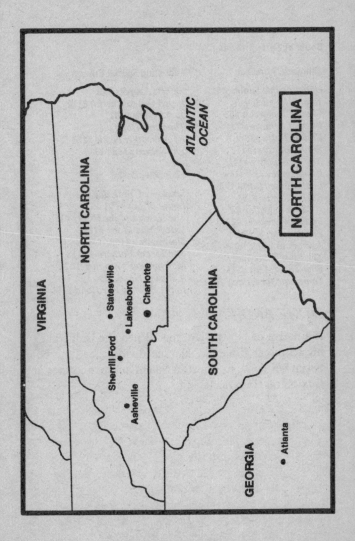

NORTH CAROLINA

Chapter One

Valentine had *definitely* seen the man before. This was not paranoia; she'd long since gotten over that stage. Besides, she was home now. Still, there was something familiar about the way he walked—that subtle flexing of his lean hips, countered by the easy swing of those wide shoulders.

"I'm losing my mind," she declared irritably. With a hundred and one things to worry about, she certainly didn't need the distraction of trying to recall where and when she'd see some strange man before, hips and shoulders notwithstanding. "What do you think, Ollie, am I turning into a dirty old woman?"

The Japanese fantail cast her a bulbous-eyed glance, flicked his veillike tail and turned his back to her.

"Fat lot of company you turned out to be," Val complained. "Serve you right if I got a cat for companionship. Oh, well, back to work."

She raised her window a few inches and spread the remains of her supper on the windowsill for any interested partakers, lingering for one last look at the man below.

He was crossing the street in front of her apartment house now. In a few seconds he'd be hidden by the dogwood tree, and once he was out of sight, Val promised herself, she'd get back to the nightly routine. Hemming another skirt, typing another page; another page, another skirt.

It was just that she hated mysteries, even one this trivial. Broad shoulders, deep chest, narrow hips and an effortless way of moving... He probably moved silently, too, even though he was a large man. Where *had* she seen him before?

Think carefully, Mrs. Scott. The driver of the van. Witnesses said he wasn't wearing a mask. Have you ever seen him before, ever seen him before, ever seen him...

The words echoed off into silence as Valentine stood transfixed by a past she'd come halfway around the world to forget. Then, from the trees beneath her window, a wren cut loose with a full-throated chorus, releasing her from the memories. She turned away, reaching reluctantly for the skirt she'd been clumsily hemming.

He was probably just someone she'd seen at work, she rationalized. The firm consisted only of Wynn Flowers, her architect boss, and Robin Chatham, the draftsman. And, as of four days ago, Valentine Whichard Scott, secretary-receptionist. But her mysterious stranger might be one of the many building contractors who regularly trooped through Wynn's elegant new offices, leaving behind trails of red mud with their waffle-soled boots. He might even be a client.

Throughout the evening, Val wondered about the man she'd watched cross the street and disappear under the dogwood tree outside the door. A gray contractor's van parked at the curb had blocked her final view, so she had no idea which direction he'd taken from there.

It was a trivial thing, but it bothered her not to be able to remember. Her nerves must still be a bit raw after all this time. Either that, or the strain of pretending to be something she wasn't was getting to her. Still, it wasn't like her to forget someone she'd once met.

Besides, he wasn't the sort of man any woman would be likely to forget, even a woman who was definitely not in the running. The way he carried himself, those aggressively masculine features . . .

Frowning at the black wool skirt she'd just taped up, Val fingered the fabric absently. Why on earth had she started with the black? Here it was summer, and she hadn't a thing to wear to work that wasn't several years out of style. So what did she do? She started with her woolens.

Practical, organized and efficient was the way she'd described herself on her job application. If Wynn Flowers only knew what a strain it was for her to appear practical, organized and efficient at the same time she was trying to appear suave, intelligent and poised, he'd laugh himself silly. Just before he fired her.

Sewing had never been Val's strong suit. When she tired of jabbing her finger with the needle, she settled herself at the rented typewriter for another go at the stack of correspondence she'd brought home with her. At this rate, the longer she worked, the farther she'd fall behind.

At eleven-fifteen she switched on the news in time for a promise of rain from the regional forecaster. Her mind drifted back to her mystery man. Who was he? A celebrity? Someone she'd seen on television? He could easily have played the part of one of those mature, dangerously soft-spoken heroes in a detective series. A newscaster? He had that look of tough competence one saw in all the best foreign correspondents.

God knows, that was one breed Valentine should recognize.

This was getting her nowhere. Unless she wanted to lose her precious job before the first week was up, she'd better concentrate on finishing those last two letters and then see if there was some way to take up the waistband of her second-best summer dress. Unfortunately, it wasn't a style she could simply gather in with a belt.

"From now on, I buy my clothes at K-Mart," she muttered, trying once more to figure out the intricacies of facing, interlining and lining, plus miscellaneous tapes, all installed with a stitch so fine it defied detection. She had stretched her budget as far as she could to accommodate the rented typewriter. It definitely would not cover a new wardrobe.

Yesterday she'd worn her stone-gray linen suit, the skirt hemmed with masking tape. The tape had stuck to her knees and come off on her nylons, and she'd hardly dared leave her desk all afternoon.

Val passed the next two evenings as she'd passed all the other evenings since moving into the second-floor walk-up, alternately hemming and typing. After a marathon session at the keyboard, she flexed her fingers, put the kettle on for coffee, changed her mind and poured herself a glass of milk. Old bones needed calcium, and at this moment, she felt every one of her thirty-eight years.

She'd almost finished her dresses. Fortunately, they were of excellent quality, the styles basic enough to be good year after year. *Un*fortunately, each outfit came with scores of memories, few of them welcome.

Kicking a path through the balls of crumpled paper that littered the bare hardwood floor, Val collapsed in her one comfortable chair, a rather hideous overstuffed thing in a particularly offensive shade of green. She was going to have to do something about this place; it definitely didn't fit in with the image she was trying to project. If that image ever faltered, she'd probably collapse like a worn out balloon. One big fizzle.

As she sipped her milk, her thoughts veered to the man with the lean hips and the wide shoulders. She'd seen him twice in the past two days, both times from a distance. His hair was a medium shade of something, either sun-streaked or graying. As for his eyes, she'd felt the strangest sort of tug—as if she were a bit of flotsam and a powerful tide was sweeping her right up on his bank.

Which was an absurd idea, even for her, and she'd harbored some pretty bizarre ones lately. But she was more certain than ever that she knew him from somewhere. Something about white...

Visions of starched white shirts drifted through her mind. The hospital at Cyprus? There'd been so many strange faces—the hospital staff, all those tight-lipped intelligence types who'd questioned her so exhaustively. And the reporters.

But if he'd been *there*, then what was he doing *here*?

Val raked her fingers through her thick leaf-brown hair. When was it going to end? After all these years she'd come home, expecting to find the same sleepy little farming community she'd left almost twenty years before. It had been too much to hope for, but oh, God, she'd needed it so desperately, the unquestioning acceptance, the healing balm of familiar places, familiar faces.

Albert's work—she shook her head in unconscious repudiation—had carried them to all parts of the world. Over the past ten years, they'd never lived in any one place for more than a few months. It had been exciting in the beginning, less so once the long process of disenchantment set in. She'd seen the insides of more airports in Europe and the Middle East than—

The airport! *That* was where she'd seen the man.

Sighing with a mixture of relief and exasperation, Val finished her milk and set her glass on the rickety table that held her typewriter. Essentially an orderly person, she hated loose ends. Sometimes it seemed to her that her whole life had been one enormous loose end, but now that she was in the process of getting it together again, she didn't want any untidy carryovers from the past.

At least this man had nothing to do with her past. They'd seen each other at Charlotte-Douglas International, and because she'd come in on the last flight and the terminal had been almost deserted, Val had noticed him.

He was the sort of man most women would have noticed: large, but not too large, fortyish—no longer young. He'd been wearing dark pants and a white shirt, and it was the white shirt she'd noticed first. Albert had been a fanatic about having his personal linens hand-laundered just so. This man's shirt had had that commercial laundry look—the collar not quite properly done, several creases ironed into the stiffly starched sleeves.

He'd looked every bit as tired as Val had been feeling, which might have explained the unexpected affinity she'd felt when they'd passed each other in the corridor. Rough-cut features, a crooked half smile, he just missed being homely, which, oddly enough, lent him a certain fascination.

Val had found herself glancing back at him, admiring the flex of a taut, narrow backside, the pull of his pant leg against a well-developed calf muscle. Thoroughly shocked at the unexpected direction her thoughts had taken, it had occurred to her, as she'd watched his easy gait, that in spite of his obvious virility, there was a rather engaging hint of vulnerability about the man.

And he'd acknowledged her awareness. Ships that pass in the night, she'd thought dismissively, half embarrassed at her frank assessment. The look that had passed between them had been less than a smile, yet somehow more than a disinterested glance.

Or had she imagined the whole thing? Her womanly instincts had lain dormant for so long they were probably rusted stiff by now. And if there was one thing she didn't need, it was *that* sort of distraction. Sometimes she felt as if she were both puppet and puppeteer, pulling at her own strings. One wrong move and she'd crumple into a defeated little heap of rags and sticks.

"For heaven's sake, don't rock the boat now, Valentine," she muttered aloud, wondering how long she could continue this charade. She'd just ruined another perfectly good sheet of paper. She was up to about twenty-five relatively error-free words a minute, and Wynn wasn't a particularly demanding employer. Still, he had hired her as a secretary.

Val had confided at the time that she might need to brush up on a few office skills, as she'd spent the past few years traveling. Minor understatement. The truth was that after her first few disastrous job interviews in Statesville, she'd learned to gloss over her inadequacies and use whatever edge she had over all those aggressive MBA's and high school graduates who'd cut their teeth on computers.

She hadn't liked it. Up front and on the line, that had always been her style. Well, survival was her style now, and if that meant pretending to a level of skill and polish she didn't happen to possess, she'd darned well set about acquiring them. Somehow.

Grace had been aghast. "A secretary? Valentine, you don't even know how to *type*! How could you get a job as a secretary?"

"Mr. Flowers thinks I'm classy. He told me so. Don't think I didn't play it to the hilt, too."

Grace's snort of disgust was loud and clear. "Hmph! He would. He's arty. Always went for that way-out stuff. Big disappointment to his folks, I can tell you, and them with the biggest chicken hatchery south of Wilkesboro."

"He's an awfully good architect, Grace. I've seen several of his houses, and even his offices are stunning."

"Offices are meant to work in, not to look stunning. What the devil did you say to make him give you the job?"

"What was I supposed to say, that I could order shirts laundered to perfection in three languages, wangle a pair of seats on an overbooked flight nine times out of ten and pack enough in a single suitcase for a two-month trip? What sort of job would that get me?"

"Travel agent?" her middle-aged cousin hazarded.

"Lakesboro doesn't have a travel agency."

"You wouldn't need a job if you'd stay here in Sherrill Ford with me. Why you wanted to move into a stuffy apartment in town when you could have lived here rent free—"

"Grace, I can't sponge off you forever. Sooner or later, I've got to start earning a living."

"But Charles—"

"And I *don't* want another husband." Charles Reedy was one of the reasons she'd moved into her own place on the other side of the lake, after spending several weeks with her cousin. Grace had presented him like a stuffed pig with an apple in his mouth just two days after Val had arrived in Sherrill Ford, exhausted, emotionally drained and with a miserable head cold.

"Charles is a decent man and he has a lovely home, and we'd be right next door to each other. I'm practically the only family you have left, Valentine."

"I know, Grace, and I can never thank you for all you've done for me, but I can't build my future around another person. Not again." And certainly not around Charles, who was probably all Grace said he was, but Val found him a touch too nosy for comfort. She'd answered enough questions to last her a lifetime before they'd allowed her to return to the States. "Besides, Sherrill Ford's only half an hour or so from Lakesboro. We'll still see each other often."

Cody slipped off his jacket and tie and stroked the late-day stubble on his chin. He'd tried calling his son again last night, only to be told by the housekeeper that there was no one at home. Anna and her husband were cruising in the Windward Islands. God knows where Eric was.

Cody had flown to Lauderdale the previous month to try to talk the boy into going to Lakesboro for a visit, but it was tough to compete with a stepfather who'd just bought a yacht the size of a city block. Anna had really feathered her nest this time. She was in her element, and Cody was glad for her. But God, he hated what it could do to his son! Eric was seventeen and determined to prove his maturity by kicking over the traces. Some of his classmates had been involved in some pretty serious trouble, and if he thought for a single minute that Eric was mixed up in anything like that...

Dropping down onto the sofa, Cody stared at the ceiling, giving way to the bitter thoughts that ate through his guard whenever he was tired. He'd been planning to bring the boy up here, where the two of them could pick out a small boat, outfit it, and then spend a few days doing some serious fishing on the lake. A kid enjoyed fishing with his old man, right?

Instead, he'd hardly seen the boy. First there'd been some friend with a weekend charter that Eric had promised to crew for. After that, there was the marlin tournament, and he could hardly pass that up, could he? A stringer of bream and crappie, or even a striper or a largemouth, could hardly compete with a few hundred pounds of fighting billfish.

"Dammit, who taught him to fish? Who bought him his first spinning rod?" For a brief moment, Cody accepted the full weight of his failure as a husband and a father. Mostly it was the emptiness that got to him. What did a man do when his wife walked out, taking his young son, his home—hell, even the friends they'd shared?

He worked. He worked his butt off trying to prove something. God knows what and to whom. And on the nights when he was too restless to sleep, he went out and raised a little hell. Those occasions were fewer and farther between these days. He'd found the price unacceptably high. Oh, he could take an occasional hangover, but waking up in bed with some stray kitten half his age had left a taste of guilt in his mouth that had lasted for weeks. Instead of rejuvenating him, it had only made him feel depressingly old.

Stirring restlessly, Cody gave up the notion of getting any real work done tonight. His concentration was shot, had been for weeks. He couldn't remember the last time he'd been able to focus his mind on the challenge of a difficult design problem. What was the point of beating his brains out to build a business when there was no one to benefit from it but himself?

Cody tried to convince himself that he was tired enough to sleep. He'd put in a solid fourteen-hour day after one more in a string of restless nights.

Casting a baleful glance at the ceiling of his ground-floor apartment, he muttered, "If that night-blooming novelist is still going strong when I get out of the shower, I'll throw the damned switch on the whole apartment house!" Raking a hand across his shirt, he felt for the cigarettes he habitually gave up.

Things weren't coming along quite as fast as Val had envisioned, but she was working on it. Wynn Flowers, her grizzled, cigar-chewing boss, happened to be both absentminded and disorganized, despite the fact that he was a respected and successful architect. He'd been desperate for someone to run his office. But for the fact that Val had been equally desperate, she'd probably never have had the nerve to apply for the job.

She'd worn her very best suit, her Italian handmade shoes with the Band-Aids on the soles and her haughtiest expression. It had worked. God knows why, but evidently Wynn Flowers, his yellow-stained beard giving him the look of a shrewd, slightly irreverent Santa Claus, had seen in her appearance something that might appeal to his clientele. She'd gotten the job.

Then she'd gone back to her stuffy, furnished apartment, carefully removed the suit and hung it in the tiny closet, and fought off the nausea brought on by an attack of sheer nerves. After that, she hadn't dared look back.

Every night since her first day on the job, she'd brought home a sheaf of scribbled notes to be translated and then painstakingly typed. Each morning she placed a neat stack of correspondence on Wynn's desk for his signature. She was coming along, all right. As long as Wynn's flamboyant young draftsman, Robin, didn't decide to go back to school, leaving her with the whole ball of wax, she'd do just fine.

Grace called on Thursday, minutes after Val had let herself into the apartment. "Come to dinner Saturday night, Val? Charles said his girls might be here for a visit, so I've invited them all over for my chicken casserole."

Val winced, visualizing an evening of unsubtle references to Charles's status as a widower and her own as a widow. With his teenaged daughters as an audience, that should be jolly good fun.

"Grace, I'd sort of promised myself to do some painting and papering this weekend. I've been so busy at the office, learning the procedures and everything, this is the first chance I've had."

"Procedures, my foot. Still trying to catch up, aren't you? Banging away on that machine night after night. What are you going to do when your famous architect brings in a computer? Think you can pick that up on your lunch hour?"

"Don't even joke about such a thing," Val said with a shudder. "Look, maybe I could come by on Sunday afternoon."

"Charles has to take the girls back to their grandparents on Sunday."

"I don't want to see Charles, I want to see *you*."

"But Charles—"

"Grace," Val said warningly. She wouldn't do it. Not even for Grace, whom she loved, would she subject herself to another deadly evening with Charles and his persistent probing. The man lead such a deadly dull life that he couldn't pass up an opportunity for a vicarious thrill, but Val wasn't the answer to his boredom, no matter what Grace hoped.

"Valentine, I've been out in this world a lot longer than you have—"

Dear God, where do you think I've been, packed in cotton wool on a closet shelf?

While the familiar lecture droned on, Val let her mind range briefly over the depressing landscape of the past eighteen years. She'd come a long way, most of it down a dead-end road. She was finally headed in the right direction, but she still had a long way to go before she would feel secure.

"Grace," she broke in gently. "I know you're only doing what you think is best for me, but it just won't work. I like Charles well enough, but—"

"And he likes you," the older woman put in quickly. "He told me his business had its best season yet last year. Orthopedic shoes, you remember? He told us all about his plant in Milwaukee."

"How could I forget?" Val quipped dryly.

"Don't be snide, it doesn't become you. Oh, honey, you know me. I just want you to be happy."

"I know you, all right," Val retorted. "You just hate to see a good man go to waste."

"Well, there's that, too. Pity he didn't take a shine to me. I've been thinking about a color rinse on my hair, what do you think? I haven't met those girls of his yet, but I could probably be a big help to him there. On the other hand, that's not helping you with your problems."

"What do you mean, you haven't met them? You've lived in Sherrill Ford ever since you left Lakesboro. You know everybody north of the 150 bridge on both sides of the lake."

"Yes, but Charles hasn't been here that long. He left Milwaukee after his wife died, hoping a new environment would help the girls get over the loss."

"Mmm," Val murmured noncommittally. Hardhearted she may be, but she couldn't seem to work up much interest in the Reedy family. "You're a sly old manipulator, you know that? All those years running Dr. McGuffy's practice really gave you a taste for power." Val had always thought Grace had been in love with the general practitioner she'd worked for as nurse, receptionist and general superwoman until he'd retired.

"Power nothing," Grace snorted. "It's only common sense. The only job you know is being a wife, and—"

Val's gentle, "I'll call you one day next week and we'll get together, okay?" cut across Grace's argument in favor of not letting eighteen years of job training go to waste.

Friday came, and Val was no longer in the mood to redecorate. What difference did it make when she got around to it? No one was likely to see the place but Grace, who, with cousinlike candor, would find something to criticize no matter what she did to the apartment.

On the other hand, it might help her to project the image she'd created for herself if her surroundings were a bit less depressing. She'd hoped that once she'd proved her worth, she could gradually go back to being her old self. She was beginning to wonder if she'd even recognize the real Valentine Scott.

She'd certainly outgrown the naive young woman who'd taken a week's vacation to see the Smithsonian and ended up engaged to a man she'd run into—literally—by the Epstein sculpture at the Hirschorn. She'd like to think she'd come a long way from the docile creature who worked herself into a nervous wreck trying to live up to the honoring and obeying part of her marriage ceremony.

Because Albert Scott hadn't been worth obeying. God knows, he certainly hadn't been worth honoring! Perhaps the man she'd married had never existed outside her own impressionable mind.

It had been an instinctive need for security that had sent her scurrying back here. Lakesboro was a small town that liked to think of itself as a resort town, in spite of the fact that it boasted neither hotel nor motel. Wynn claimed that Lakesboro's most popular sport was sitting around talking about going fishing, and Val had to admit that he wasn't far off the mark. A sleepy southern community, it hardly even rated small-town status.

But it was home, and that was what counted. She'd spent too many years living in foreign lands, where, even with her knack for languages, she'd always been a stranger. There'd been many years of watching ambition turn to greed in the man she'd married, and greed erode into something even more frightening.

Then, in the space of a single instant, her whole world had gone up in smoke.

Val had desperately needed the security of home and family at that time, but even so, it had been months before she'd been able to get away. For that matter, the only family she had left consisted of a scattering of distant cousins, her only real home a sense of belonging that persisted in spite of the new highway and all the new construction that had changed the face of her old hometown. Grace had still been here, welcoming, comforting and maddeningly meddlesome, as always.

Now all she had to do was to prove to herself that her judgment wasn't as seriously flawed as it seemed. She'd made a mistake, and it had cost her dearly, but she'd already picked up the pieces and was well on the way to putting together a satisfactory life for herself.

At the end of her second week, Val banked her paycheck and congratulated herself on her progress. Today she'd managed to do almost half the typing before she'd left, leaving her only six short letters and a three-page detailed statement to do tonight.

Unconsciously, her eyes searched for a glimpse of the man from the airport. He'd been coming in just as she'd hurried out this morning; this time, they'd almost smiled.

She let herself into the cheerless apartment, greeted her goldfish and stepped out of her shoes. The air conditioner was acting up again. She could always open her windows and hope for a breeze, but what would she do in the winter if the furnace gave as much trouble?

Face the problem in the winter, she dismissed. No point in borrowing trouble.

She really *did* need to get out more. A place of her own was all very well, even if it was a furnished apartment with dreadful prints on the walls and not so much as a scatter rug on the floor, but she was getting stale. The trouble was, she didn't know anyone anymore except for Grace, and Grace was bound and determined to see her married again.

When Val had first come back, she'd stayed with Grace in Sherrill Ford, content to cocoon herself in the old farmhouse until she felt ready to face the future.

It had been hopeless. From the second day on, there'd been no letup. *Poor Charles, rattling around in that big brick house with two daughters to bring up. What he needs is a wife. Poor Valentine, widowed at thirty eight.... Still a lot of good years left in her for the right owner. All Val knows is being a wife. All she really needs is another husband.*

"Darn," Val muttered, dragging the cover from her portable. She rolled in a sheet of paper and began a furious attack. She'd get her speed back up if it killed her! She'd make herself so indispensable to Wynn Flowers that he wouldn't dare fire her, even when her designer clothes wore out and she no longer complemented his fancy offices.

Cody's feet hit the floor as he voiced a searing oath. He'd been almost asleep—the first time he'd made it before midnight in weeks, and it had started again. He'd complained to the management three times, and this was where it had gotten him. If he wanted anything done, he'd have to do it himself.

"I'll throw a scare into that hack he won't soon forget," he promised himself, sucking in his breath to zip himself into the khakis he'd shed earlier. The super was supposed to handle complaints, but, as usual, he was nowhere to be found.

There'd been two vacancies in the six-apartment building when Cody had left for Lauderdale. According to the super, they'd been filled by a college kid who was supposed to be working on his thesis, and a woman. He'd seen the woman. She was a knockout in the very best sense of the word. Ashley Pellerini, according to the pair of new cards that had sprouted by the mailboxes.

The college student must be V. Scott, but if V. Scott thought he was going to earn his degree at the expense of Cody's mental health, he was in for a powerful dose of the real world!

Cody burned off some of the adrenaline by taking the stairs two at a time. His bare feet made no sound as he bore down on the door of the apartment above his own.

"All right, V. Scott, either you give 'em a rest or I chop 'em off," he threatened softly. Leaning on the buzzer, he focused his wrath on the erratic clatter that came clearly through the paneled door.

At the shrill intrusion, Val felt her heart slam against her rib cage. As her fingers hovered over the keyboard, she searched her mind for anyone who might be calling on her at this hour. "Who is it?" she called out timidly.

There was no mistaking the repeated sound of knuckles on the door, especially when they were applied with almost enough force to go through the wood. The buzzer sounded again, and, shoving her hair back from her face, Val hurried to the door, checking to be sure the chain was secured. "Who is it?" she demanded, trying to disguise the tremor in her voice. Should she dial the sheriff? What could she tell him? That someone had just rung her doorbell?

Cautiously, she slid the bolt and opened the door a crack. "Yes?"

Cody, fist poised to strike again, held his fire as he examined the single enormous brown eye that showed in the narrow crack. "V. Scott?"

His scowl changed slowly to a puzzled frown. He recognized the eye and the high, pale cheekbone almost immediately. Disappointment registered in the back of his mind. So his night-writing neighbor had turned out to be the woman instead of the student. Tough. Under other circumstances, he might have enjoyed getting to know her.

"Uh, about your writing," he began, swallowing the dregs of belligerence. How the devil could he stay angry with a strip of wavy brown hair, a frightened-looking eye and a cheek that could have been carved from ivory?

"My what?"

"Your writing. Your book, your love letters—whatever."

Val's eyes dropped from the aggressive jawline to the expanse of dark hair curled across a broad, naked chest. Oh, Lord, it would have to be her stranger from the airport. Somehow, he didn't look nearly as nice and safe up close. "My what?" she repeated, wondering about the protocol for late-night complaints.

"You're the one who's been typing every night for the past two weeks, right?"

Guiltily, Val nodded, her gaze never leaving the tanned and rugged features. His eyes were set in a network of crow's-feet, and he looked tired. He'd looked tired the first time she'd ever seen him. She had an irrational urge to smooth away the lines that sprang up like parentheses just above his nose.

Cody shifted uncomfortably. "Say, do we have to talk through the crack in the door? Actually, I'm harmless." Why the hell hadn't he taken time to put on his shirt? "Look, I'm your downstairs neighbor. I, uh..."

"Oh dear," Val whispered.

"My name's Macheris, Cody Macheris, Ms. Scott. And you're...?" He waited for her to provide a name to go with the initial, but she only nodded again.

Val had hesitated over what to put on her door, not wanting to advertise her gender. V. Scott had sounded about right—ambiguous, but with a certain flair. At the moment, she felt anything but flairish.

"Well? Do we stand here all night, or may I come in, Ms. Scott?" Cody's patience was in short supply, even for attractive, mysterious women with world-class ankles.

"I'm not receiving, Mr. Macheris," she said.

"I'm not giving, Ms. Scott." Cody was amused, in spite of his irritation. She had style, he'd give her that. Even in rumpled pajamas, she came across like a duchess.

"Then may I inquire—"

"You may do anything you please, Ms. Scott, as long as you do it quietly. That's Q-U-I-E—"

"I can spell, Mr. Macheris." Val's fingers tightened on the door. She could spell, all right. What she *couldn't* do was type. "If I've disturbed you, I apologize. It won't happen again."

Cody found himself at a loss for an exit line. She'd disturbed him, all right. She'd been disturbing him for weeks, ever since he'd passed her outside the Piedmont gate at the airport. He'd be willing to bet that V. Scott was not the sort of woman who usually gave a man the come-on, but all the same, there'd been something in the look she'd sent him. Something almost...

Well, if not exactly inviting, then at least exploratory.

As tired as he'd been—hell, as tired as he was now—every male element in his body had snapped to attention.

Cody still wasn't certain what it was, but there was something about V. Scott that made him suspect he was in for another long, restless night. Whether or not she ever got around to putting away her machine.

Chapter Two

A muscular forearm rested on the drawing board the following morning as Cody lifted his eyes from the alarm system he was working on for an automobile showroom. His office was in Statesville, but he did a lot of the design work in his apartment.

V. Scott, hmm? Would that be Virginia? Valerie?

Victoria. He'd be willing to bet on it. He yawned widely and attempted to concentrate on the overdue project, but his mind kept straying back to a pair of elegant legs, a set of aristocratic cheekbones and a waist he could have spanned with his two hands. An intriguing woman, V. Scott. Hardly the sort one expected to see in a place like Lakesboro.

From a distance, she had the touch-me-not look of mature elegance. Seen late at night through the crack of her door she looked younger, somehow more vulnerable, but still, she was no kid. There was a quality of reserve about her that hadn't come without experience, and not all of it pleasant, he suspected.

Odd, the way she stood out in his mind. Strictly speaking, Anna had been prettier. He could name a dozen women who were probably as beautiful, but this one was somehow different. Her clothes didn't fit as well as he'd first thought, but she had a way of carrying herself that made the fact irrelevant. Her hair was nothing extraordinary: medium brown, medium short. But it moved when she walked, waving back from her face as though she'd just raked her fingers through it.

Cody found his own fingers itching to explore the thickness and the texture of that warm brown hair. And the legs—she had the finest set of legs he'd ever laid eyes on. Yet there was more than that.

His analytical mind was no help to him here. It was her face that captured his imagination, but for the life of him, he couldn't say why. He only knew that there was something about it—a quiet sort of beauty that struck a responsive chord deep inside him. Even late at night, seen through a crack in the door, she had an indefinable quality of... well, for want of a better word, *quality*.

Valentine made arrangements with the town's only professional typist to drop off rough drafts of Wynn's correspondence on her way home and pick up the finished work the following morning. She groaned at the cost, but it would only be for another week, at the most. By that time she should be able to tackle the full load during working hours. Meanwhile, she'd practice diligently during her lunch hour and every minute she could steal when there was no one else in the office.

So far, she hadn't met a single one of her old friends. Either they'd all moved away, which was probably the case, as Lakesboro had no industry and few jobs opportunities, or else they'd married someone whose name she didn't recognize.

At any rate, she'd hardly have much in common with anyone she'd known so many years ago. Without meaning to be hurtful, they'd have brought up things best forgotten, and Val wasn't ready to talk yet. Not even Grace knew the whole story.

Grace called again on Saturday morning with another invitation to dinner and Val was almost tempted. "Could I take a rain check, Grace?" she begged. "I promised myself I'd go shopping for paint and get started on the living room. Robin worked out a complete decorating scheme for me, one he vows will make my living room *look* cooler, even if it's not. If I don't do it now, I'll lose my nerve."

"Who—or what—is Robin?"

"Wynn's assistant. He's a draftsman by trade, but I think he'd really rather be an interior decorator. He's awfully sweet. He showed me how to change a ribbon and what to do when the copier starts blinking red lights at me. Actually, he saw through me in a minute, but he thinks it's all a marvelous joke."

"Huh! Some joke, with your whole career based on a falsehood!"

"Grace, it's not that bad. I only...exaggerated a bit. Anyway, my abiding fear is that Robin will decide to go back to school and leave me to sink or swim on my own. It's all I can do to keep my head above water as it is."

"Can't say I didn't warn you," Grace mocked. "Oh well, Charles'll be disappointed, but maybe I can fix something up for next weekend."

With a sense of impending doom, Val got away without committing herself to anything definite. She'd been widowed less than a year, but under the circumstances, she could hardly use that as an excuse. Grace was well aware that Val had left Albert long before the bombing.

She'd gone back to Rome and moved in with the wife of a young career diplomat she'd known for several years. Ivanna, who already had two-year-old twins, was pregnant again and having problems, and both she and her husband, Piet, had welcomed Val into their home. It had been an ideal solution for all concerned, for Val had needed time to heal, time to plan for the future, before she tackled Albert about a divorce. He'd refused even to discuss it after the final break, telling her she'd change her mind in a few weeks.

She hadn't. She'd waited for months, until Ivanna and Piet had brought their new son home, before trying to contact Albert again. Of course, she could have gone back to the States and eventually gotten a divorce on her own, but she'd wanted it over within the shortest possible time so that there could be no chance of his showing up on her doorstep and disrupting whatever future she was able to construct for herself.

It had taken weeks to track him down, even knowing his favorite hotels, the places he was most apt to stay in any given country. Albert had agreed to meet her to discuss a divorce, but he hadn't made it easy. She'd had to go to him, and flying from Rome to Beirut was an expensive, exhausting proposition under the best of conditions.

Eighteen years of her life had gone into their marriage and even though what she'd walked away from had been a hollow mockery, Val had felt compelled to end it with as much dignity as possible under the circumstances.

Beirut had been quiet for months. She'd flown in and out of the airport there countless times in the past, and Piet, who'd helped make arrangements for her flight, had assured her there was nothing to worry about.

The flight had been tiresome, but uneventful. Albert had greeted her with a sardonic smile. His dark mustache and his blond hair were as flawlessly groomed as ever, his tropic-weight suit looking as though a valet had just that minute eased him into it.

They'd been on their way to Albert's white Mercedes when a van had swerved toward them. Later, Val seemed to remember two shots ringing out, but they'd been swallowed up instantly in the explosion.

A single act of terrorism had changed her whole life. Albert had been the target, only, of course, she hadn't known that at the time. She hadn't known anything at all. She'd been flung against a concrete wall, several ribs had been broken, she was badly concussed and a piece of reinforcement rod had been driven through the fleshy part of her left shoulder.

Albert had been unconscious when they'd been flown to the British Hospital at Akrotiri, Cyprus. He'd still been in a coma when Val had become ambulatory, and she'd insisted on remaining at his bedside. Heedless of the comings and goings of hoards of intelligence people, reporters and hospital staff, she'd stayed there, leaving only when the nurses had insisted that she sleep for a few hours. Sometimes she'd thought about the way it had been in the early years—the plans, the excitement, the love. But mostly she hadn't thought at all. Thinking had been too painful.

Ironically, she'd come to feel closer to Albert Scott in those final weeks than she had in all the years they'd been married. Perhaps for the first time she'd been able to see him as he was: ego, ambition, insecurities and all. Even the pain she'd suffered when she'd learned of his long-standing infidelities had drained away by then, to be replaced by an overwhelming feeling of failure.

She'd finally understood that the man she'd married had existed only in her mind. Perhaps he really had loved her...once. She'd been useful to him. God knows why, but he'd seemed to need her.

In that last week before she'd left him, he'd actually bragged about his infidelities, but he'd never once hinted at the other thing. She'd like to think he'd been trying to protect her, but she would never know. She had later learned that one of the women she'd unknowingly been sharing him with all these years had been a part of the arms-smuggling operation he had been mixed up with. The intelligence people, including Meekins, the agent Val had come to think of as her roommate, had been remarkably closemouthed about the whole affair.

Albert had died without ever regaining consciousness, a fact that had frustrated the governments of at least three countries to an extreme degree. Val had finally been cleared of any involvement and sent home to pick up the pieces of her shattered life.

After a few false starts, she was succeeding quite nicely.

Letting herself into the small lobby, Val juggled her dinner, a stack of wallpaper sample books and her purse as she dug for her keys. When the outside door opened behind her she jumped to one side.

"Uh-oh, sorry," said Cody, easing himself through the opening. "Did I bump you?" In one hand he carried a jacket, in the other a bag identical to the one Val held clamped between her teeth.

"Nffp," she mumbled. Removing the bag, she apologized. "My fault. There's scarcely enough room down here to turn around."

"I see you've discovered our one-star burger joint. They're better if you douse them with horseradish and extra catsup."

"Leakier, too, no doubt. My dry-cleaning bills are high enough, thanks."

Cody eyed the thick books under her arm. "Been to the library?"

"Wallpaper samples. I borrowed them from the place where I work."

Cody leaned his back against the cool green plaster wall, admiring her easy grace, even loaded as she was with more than she could carry. "You work?"

"What do you mean, 'I work'?" Val laughed. "Of course I work. How many independently wealthy woman do you know living in a place like the Country Club Apartments?"

"Oh, I don't know, it would be a good low-profile cover for when the cost of fame and fortune got to be too high. Who'd ever expect to find a best-selling novelist living in a dump like this?"

Val planted one foot on the bottom step, balanced her sample books on her hip and sent him a look of amusement. "I hate to disappoint you, Mr. Macheris, but I'm not a novelist, bestselling or otherwise. I'm a secretary."

"I wish you hadn't told me that. I could have rationalized all those sleepless nights when I thought you were up there putting together a future best-seller." He grinned, somehow managing to look sweet and decent and dangerous at the same time. "If I'd known it was only a sales report or the minutes of the last board meeting, I might not have been so polite."

"Were you polite? I hadn't noticed."

"Yeah, well . . ." The grin took on a slightly shame-faced quality as Cody skimmed the elegant length of her with an appreciative glance. "My secretary should be so dedicated."

"Your secretary probably already knew how to type when you hired her." Val hadn't missed the look. She'd done some looking of her own, slightly shocked at her reaction to a man to whom she hadn't even been formally introduced. When she had first seen him that night at the airport, she'd been drawn to him instinctively. If she'd had to make a snap judgment, it would have been that he was both essentially masculine and essentially decent.

While Cody searched for a polite way to put the question that was obviously on his mind, Val hurried over an explanation. "I was a bit rusty at first. Everything's under control now. You don't have to worry."

She'd been right all along about him. He wasn't nearly as tough as he'd sounded that night he'd come pounding on her door. It occurred to her that there was something rejuvenating about being in the presence of an attractive man, and this one was definitely that, even in rumpled khakis and a white cotton shirt that some laundry had mutilated. The warm, clean scent of his body reached her nostrils, unalloyed by colognes or scented after-shaves, and Val felt her pulses quicken in a totally unexpected way.

"I'd better go feed my goldfish," she murmured, turning away. "Ollie hates to be kept waiting for his dinner."

"Hey, V. Scott," Cody called after her. "Wait a minute, will you?"

From the second step, Val glanced over her shoulder, head held high in an unconscious effort to counteract an inexplicable melting sensation. Something told her it wasn't due entirely to the warm weather. He was still leaning against the wall, one hand in his pants pocket, the other holding a paper bag. Under the harsh over-head light, he looked homelier than ever. And remarkably attractive.

"Have dinner with me?" With a beguiling grin, Cody held up the bag. "I could grab us a couple of drinks and we could take the works to a park I know about. Coolest place in town."

Startled into remembering a place she hadn't thought about in years, Val descended the two steps and then paused. "Riverside Park? I thought that had been paved over or turned into a cottage development by now. There used to be a shortcut."

"Through the cemetery behind the Methodist church," Cody supplied with an eagerness that lent an almost boyish look to his craggy features.

Val glanced at the stack of wallpaper books she'd borrowed from the office. Was she really ready to tackle another decorating project? The last one had proved to be a disaster. Robin had sworn to her that navy-blue walls would be stunning. So far, they'd only proved depressing. "I'd almost forgotten Riverside Park, but it used to be one of my favorite places."

"Dump your books, put on your walking shoes and I'll get us something to drink, okay?" Cody was struck by a feeling of excitement all out of proportion to the small triumph. *Take it easy, old man. Remember your basic survival training: the more tempting the bait, the more dangerous the hook.*

As he paused in the open door, he allowed his gaze to narrow on the halo effect of an overhead light on the flyaway strands of her short brown hair. To hell with caution; she was an extremely good-looking woman and he was old enough to take care of himself.

"Beer or something soft?" he asked, and when she hesitated, he knew a moment's fear that she was going to back out on him. The strength of his disappointment shook him rather badly. "Leave it to me," he tossed off. He was gone before she could call him back, loping down the sidewalk as easily as if every muscle in his body hadn't been dragging just five minutes earlier.

Val gazed after him until the automatic door-closer robbed her of the view. Leave it to him, he'd said. Remarkably, she wished she could do just that. He really was the last thing she needed at this point in her life, just when she was learning to stand alone. Still…as long as she kept her wits about her, where was the danger in a simple impromptu picnic? Good Lord, she was no giddy girl, hero-worshiping the first set of broad shoulders that came her way.

In the few minutes it took her to drop her things and wash her face and hands, Val considered changing into her oldest pants, a baggy shirt and the pair of soft leather flats she'd always worn when she traveled because they were great for the inevitable mad dash between terminals.

She'd have been more comfortable, but every instinct warned against it. Once she started letting down the barriers, who knew how far she'd go? It might not be easy getting them back up should the need arise.

Besides, there was nothing wrong with the tan jacket dress she'd worn to work that day, aside from a few wrinkles and a slight pucker at the hemline. Before hurrying back downstairs to join Cody, she replaced the belt with a colorful silk scarf and took the time to touch up her lipstick and splash some light cologne on her wrists and the backs of her knees.

Riverside Methodist church, and the tiny park and cemetery adjacent to it, had changed remarkably little. A lifetime ago Val had played among these same mossy old stones, stroking worn granite lambs, gazing up the rigid robes of gentle-faced angels and patient shepherds. She could almost hear the sounds of the church choir practicing for the Sunday service, her mother's alto rounding off the sharp edges of a rather nasal soprano. For years Val had thought the alto part was the lead.

"Watch that root," Cody warned, taking her arm as they skirted around the base of an enormous magnolia tree.

"Did you ever play in cemeteries when you were a boy?" Val was a little startled at her own physical reaction to his touch. As soon as she gracefully could, she eased her arm away.

"I seem to remember being chased away by guards in the middle of some Halloween prank. Did you play here as a kid?"

"It was my favorite haunt, especially in the summertime."

Cody gave her a pained look. "Your favorite *haunt*? That was pretty bad."

"Sorry, strictly unintentional." Val smiled, and the smile broadened into a grin. When was the last time she'd cracked a joke, even inadvertently? "Seriously, with all these trees, the cemetery was the coolest place in town. I loved playing hide and seek here."

"Kids still do, come to think of it, even with Duke Power State Park close by."

"That's why they squeezed Riverside Park in on the other side—it was everybody's favorite meeting place, anyway, from kindergarten on through courting." With the late-afternoon sunlight softening the few fine lines in her brow, she turned to smile at him. "You know, I was never really frightened by ghost stories, even as a child. Could it be because we were all on such friendly terms with all the ghosts in town?"

"An odd way of looking at it, but I guess it's as good a reason as any."

By mutual consent they settled onto a stone bench overlooking an arm of Lake Norman. Val opened her bag of French fries, which were now quite cold. "Did you know most of that used to be corn and tobacco fields?" She nodded to the gleam of pale green water that glistened through the darker green of the pines.

"Impressive, the effect of one well-placed dam, isn't it?" Cody opened another bag and withdrew a bottle of inexpensive red wine. "Screw-top. I grabbed the first bottle I could find. Hope you weren't expecting anything too fancy."

Amused, Val watched his hands as they twisted the dark-green metal cap to break the seal. For such a rough-cut man, they were surprisingly well-kept hands—large, long fingered, with neat, square-tipped nails and a smattering of dark hair on the backs. Her gaze strayed up his muscular forearm to the creased roll of his shirt-sleeve, which was damp now from perspiration.

A thrill of something almost like fear shot through her. Nice hands or not, she didn't know the first thing about this man, yet here she was sharing cold fries and lukewarm wine with him. What on earth had possessed her? Valentine Whichard Scott, the original don't-make-waves gal.

As she searched her mind for a polite excuse to cut the evening short, Cody handed her a plastic wineglass. "There you go," he said with an engaging smile, and she forgot all about excuses.

"Wine *and* wineglasses? I'd expected a canned soda."

Cody lifted his glass to touch the rim of hers. "Compliments of Suzie's Deli. Suzie thinks she owes me a favor, so now and then she throws in something extra. This time it was the glasses."

"A real delicatessen? In Lakesboro?" Val sipped cautiously. "Mmm, this isn't bad at all."

"Lakesboro might look like a sleepy little farm community, but we *are* a lakefront resort, after all," Cody informed her, a gleam of laughter lurking in eyes that were neither blue nor brown nor gray, but a dark mixture of all three.

"You seem to know more about this place than I do, and I was born here. I don't remember seeing a deli around here. But then, I'm still relearning my way around. The town's tripled in size since I left home."

"Around the corner, next block, two doors down. Blink, and you'll miss it. The sign still says Sandwich Shoppe—two *P*'s and an *E*. Suzie's having another one painted."

"That wouldn't be Suzie Boger by any chance, would it? Her parents used to have a diner next to Raymond's. Long, pale blond hair, pretty, sort of bubbly?''

"Suzie Pauley. Married Ralph Pauley from the Exxon station, two boys on the high school track team. Short brown hair, nice smile, still bubbles if you catch her early in the morning when her feet aren't bothering her.''

"Oh, no,'' Val murmured around a bite of cold, dry hamburger. "Suzie always said she'd dye until the day she died.'' As classmates, they'd been casual friends, never all that close. Suzie had been a real party girl, head cheerleader, voted most popular girl in their senior year.

Val hadn't been voted anything. Tall, thin and painfully shy, she'd even been absent the day the yearbook pictures were taken, suffering from a stomachache that had cleared up with remarkable promptness the very next day.

"Are you a teacher at the new high school?'' He didn't look like a teacher, but then she couldn't imagine what a man like Cody Macheris would be doing living in a place like Lakesboro.

"No, I'm not a teacher,'' he said with a slowly widening smile. Without asking, he topped off her glass.

"Whoa—two's my limit.''

"We haven't even started in on the toasts yet.'' Cody lifted his glass to hers.

What a neat way he had of evading questions. Val could have used his expertise at one time in her life. "What did you have in mind?'' Infected by a smile that did remarkable things to his uneven features, she allowed her curiosity to go unsatisfied. She didn't need to know anything about him. In fact, the less she knew the better.

"How about a toast to ships that pass in the night—at airports?"

"You remembered?"

"Didn't you?"

"Well yes, but—" She twisted the stem of her wineglass, the contents spinning dangerously near the rim.

Cody watched her. With an expression that defied analysis, he gazed at her face, her hair, her clothing, noted the slender, ringless fingers that gripped the fragile stem. A portion of his brain that had been trained for just such things clicked into operation, instinctively processing minute details and adding them up.

Excellent clothes; expensive, but not new. Bought either for someone of a larger build or at a time when she'd been filled out more. No jewelry, although she'd worn rings, probably two of them, on her ring finger, left hand, until fairly recently. The indentation was unmistakable.

Silk scarf, not bought at a chain store, lizard-skin shoes—the real thing, too. Both first class, but showing signs of wear.

And her mannerisms, something about the quick, half-fearful way she looked at him now and then . . . V. Scott was hiding inside a very carefully cultivated exterior, hiding inside and peering out to see if it was safe to emerge. But hiding from whom? Or what?

Thoroughly fascinated, Cody continued to toy with his wineglass as his peripheral vision took in the guarded way she sat, feet tucked together, back straight, ready to jump and run at a moment's notice. Damned if he wasn't intrigued—almost as much by his own reaction to her as by the woman herself.

Val's spine grew more rigid as the silence spun out between them. She'd been enjoying herself, and then he'd begun to look at her in a certain way. She *hated* being watched! Even when it had nothing to do with that awful business.

Besides, she'd walked home in the blistering heat after a grueling day at the office, and she knew she was wilted, knew the location of every line in her face, every strand of gray on her head. "You don't seem like the sort of man to fit into a place like Lakesboro," she blurted when she could stand his scrutiny no longer. "Not even in Statesville, really."

"Oh? What sort of place do you think I'd fit into?"

"Well, certainly something more...cosmopolitan." She was feeling her way, evading his curiosity, inviting him to satisfy hers. "I should think you'd find the pace here too slow. There's not a lot to get excited about, unless you like water sports. Or, as my boss says, you enjoy sitting around talking about going fishing."

Cody liked her smiles. They were rare, seldom lasting more than a few moments, but well worth waiting for. She had a sense of humor; he'd already discovered that much. How much more was waiting to be discovered? He found himself wanting to hear her laugh, and he wondered what sorts of things delighted her.

"As to that, I even go so far as to wet a hook now and then," he allowed, his interest quickly concealed under a lazy-lidded smile. "This pace suits me just fine. If I get restless, I can always drive up to Barium Springs. But what about you? A woman with your looks, style— somehow I can't picture you settling down in Lakesboro."

"It's home to me. I have a cousin who lives across the lake in Sherrill Ford."

"You came here just to be near your cousin?" His tone was openly skeptical.

Her gaze fixed on the lengthening shadows that followed the sloping hillside up from the grove of pines at the water's edge, Val was torn between the need for caution and the need for companionship. He was just too easy to talk to, darn him! She wasn't the sort who made friends easily, but there was something about Cody Macheris . . .

"We were speaking of you and how you came to live in Lakesboro," she reminded him. "I don't even know where you came from, much less why." So much for subtlety. After all those years of hobnobbing with high-ranking officials of various governments, of spending endless hours engaged in small talk, always careful to give neither offense nor information, here she was asking a stranger point-blank to explain himself.

Cody exhaled decisively, as though awarding her this round. He hooked his arms over the back of the bench and extended his legs, crossing them at the ankles. "Denver, Chicago, Atlanta—Nam, Stuttgart, New York. Plus various army bases and government installations."

"Goodness!" Val felt a twinge of uneasiness that disappeared almost instantly. "And you ended up in a place that's not even on the map?"

"One of the major attractions. Actually, I'd been headquartered at Fort Bragg with the Fifth Group, Special Forces, back in my service days. So you see, North Carolina wasn't exactly new to me. Then, a few years ago I designed a security system for Blackhart Industries in Statesville. The area appealed to me." He lifted his shoulders carelessly, his expression noncommittal. "I decided it was time to put down roots."

The fact that he'd recently been divorced by his wife, lost custody of his son, lost the home he'd just built for them near Atlanta—not to mention a considerable chunk of any future income he might earn—had had something to do with it. All he'd wanted to do at that point was find a hole and crawl into it. Lakesboro had seemed a likely hole.

Val no longer made a pretense of disguising her curiosity. "That's what you do, design security systems?"

After a moment he nodded, and she caught the soft sound of his exhalation, a sound that in someone else might have been considered a sigh. She put down to a trick of lighting the bleak look that crossed his rough-cut features.

"My outfit's called CMS, for obvious reasons. We specialize in industrial security systems. I have a crew that does the actual installation, and a small office staff, but I handle the design and the inspections. Quality control's an important factor in my line of work." His grin was faintly self-deprecating. "Too many false alarms, and you lose your credibility. Your turn, V. Scott. You grew up here in Lakesboro, then what? College? Marriage? Career?" Dropping one arm to his lap, he turned to face her.

Avoiding his gaze, Val watched the coppery glints reflected on the waters below as the sun sank behind the opposite shore. "Did you know the town was called Pinesboro until Lake Norman was in the works? The community got together and decided that since they were about to become a lakefront resort, the name Pinesboro would have to go. They changed it officially to Lakesboro. I used to wonder why they didn't pick something a bit more imaginative while they were at it."

"If it's imagination you want, what about your own address, the Country Club Apartments? I know for a fact that the nearest country club is in Statesville, unless you count the farmer's exchange."

"Be thankful for small favors. We might have been living at 1010 Grubbenpheltzer Arms. That was the developer's name, and he wanted a memorial, but his backers threatened to pull out. I was seven when the first building was finished. I remember being awfully impressed with all that yellow brick. I'd probably just seen *The Wizard of Oz.*"

Having heard the age of the apartment complex from the super, Cody was able to do the arithmetic in his head. So she was thirty-eight. It showed only in a certain gravity of expression now and then. She had the skin of a young girl, a figure any woman would envy. Thirty-eight was a good age for a woman.

"It looks as if our town fathers overestimated the need for housing," Val observed. Indicating the neck of water below where they sat, she said, "As a resort, Lakesboro sort of fizzled. Sailboats can't come under the bridge, and except for a bait and tackle shop, we're still pretty much a farm town."

In companionable silence they sipped wine and watched the shadows deepen under the massive cedars and magnolias. Now and then Cody glanced at the woman beside him, taking in the pure line of her profile, the way her short brown hair flowed back from her face and curled into her nape. She was an enigma; an intriguing blend of poise and shyness, of maturity and vulnerability. He rested the urge to trace the line of her delicate jawbone up to a small, flat ear.

Bits and pieces of her were coming together in his mind to form the woman who was— Hell, he didn't even know her first name!

"You mentioned being at Fort Bragg with the Special Forces." Val knew little about the fabled group except what was covered in the news reports. "Is that where you got started in security work?"

Cody nodded thoughtfully. "Generally speaking, we were trained in five basic specialties, including medical techniques, engineering, communications and intelligence. Security—how to make it, how to break it—was just one more factor." Cody had learned a hell of a lot more than the things he'd mentioned, but it was not a topic he cared to discuss, especially with a woman he scarcely knew.

He'd already said more about that portion of his life than he'd ever said to Anna, and Anna had been a part of it. An unwilling, complaining, rebellious part of it. She'd hated everything about the army, but he'd been a soldier when he'd married her. He was a man who believed in honoring his obligations.

"I got a degree in electronics, thanks to the army. Otherwise, my business would probably consist of a few Dobermans and a stack of Beware of Dog signs."

"Could you have taken a degree in something else if you'd been interested?" Val was openly exploring the various facets of his mind.

"You mean like ancient history or microbiology? I might have, if I'd been interested. But by then I was getting on in years. I'd collected a few responsibilities, too, and it seemed sensible to go on with what I'd been doing in the army. Besides, I've always enjoyed problem solving."

Clasping his hands behind his head, he grinned engagingly, and Val resisted the temptation to offer him a few of her own problems to enjoy.

"So that about sums it up. I learned a trade in the army, I'm still working at it. End of story."

"But—"

"Now for dessert," he announced abruptly, fishing into the deli's paper bag to produce two doughnuts. "Plain. I could have got the chocolate iced ones, but for a first date I thought plain would be more appropriate."

Val's lips quivered. She shot him a quick look to see if he was serious. "Infinitely so," she agreed soberly, taking the confection and licking a grain of sugar from its surface. "Is this a date?"

"Well, isn't it? A dinner date? I asked you out to dinner and you accepted, so what else would you call it?"

A battered yellow convertible pulled noisily up at the far edge of the small park and cut the engine. Both Val and Cody watched with amused indulgence as two heads immediately met in middle of the front seat and sank from view.

"You ever come courting here?" Cody asked, glancing at her as if trying to picture a younger version flushed with desire.

"Didn't everyone?" Val responded. But she hadn't dated all that much. A late bloomer, she'd been just exploring the fringes of passion with her high school boyfriend when her father had died of a heart attack. Her mother had battled acute depression for almost two years before she'd felt strong enough to be left alone. Val had been emotionally exhausted when she'd met

Albert Scott. Perhaps if she hadn't been, she might not have rushed into marriage so quickly.

Cody fell silent, and Val relaxed and let the cool fragrance of the evening wash some of the tension from her body. One foot eased out of her high-heeled pump, and she curled her toes into the damp grass, startled at the sensations aroused by the brush of bristly stalks on the sensitive sole of her foot.

From nearby, a thrush caroled four short bars, and Cody repeated the notes in a melodious whistle.

"That's wonderful," Val exclaimed.

Across the park, heads popped up in the front seat of the old convertible, first one and then the other. A moment later the engine caught. Two quick backfires, a squeal of tires and they roared off.

Val's sharp, instinctive cry rang out against the guttural sound.

"Ms. Scott? What the hell!"

Bent double, Val tried to cover her face with her hands. She was totally unaware of the muffled whimpers that escaped her, the soft, "No *please*, no!"

Strong arms gathered her up roughly, held her, caught at her fists. It had started just this way before—two quick shots then the explosion and the madness. The stark, terrible madness.

"For God's sake, what's wrong?"

She burrowed her face into the wall of solid flesh, clutched at the rock-hard shoulders as she swallowed the metallic taste of fear that rose inside her.

"Is it over? Have they gone?"

Reality drenched her like a cold rain. "Oh, I'm sorry. I'm so embarrassed." This was Lakesboro. She was home among friends, not half a world away.

"Hey, snap out of it," Cody urged, his puzzled re-assurances gradually getting through her unreasoning fear.

"I'm all right," she whispered, more for her own benefit than his.

"It was just an old jalopy with bad plugs, that's all. A couple of high school kids who discovered that their private spot was more public than they'd realized."

"Oh, Cody, I'm such an idiot."

He held her away, the hands that bit into her arms gentle in spite of their strength. "Look, would you mind telling me what is going on? And what the hell is your name, anyway? I can't very well go on calling you Ms. Scott."

The laugh wasn't entirely successful, but it was the best she could do at the moment. Val felt like a fool and knew she must look like a wreck. The last of her doughnut was still clutched in her fist. A moment before, it had been pressed tightly against the side of her face.

"I'm all sugary," she said shakily, brushing ineffec-tually at her right cheek.

"Forget your face, just tell me what's the matter," Cody ordered, his voice gruff with concern.

"I think it must be because I was so relaxed," Val said hesitantly. "Evidently I've been, uh, more tense than I'd thought." She frowned at the glisten of sugar on her fingers.

"Name?"

"What, you mean mine? Oh—Valentine Scott."

"Valentine. I've been calling you Victoria in my mind. Now, Valentine, why were you so tense and why were you so relaxed? And why the devil did you react like that to a noisy muffler?"

Chapter Three

Val was sorely tempted to pour out the whole story over those accommodating shoulders. From the very beginning, she'd trusted him instinctively, which was little short of a miracle. God knows, if any woman had reason to distrust men, she did. But the first time she'd ever seen Cody Macheris, it was almost as though she recognized him. Not physically, although she was far from indifferent to his tough masculinity.

It went much deeper than that. The night at the airport, when he'd sauntered along the empty corridor toward her, some element beyond the physical had reached out and touched a responsive chord inside her at a moment when she'd been at her lowest ebb. For an instant it was as though she'd actually tapped the strength of another person, someone she didn't even know.

It was happening all over again. Wordlessly she gazed into his eyes, warm now with the afterglow of a setting sun. They were kind eyes, although she sensed that they could be as unyielding as steel. They met her own gaze readily. They might conceal, they might even evade— but they would never lie. Somehow she was certain of that.

It was the genuine concern she saw there that bothered her. It would be so easy to lay her burdens down. So easy and so wonderful.

She'd fall in love again, and for a little while, she'd feel secure. This time, it might even work out. She was older, a better judge of character. But what if she was wrong again? Could she pick herself up and start over once more?

It wasn't worth the risk. Her security, both emotional and financial, was her own responsibility. She was getting there. She almost had it together, but if she lost control, even for a moment, she might never find the courage to try again.

"You're not going to tell me, are you?" Cody said resignedly.

"There's nothing to tell, nothing you need to know. Some women scream at mice, some at—"

"Valentine," he warned softly, his hands closing over her shoulders once more.

"Cody, please." Val shook her head, not trusting the intensity of these strange new feelings. Feelings were a mirage. You could follow them forever and never quite catch them, because they weren't real—a trick of the mind, an optical illusion.

"All right, but at least let me clean the doughnut from your face. You're just transferring it from your face and hair to your hands, and then to my shirt."

From his hip pocket he removed a handkerchief that smelled faintly of laundry detergent and proceeded to dab at the stickiness on the side of her face. Val found herself trembling as his body heat began to thaw the chill from her bones.

"This smears. Feel like a hike down to the lake?" he queried.

"Not particularly." Her knees still felt like cooked spaghetti.

"I was never a Boy Scout but I did manage to pick up a few emergency tips." Before Val realized what he meant to do, he was doing it; holding her face between his hands, he lowered his mouth and gently began to lick the sugar from her cheek.

Lightning streaked through her, pressing the air from her lungs. Desperately, she clutched at his wrists, pulled at his hands. It was like pulling on iron bars. The coercing rasp of his warm, wet tongue continued to caress her cheek, moving to her temple and skirting dangerously close to her right ear.

"Cody, stop that," she panted when she remembered how to breathe again.

"Can't stop now," he whispered, the current of air chilling a rash of goose bumps down her flank. "Piece of sugar crust stuck to a curl right . . . here."

Her hand flew up to hold the place where he'd tugged at her hair. They were sitting knee to knee, and Val was leaning forward, held by the clasp of his hands. If he released her, she'd probably tumble right into his arms. Heaven help her, at that moment, there was nowhere she'd rather be!

"Cody, this has gone far enough," she managed, jerking herself free when he began a foray to the vulnerable place just under the jaw.

"Not nearly far enough," he countered, letting her go, but pinning her with a look that was almost as physical as his touch. "It'll do for a start, though."

"A start, nothing," Val declared shakily. She jumped up and had moved several steps away before she realized she was wearing only one shoe. "Look, neighbors we may be, but that's the extent of it. I really don't have time for—for the sort of thing you seem to be looking for."

"You mean friendship?"

"Is this the way you treat your friends?" Val found her shoe under the bench and jammed it on, ignoring the bit of gravel that clung to one foot of her nylons.

"Only the sweetest ones," Cody assured her. His grin was irresistible. Arms once more hooked over the back of the bench, he returned her frown with a look of open interest.

Val was torn between a desire to wipe that crooked grin off his face and an even more compelling one to respond to it. "Look, Cody, this has been nice. Strange, and a little embarrassing, but . . . nice. Now I really do have to run."

"More overtime?" He gathered up the remains of their impromptu meal and stuffed them into the crumpled bag.

"Overtime?" Val repeated.

"The typing you're always doing after hours."

"Oh, that. Don't worry, I've already turned in my rental machine, so you'll be able to sleep nights."

"Can you guarantee it?" Cody had a feeling that his insomnia might be entering a new phase. He caught at her hand to help her past the gnarled roots of the magnolia tree, and Val felt an immediate jump in her body's voltage. It had been so long since she'd engaged in this sort of byplay, she'd forgotten the rules. Was she reading the signals all wrong?

"You could always try warm milk," she suggested dryly.

Cody kept the hand, in spite of her polite effort to retrieve it. "Cold showers might be more appropriate," he muttered.

Val yanked her fingers from his grip. Things were moving too fast. "Look, Cody, there's got to be a more graceful way of going about this, but at the moment I can't think of it. So I'll lay it on the line. I'm not interested in getting involved with you. Or with any other man."

"I noticed you're not wearing rings."

"That has nothing to do with it. My—" She broke off. What could she say without dredging up the whole wretched affair? It would be like handing him an intimate part of herself, and she didn't dare. He had enough of an advantage as it was. "My work," she hedged. "And I'm redecorating my apartment. I have to return those sample books tomorrow."

It was astonishing how much mockery could be conveyed by one slightly elevated eyebrow. Bracing herself against his obvious skepticism, Val tried another tack. "Look, we happen to live in the same apartment building. At least a dozen other people do, too. That doesn't constitute grounds for a personal involv—"

"Knock it off, Valentine. It's a hell of a lot more than that, and you know it. In case you're interested, I'm not exactly in the market for a wife, either."

"So there you are," she pronounced, triumph struggling against something slightly less pleasurable.

He shot her a look of mild derision. "But that doesn't mean we didn't strike sparks off each other from the very first. I don't think it'll go away anytime soon, either."

"It will if we let it."

"With both of us living in the same apartment building, seeing each other every day? Come on, honey, act your age."

"So why don't you move?"

"Who, me? You forget, I've got seniority."

Checkmate. The gentleness that had struck Val earlier was nowhere in evidence now. "Well, *I* certainly can't move. Besides, there's not that much to choose from."

"Maybe your boss, the architect, could design you a house."

Val wrapped her arms around her and turned toward the rusted wrought-iron fence that separated park from cemetery, and Cody fell into step beside her. "I can't afford that and you know it," she grumbled.

"I do? How could I know your financial situation? How could I know anything about you except that you once lived here and you still have a cousin in these parts? Oh—and that you're a secretary. But you told me you'd never been a secretary before, so maybe you got bored and—"

"You want my credit rating, is that it?" Val snapped.

"I don't want anything you're not willing to give," Cody said with ill-concealed impatience. "I'm only pointing out that so far I don't know much about you." He knew more than she'd told him . . . far more. The trouble was, the more he knew, the more he wanted to know.

"I seldom hand out my biography on a first date."

Catching the dry note of humor in her tone, he breathed easier. Dicey proposition, this business of getting to know a woman. He said as much. "Twenty years ago, this would have been a damned sight easier, you know? I mean, how much living can a man or woman do in the first twenty years?"

"Rather a lot, in some cases."

He nodded thoughtfully. "What I'm trying to say is that I don't want to trip any hidden mines, Valentine, but it's hard to get to know you without risking a few."

It had to be accidental, the phrasing. If he'd known anything...but he *couldn't* have known anything. There'd been only two photos published before Meekins had clamped the lid on, and neither of them had been very good. And who remembered a name that had cropped up in the news for a couple of days several months ago?

"Valentine? What's going on behind that smooth ivory brow of yours?"

She gave up. With a look that was half impatient, half bemused, she measured out a few statistics. "Valentine Whichard Scott, native Tarheel, home again after years of living abroad. Brow, incidentally, not as smooth as it once was."

"That's it? You're not telling me much I don't already know."

"Bad typist, fair linguist, excellent receptionist...I think." And at Cody's encouraging grin, she added, "Widowed, no children. There, does that solve your problem?"

They were strolling slowly across the lush grass as fireflies emerged to light shadows of the summer evening. Kitchen lights went on along the street beyond the church as women began to wash up after supper, and porch swings began to creak as men wandered outside to digest. It was a time of day Val had always loved, and not even the advent of dishwashers and air conditioners had changed it all that much.

"I think I've forgotten the original problem," Cody confessed, and Val swung around to shake her head at him.

"You told me I'd have to move out of the apartment because you had seniority, and we couldn't go on meeting this way," she reminded him, a hint of laughter in the tone of her voice.

"Oh, yeah...that problem. Seems to me we'll have to come to some sort of compromise. There's always the traditional way."

"One of us goes on an extended cruise, you mean?"

"*Both* of us go on a cruise," he corrected gently. "Single cabin, double occupancy."

Val marveled at the fact that she could go so easily from panic to playfulness. Whatever else Cody did for her, he was definitely good for her in that respect. "Why don't you commission Wynn to design you a house of your own so you won't be bothered by your inconsiderate neighbor? There's still some lovely property available right on the lake."

"Now what would I do with a house? Do I strike you as the domestic sort?" Cody closed the rusted gate after them, and they strolled slowly past the old white frame church where Val had earned a perfect attendance pin when she was eleven.

"As a matter of fact, you do," she said frankly. "Cody, do you know what struck me about you that night in the airport?"

"I'm afraid to ask."

"That you looked nice. Not *handsome* nice, but *nice* nice."

"Nice nice, huh? Move over Lawrence Welk, you've got competition."

Without thinking, Val tucked her hand under Cody's arm. "Oh, for goodness' sake, you know what I mean."

"Yeah, I'm afraid I do," Cody agreed, covering her hand with his. "Which is why I think alternative number two is the best bet for us."

"I'm almost afraid to ask," Val teased. They reached the apartment, and as if sensing that the tenuous spell would be broken once they entered the building, they lingered outside the door.

"Friends," he said flatly. "I have a feeling we could both use a nice, uncomplicated friendship, don't you?"

Uncomplicated? At the moment, things felt extremely complicated to Val, but she could hardly tell him that. Not when she was still fighting this unlikely compulsion to curl up in his arms.

"Well?" Cody prompted after several moments had passed. "Have we got a deal, or do you start looking around for new quarters?"

Leaning against the yellow brick wall, Val tried to concentrate on her view of Lakesboro's modest skyline, which consisted, from her vantage point, of hundreds of treetops, three steeples, a corner of Marshall's Pharmacy and the roof of Raymond's Variety Store.

Instead, she kept seeing Cody's broad shoulders leaning against the dogwood tree, the lower branch almost touching his thick, untidy hair. At close range she'd discovered that it was neither sun-streaked bronze nor graying blond, but a mingling of colors, as were his eyes. Those lazy-lidded eyes that were neither blue nor brown nor gray, but a mixture of all three.

Darn it, she'd *promised* herself she wouldn't jump into anything—or at least she would have promised herself if the likelihood had even occurred to her. Yet here she was, getting ready to jump into...

"Friendship?" she echoed uncertainly.

"Friendship," Cody confirmed, launching himself from the support of the tree to extend his hand.

Reluctantly, Val placed her hand in his, liking the firm, dry contact. "I'm not sure just what I'm letting myself in for," she ventured.

"Nothing you can't handle. We might even lay down a few ground rules, if it'll make you feel more comfortable. For instance, if I ask a favor, I'll give one in return, okay? If either one of us gets tired of his own company, we just send up a flare. For my part, I'm a good listener, a great handyman and a passable cook. I don't borrow records, I always return borrowed books, I won't intrude when you're entertaining and I promise to let you pay your own way if we go out to dinner. Can't get much fairer than that," he ended smugly.

Val was laughing by the time he finished, and Cody joined her. Slowly, his smile faded and he studied her thoughtfully. "Why do I get the feeling that you haven't been doing too much of that lately?" he asked.

With the sun truly gone, the air was growing cooler. Rubbing the sudden chill from her arms, Val evaded his question. "Who, me? All you have to do is say something mildly funny and I'll crack up. That's what friends are for, isn't it? To laugh at each other's jokes?"

He sighed. "Yeah, you're right. But right now I've got some work to do that's no laughing matter." He ushered her through the door and turned toward his own entrance. "Keep in touch, hmm?"

The navy-blue would have to go. Robin could paint his own rooms any color he chose, but Val couldn't live with navy-blue walls, even with the help of the yellow carpet, the white wicker furniture and the jungle of houseplants he'd proposed. Thank goodness she hadn't yet invested in anything more than a few cans of paint and several hours of hard labor. The trouble was, it would take hundreds of coats of *anything* to cover those dark walls.

"A little ingenuity, that's what we need here," she muttered to herself as she held a sample of yellow-and-white striped wallpaper against a corner. She'd painted all four living-room walls and the tiny hallway, after getting special dispensation from the super and signing an agreement to return them to their original state of drabness before she moved out.

The trouble with wallpaper was all that pasting and holding and sticking. Perhaps she'd do better to use something other than stripes. She'd do well just to get it on the walls, without having to worry about getting it on straight. On the other hand, the jungle butterfly print would cover a multitude of errors. It was wild, but it was cheerful.

She hunted up the price code and groaned in dismay. These few rolls were leftover ends that Robin had given her as samples; she might have known they'd cost the earth.

What had possessed her to listen to Robin Chatham in the first place? He wore pink pants and plastic sandals to work, for goodness' sake!

Val dropped into the ugly green chair—uglier than ever now—and stared dismally at her bungled effort at a chic decorating scheme. She should have followed her first instinct and gone with a pale creamy pink and lots of neutrals.

"Ollie, we goofed," she said dolefully.

Acting on an impulse, she stamped on the floor. Within minutes, she heard Cody's footsteps, surprisingly soft in a man so large, on the stairway outside her door.

"You rang?" he said through the closed door.

"C'mon in, it's not locked," Val invited, not stirring from her chair. Might as well let him know the worst. If that didn't turn him off, nothing would.

"Do you normally sit around with your door wide open to anyone who walks in off the street?" Cody, looking slightly rumpled, but nonetheless wonderful in khakis and a knit shirt, glared at her.

"It wasn't wide open, and no I don't," Val returned. "My hands were full of wallpaper when I let myself inside, and I forgot."

"Well, don't—"

"Look, if you're going to lecture me, just go home. This is Lakesboro, remember? Crime rate zilch. Even so, I'm normally not so careless. So drop it, will you?"

"Sorry, professional bias, I suppose."

"Yesterday you indicated that you were available for listening," Val reminded him, trying to ignore the look of fascinated horror on his face as he examined her living room for the first time. "Okay, *friend*, I need to talk, so start listening."

Uncertainty clouded her eyes. "But maybe you're busy?"

Cody's gaze slowly worked its way around to the lumpish chair where she sat, elbows on her knees, surrounded by unfurled rolls of wallpaper in several designs. His eyes widened slightly, but in no other way did he indicate that he noticed anything different about the way she looked.

Val had changed into a pair of baggy yellow slacks that should have been discarded long ago, and a pink tunic she'd bought in Marrakesh once when her luggage had gone on to Lisbon. She was barefoot, the bulk of her hair twisted into a knot and secured with a pencil, with a short fringe curling around her slender neck.

"All right, get if off your chest," she said, resigned to his derisive appraisal.

"*My* chest? I thought it was *your* chest we were supposed to be airing." His glance dropped to the front of her shirt, where no hint of her modest curves broke the smooth fall of pink cotton.

"This place. It's a mess, isn't it?" Val challenged.

"You want honesty or tact?"

"You don't have to tell me," she said morosely. "I goofed. Now I'm afraid I'm going to goof again trying to fix my first goof."

"Then you want a scapegoat, is that it?" Gingerly, Cody lowered himself to a plastic-covered sofa that looked as if it had served time in the waiting room of a busy pediatrician.

"No, that's *not* it, dammit, I—" Val charged up out of her chair, unable to put into words the impulse that had made her summon him. "Oh, Cody, how do I know what I wanted? Absolution? A paperhanger? You said you were a good listener, so just listen, will you?"

She continued to prowl, saying not a word as she stepped over the ends of wallpaper, several decorating magazines and the shoes she'd kicked off earlier. "Meet Ollie," she muttered, waving a hand in the direction of the dime store goldfish bowl. "Ollie, my friend Cody."

Putting aside the thought of the unfinished estimate he'd been working on downstairs, Cody concentrated on the woman before him. The more he saw of her, the more she fascinated him, a situation not without inherent dangers. It had probably been a mistake to suggest this friendship thing, but he'd been playing for time.

Face it, he'd also been lonely as hell. Valentine Scott was the first woman in a long time who interested him enough to make the effort. Unfortunately, she was beginning to interest him entirely too much.

"At least I don't have to pretend any longer," she said with a sigh. "Not with you, anyway. You have no idea how tiresome that can get, but what else could I do?"

"Do you know," Cody said mildly, "I haven't the foggiest notion what you're talking about."

Val stopped and turned to him, gesturing to herself and the offending room. "Me," she exclaimed. "This!" She waited expectantly, and when no comment was forthcoming, she plopped herself back in the green chair and planted her chin on her fist. "It was all I had to fall back on. Heaven knows, it wasn't much, but it was all I had. You see, I got the idea from an ad I read for a mature woman with no experience who could meet the public."

As though what she was saying made perfect sense to him, Cody nodded thoughtfully. Hadn't he claimed to be a good listener? A mature woman with no experience, she'd said. Somehow, he'd have thought tne two terms mutually exclusive.

"Unfortunately, that job was taken, and the only other one that advertised for a mature woman called for a car and a lot of driving. Mine gets me back and forth to work on rainy days, but it's got a serious drinking problem, and it's beginning to smoke, too."

Cody had seen the gas guzzler she drove; it needed a ring job. He tactfully refrained from mentioning it.

"Anyhow, I had two things going for me: maturity and no experience. I'm certainly mature," she admitted dryly, "and the only job I ever held lasted all of seven months, and that was almost twenty years ago. But I read this article about job hunting—that was after I'd already applied and been turned down for every job opening in Statesville. Analyze your skills, it said." She grimaced. "Unfortunately, mine aren't all that impressive. Self-presentation was the next heading, and it seemed like a better bet, so I concentrated on doing it."

Cody made himself comfortable. This was a new Valentine he was seeing tonight, and he found himself more fascinated than ever.

"My clothes are good, and I've traveled widely," Val went on. "Living out of a suitcase as I did for so many years, I soon learned that it's better to have a few really good things than a lot of cheap ones. They travel better. Even the best things go on sale eventually, if you know where to look." She smiled engagingly. "Minus the labels, of course."

Cody felt a gnawing tenderness begin to grow inside him. He felt like racing out and buying her a trunkful of clothes, labels and all.

"So," Val continued with an airiness that concealed a multitude of uncertainties, "I put on my twelve-year-old Galanos suit and my Bruno Maglis with the Band-Aids on the soles, and I played it to the hilt. It worked. I got the best job available, and I think Wynn even offered me a larger starting salary than he'd intended because he thought I wouldn't consider taking less. He'd just spent a fortune decorating his new office, and according to Robin, I was the perfect accessory, the pièce de résistance."

The crow's-feet at the corners of Cody's eyes crinkled as he began to smile. "So you led with those classy cheekbones of yours and came up a winner, huh?" He was beginning to fit together a few pieces of the puzzle that was Valentine Scott. "You say you've been out of the job market for twenty years?"

"Eighteen, to be precise," Val admitted, curling up her long legs beside her so that she could turn and face the sofa. "Talk about culture shock! Cody, I had no idea... I mean, I'd taken a course in personal typing in high school, but... And filing? You put things in alphabetical order, right? What could be so complicated about that?"

"What indeed?" he echoed gravely.

"Well, darn it, the ad said secretary-receptionist, and at least I'm good with people. Believe it or not, I'm tactful and diplomatic and—"

"How's your shorthand?"

Val groaned. "Don't ask. I invented a system that's got me by so far, but only because Wynn's a slow talker. If he'd been born north of the Mason-Dixon Line, I wouldn't have lasted the first day."

"So what's with the chamber of horrors here?" Cody gestured broadly at the freshly painted walls. "A little self-inflicted penance for getting away with murder?"

"I was trying to beef up my act. In case Wynn ever had occasion to drop by, I'd hate for him to think I lived in a dump."

"Even when it's the only dump in town?"

"Even then. Besides, it was depressing. It's hard to get into your role when the setting's all wrong. So I thought that for the cost of a few cans of paint I could turn this place into something really chic and extraordinary." Val toyed with a loose thread on the arm of the chair, looking up only when she heard his low laughter.

"You succeeded. It's about as extraordinary as anything I've seen in a long time. What made you choose this color?"

"Robin Chatham, damn his hide," Val muttered. "I told him I wanted something really striking for as little money as possible, and this was what he came up with. Bold, he called it." She snorted. "The trouble is, I can never tell when Robin's pulling my leg. This is probably his idea of a joke."

"And you fell for it? Honey, where's your gumption?"

"I used up most of it just landing my job," Val confessed. "What little I have left over goes to cover the fact that I'm in way over my head and I can't swim a stroke."

Cody rose in a fluid movement and caught her hand, drawing her up to stand before him. Barefooted, the top of her head came only to his chin. "Hey, little friend," he said, his hands coming down on her shoulders to shake her gently. "The first thing we need to do is put a little distance between you and your problem. Gain a little objectivity, you might say. It just so happens that I know where there's cold beer and half a jar of pickled sausage. If you've got some crackers, we could pool our resources while we work on a solution."

Too disheartened to be wary of the powerful tug of his masculine attraction, Val nodded gratefully. "I can even throw in some cheese."

She turned toward the kitchen, which was still in it's original shade of faded tan, Cody noted. He gazed after her, taking in the drape of soft yellow fabric over her slender hips, and the oddly touching projection of her shoulder blades under the filmy cotton shirt. She was too thin. It might be fashionable, but he'd feel a damned sight better about her if she'd put on a few pounds.

He caught himself up sharply. Why the hell should it matter to him? In spite of the game they were playing—and it was a game, whether she wanted to admit it or not—they were no more friends than he and Anna were friends. Less so, in fact. He and Anna had twelve years and a son in common. With Valentine Scott, all he had was an itch that couldn't be scratched and a bothersome feeling of something just beneath the surface, something that he hadn't yet reconciled in his mind.

Chapter Four

If Val had entertained a few worries about Cody's forgetting the boundaries of their relationship, she soon forgot them. Over beer and sausage, crackers and cheese, in a kitchen identical to her own, they explored and discarded as impractical several solutions to her decorating problems.

"The trouble is, I've already shot my budget for the month," Val explained, hooking her feet around the legs of a varnished, slat-back chair. "Robin said I should go for the broad effect first—the walls. I thought I might find some inexpensive wicker pieces and spray them white, pick up a few houseplants, and then, once I've stopped subcontracting my typing, I'll see about carpet and then visit a few galleries to find something for the walls."

"Subcontracting?" Cody opened another bottle of beer and poured half in Val's glass, drinking his half from the bottle.

She hadn't meant to mention that. Still, why not? She'd already laid bare her conniving little soul, and he hadn't yet turned away in disgust. "I told you about that, remember? About my job and why I had to stretch the truth to make up for—"

"What do you mean, subcontracting?"

Moving her glass to one side, Val trailed a finger through the ring of moisture and formed a square within the circle. In the center, she carefully traced her initials, the initials she'd been teased about as a child. *V. W.* She'd been called Beetle by half her graduating class. "Lucy's Letter Shop," she elaborated. "What I can't get done during the day, I drop off there after work. It's ready for me the next morning, no questions asked. My cousin Grace used to live around the corner from Lucy McIntire."

"You get family rates, I hope," Cody said dryly, recalling the few times he'd had to depend on Lucy's services.

"If a dollar a page is considered family rates."

"Oh hell, is that what I pushed you into? Why didn't you tell me where to get off?"

Val tilted her head and examined the elaborate monogram she'd fashioned on the Formica tabletop. "You were right to complain, I just wasn't thinking. My neighbor across the hall is a private duty nurse who works nights, and it simply didn't occur to me that without a rug, the noise would go right through my floor."

"And my ceiling."

A smile teased at the corners of her mouth. "Actually, you sped up my learning process. Lucy costs more than the rental on the machine, so you might say I'm a lot more motivated now."

"I feel like a heel."

"Good. You can make it up to me by helping me figure out what to do about that mess upstairs."

"You could always sublet it for a darkroom."

"Be serious."

"On sausage and cheese? That was just an appetizer." He glanced at his watch, a practical, leather-banded affair that nestled in the gold-tipped hair on his wrist. "Why don't we go out for a steak? Afterward I promise to work out a solution to all your problems."

"*All* my problems? Just tell me how to undo all those gallons of the wrong shade of paint. I'll settle for that."

"Over dinner."

Val groaned. "Don't you ever think of anything but food?" Getting nothing but a leering grin for her efforts, she said, "Cody, I'm too tired to change, and I certainly can't go anywhere like this."

"You look just fine to me," he assured her, meaning it. She was the sort of woman who made the clothes rather than the reverse.

"Why don't you go have a steak, and I'll see you afterward?" She hadn't forgotten what he'd said about paying for her own dinner in case they went out—not that she'd have had it any other way—but she'd already shot her month's budget for that darn paint.

As if divining her thoughts, Cody pushed himself away from the table. "Go on, slip into a dress if it'll make you feel more comfortable. My treat tonight, okay? You can pay me back next time."

For reasons she was at loss to explain, Val dug in her heels. "Cody, I really don't want a steak, and I don't feel like getting dressed to watch you eat one. If you're not going to come up with any decent ideas about my living room, I'll go back upstairs and look through those magazines again. Maybe *something* will ring a bell."

"All right, you win. Who needs steak when he can dine on pickled sausage and cheese?"

"I've dined on far less and been glad to get it."

They adjourned to the living room, where Val accepted his invitation to settle on the couch. Cody's couch was an oversized leather-covered one that obviously hadn't come with the apartment.

"Now, tell me about all those times you dined on less and were glad to get it," Cody prompted.

"A figure of speech," Val retorted. "Have you ever had *prsut*?"

"Is it contagious?"

"It's Dalmatian ham. Once on the island of Pag in the Adriatic, we ate nothing but *prsut* and *paski sir*—that's a local cheese made from goat's milk—for three days. I drank Prosek, the red wine. Talk about a headache! But it was either that or warm goat's milk, and that is definitely not my favorite beverage." In light of what she'd later learned, Val suspected that far from the second honeymoon Albert had claimed, he'd been hiding from someone. It certainly hadn't been much of a honeymoon; he'd been so short tempered the whole time they'd ended up fighting bitterly.

After the briefest of silences, Cody went on to mention a few of his own favorite foods. Neither of them brought up the four dark blue walls, the two awkwardly placed windows and the bare floors upstairs, and somehow it didn't seem to matter. Val felt safe and comfortable and relaxed, the mess she'd left upstairs unimportant for the moment.

After a while, her feet found their way up onto the sofa beside her. She curled up against a cushion and listened, fascinated, as Cody told her something about his work.

"Nothing's foolproof, of course. Dogs can be drugged, fences can be climbed, rammed, or shorted out. Electronics are good, but they can be a pain in the butt. I've seen one of the most elaborate systems on the market knocked out by a single housefly."

"So maybe the best bet is not to have anything worth stealing."

"Or at least to give that appearance," Cody agreed. "Hardly practical for a retail outlet or a warehouse."

While he went on to relate an incident concerning a system he'd installed that kept sending out false alarms at exactly 11:05 each night, Val filled her eyes with the lean, tanned strength of him, the jutting nose and the stubborn jawline that hinted at a late-day beard. Her gaze fell to the open neck of his shirt, where a tuft of dark hair brushed against the hollow at the base of his throat.

"Didn't that fly teach you anything? You have to work the bugs out of a system *before* you install it, not afterward."

"Are you sure you weren't one of the original Marx brothers?" Cody shook his head. "Matter of fact, it turned out to be an overamorous security guard this time. Seems he had a new lady waiting at home, and at the end of his last round each night, he used a CB mobile unit to check in with her and let her know he was on his way. His calling frequency just happened to be one that would trigger our alarm.''

Val's laughter spilled out, and he beamed at her, as if her happiness were his goal in life.

Suddenly she turned away, startled by a feeling that cut too close to the bone. She stood up and moved across to a cluttered desk. ''They didn't fire him, I hope.''

If Cody thought she was behaving erratically, he was tactful enough to ignore it. ''Nope. Did suggest that he use the phone from now on, though.''

''I like this room,'' she said abruptly. It was neutral, nothing out of the ordinary. Nothing went together, and yet it all melded, reflecting a complex, understated personality.

She lifted a small framed photo of a young man who bore a striking resemblance to Cody. Before she could voice the question, he answered it.

''My son, Eric. He lives in Fort Lauderdale with his mother.''

''You must be proud of him. He looks nice.''

''Like father, like son,'' Cody quipped in reference to her earlier observation.

As Val brushed aside a long curl of calculator tape to replace the photo, a dozen questions arose in her mind. She chose the least personal. ''Cody, did I interrupt your work when I stamped on the floor?''

''Hey, now, what are friends for?'' Cody chided gently. He'd been doing some preliminary figuring, trying to decide whether or not to follow up on an idea he'd had concerning one of his equipment suppliers. It could wait. He'd learned the hard way never to move on important matters without carefully considering all angles first.

"Not for unloading one's troubles on, I'm sure," Val countered with a rueful shake of her head.

"Unload all you want to. I told you I'm a good listener."

"Any barkeep could listen. What I really need is a good decorator."

Moving to stand beside her, Cody reached out to touch the translucent shadows beneath her eyes. "As your friendly, decorative neighborhood barkeep, I'd say that what you really need is a vacation."

Val sighed. "I'll keep that in mind. Meanwhile, it's late, and I am tired, and we still haven't decided what I can do with that misplaced dungeon up there." She braced herself on the edge of his large, littered desk.

"We'll both sleep on it, hmm? You'd be surprised how many problems can be solved when your mind's in a relaxed state. But honey," he cautioned, hollow cheeks crinkling in a slow smile, "I think I ought to warn you, my decorating is strictly utilitarian. I shop for furniture by trying it on for size. If it fits and feels good, I buy it."

Val measured his large, muscular frame with a skeptical look. "Oh, great. You're going to be an *enormous* help—and that's no pun."

He opened the door for her, but when she would have passed through, he caught her hand. "I'm pretty good with a paintbrush. If you want me, I'm all yours this weekend. Meanwhile, may I suggest that you invest in a few two-hundred-watt bulbs and a coal-miner's hat?"

"Sure, and on my way out every morning, I'll leave a trail of breadcrumbs, too." She shot him a withering look, but before she could slip away, Cody captured her face in his two hands. Framing her jaw with thumb and fingers, he grinned down at her. His eyes took on a distinctively amber tone as he leaned over to touch his lips to hers.

Val was momentarily paralyzed. It was as if she hung suspended from the touch of his hands, his lips, held there by the very force of his personality. He demanded nothing of her with the soft brush of his lips, nor did he seek to deepen the kiss.

When it was over, she stood for a long moment, breathless, more than a little shaken. Neither of them spoke. Val stared into his shadowed face, searching for—

She turned away and hurried up the stairs. Searching for something she had no business even thinking about!

Suzie Pauley at the deli had doubled her weight and let her hair go natural, but the dimpled smile was still the same. "You remember Richard, his father kept bees."

Straining her memory, Val recalled a tall, silent boy who never seemed to hang around for extracurricular activities. Val had watched him and his father, both heavily veiled and wearing gloves that reached to their elbows, capture a swarm from inside the church steeple one spring evening just before dark. At the time it had all seemed terribly mysterious, a rite of exorcism.

"He works the Exxon now?" She licked her triple vanilla. Not all delis sold ice cream. Suzie's did.

"Manager. We've been living in Pawpaw's old place, but we just built an A-frame right on the lake, and we're planning to move as soon as the boys are out of school for the summer."

Val murmured her congratulations, and Suzie beamed. "Beetle Whichard! Who'd have thought you'd come back here after all—I mean..." She concentrated on a stubborn spot that marred the plastic perfection of her counter. "Gee, I was real sorry about your husband, Beetle. I don't read the papers much, but Richard said... I mean, it was on all the local stations. Something about something happening to this woman from Lakesboro over in one of those places in the news. Some sort of terrorist hijacking or something like that, wasn't it?"

It certainly wasn't the first time Val had been faced with the direct question. She found she still wasn't ready to answer it, even though this time, at least, it had been prompted by friendly concern instead of morbid curiosity.

She looked for a place to dispose of the rest of her melting cone. "Something like that, Suzie. This is great vanilla, but I should have started with a single and worked my way up."

"Oh, hey, me and my big mouth." In a deft sweep, the cone was taken, the counter wiped clean and Suzie propped plump elbows on the fake black marble. "You back in town for good, Beetle? I heard you were working for Wynn Flowers. Tricia Canfield was dying for that job. You remember Tricia, don't you? Two years ahead of us, married that Canfield boy who used to race hydroplanes? She's been there in the office at Raymond's Variety ever since he ran off and left her, but with the new mall out on the highway, that old place is on its last legs. I know for a fact that she was wanting to take over Mary Lee's job with Wynn, but you beat her to it."

"Should I apologize?" She had no intention of doing so, but the revelation seemed to call for some sort of acknowledgment.

"Oh, heck no, honey, I was just filling you in on the news." Twin dimples flickered in her rounded cheeks. "Say, wasn't that you I saw out walking with Cody Macheris the other night? Boy, talk about a class act, he's something else! If I didn't have Richard, I'd climb all over that man."

Val wiped her sticky fingers on a scrap of embroidered linen and crammed it back in her purse. "Cody? We just happened to run into each other on the way home, that's all." Val turned toward the door, feeling almost as if twenty years had dropped away and she was being teased about some boy she'd been seen with on the school grounds.

"Hey, look, I think it's great! I mean, it's been—how long *has* it been since you lost your husband? Stuck here in the store every day, I lose all track of time."

Parrying the question as she'd done before, Val peered through the moisture-beaded glass front counter that ran along the side of the narrow room. "Oh, is that summer sausage? Let me have about four slices, will you, and two of those big dills. By the time I get home after work, I'm usually too tired to cook."

"You and Tricia are about the only ones of the old gang still single. Well, not exactly single," the round-faced woman corrected. "I mean, at least not *still* single."

Val's lips quivered. She could remember a time when Suzie's tactless remarks had made her cringe. Now, they triggered only amusement, and a certain amount of sympathy. How many feet could one mouth hold?

"Just between you and me, there's many a married woman around here who'd love to park her shoes under his bed, if you know what I mean. Some men just have it and some don't, and boy, has Cody Macheris evermore got it!''

Boy, he evermore had, Val conceded silently.

"Of course, Richard has it, too. I remember once under the grandstand during a game—''

Richard? Lanky, silent, beekeeping Richard? Maybe they weren't talking about the same "it."

Later, munching her sandwich with a decided lack of appetite, Val stared out the window into the soft summer evening. The rich scent of roses mingled with the sultry perfume of moon-pale magnolia blossoms, heavy with their own weight. Overgrown crepe myrtles buckled the sidewalks with twisted roots and scattered their colorful confetti on the top of the gray builder's van that was parked at the curb.

Val was restless. The combination of unstable weather and Suzie's gossip had got under her skin, and now she felt herself sinking into a past she thought she'd put behind her.

Albert was gone, she reminded herself for the thousandth time. Val had flown directly to Nebraska for the memorial service and then stayed on another month with his shattered parents to be sure they were going to be all right. Of course she'd never told them that her marriage had been over long before Albert's death.

Suzie had asked how long it had been. How long since which milestone? Since Albert had slipped away without ever recovering consciousness in the hospital at Akrotiri? How long since Val had walked out on the shell of her marriage and gone to Rome to try to pull herself together? Or how long since she'd first discovered that the word "faithfulness" had no place in Albert's vocabulary?

God, just when she thought she'd succeeded in putting the past behind her, a simple thing like a backfiring car or an innocent question could bring it all back again! How could she ever hope to achieve any sort of security at this rate? She'd thought financial security would be her biggest problem, but without emotional security, what good was anything?

"I am going to *do* something about this place," Val declared fervently, feeling a sudden need for physical action. She scowled at the offensive walls. She could either buy enough paint to cover them completely in a lighter color—it would take at least three coats—or enough wallpaper to achieve the same ends. With her luck, she'd botch either approach, and she'd still be stuck with this dismal furniture.

So much for fair-weather friends. Cody had said he'd help her this weekend. Here it was the middle of Saturday, and she had yet to hear a peep out of him. It wasn't the lack of help that bothered her so much as the fact that he'd gone back on his promise.

At least she didn't need help to paint the window trim a bright, fresh white. Somewhere in this town she should be able to find a few grass mats that would do until she could afford the yellow carpet. Robin had wanted her to do the entire window wall with white linen draperies screen-printed in a tropical design, to disguise her oddly placed windows.

Sheer white café curtains at a fraction of that wouldn't have the same impact, nor would they disguise anything, but at least they'd let in lots of sunlight. As for the plants, she'd just try for big and never mind beautiful. If necessary, she'd go out and dig up her own! Now that she'd blundered this far, she might as well go the distance. It would end up costing twice as much to go back to the beginning and start over again.

Statesville, or even the mall out on the highway would have a better selection, but Val decided to settle for Raymond's, which was within easy walking distance. Her car had recently developed digestive problems, along with its other assorted complaints. She'd bought it for practically nothing from a friend of Grace's, and she hated to accuse the man of being a crook, because Grace would get wind of it and feel responsible. But the man *was* a crook. Val had been taken again.

She owed Grace a call, come to think of it. As soon as she'd brightened up her dismal living room, she'd invite her to a celebratory dinner. After that, she'd make a real effort to look up a few more old acquaintances. It was high time she did something about her lack of social life.

Cody stashed his briefcase, tossed his rumpled coat at a chair and poured himself a short drink. It had taken all of Saturday and most of Sunday but he'd made up his mind now. On Monday he would put in a bid on Centry-Ward, a small outfit that manufactured one of the most promising security components on the market. God knows how he'd swing it, but he'd always managed before. Bite off more than you can chew and you either chew a damned sight harder or you choke to death.

At the sound of something scraping overhead, his glance flickered up to the ceiling. She was still here, then. Stuck in Atlanta all weekend, he'd harbored an irrational fear that she might have packed her bags and moved out. After a couple of stiff drinks last night, he even wondered if he'd simply imagined her.

He probably should have left a note under her door before he'd left town. He'd tried to call her at work, but the line had stayed busy for so long he was afraid he'd miss his flight. Once in Atlanta, he'd thought about calling her from the hotel and decided against it. No point in making a big deal out of few days' business trip. Besides, they hadn't had any concrete arrangement. He wasn't obligated to report his comings and goings to her.

His first impulse on getting home was to go upstairs and see if V. Scott was merely a figment of his imagination brought on by too much worry and too little sleep. It was the itch of his late-day beard and the wilted state of his suit and shirt that brought him to his senses. He decided to take the time to shower first, then he'd see if she was still up there. If she was, he might see how she was coming along with her redecorating. He might even mention casually that he hadn't had dinner yet. If she hadn't, either, then...

"Valentine, you're a cool lady, but you play hell with a man's concentration," Cody murmured as he peeled down for a much-needed shower. She was definitely *not* the sort of woman a guy put the move on. Not if he wanted to get somewhere with her.

Did he want to get somewhere with her? Somewhere other than bed? He certainly wanted that so bad he ached with it. Without even trying, he'd memorized every line of that elegant body of hers. For the past three days while he'd gone over every square inch of Centry-Ward property with the Wardner brothers who owned it, her face had drifted in and out of focus at the most inopportune moments. There was still so much he didn't know about her. Yet it was almost as if he'd known her all his life.

She'd hung over his shoulders while he'd examined every facet of the five-man manufacturing operation in Atlanta. Dead tired, he'd go back to his hotel, only to find her waiting there like every man's favorite hallucination, part seductress, part innocent. Always just out of his reach.

What *did* he want from her? At this point, he was damned if he even knew. All he was certain of was that there was something between them that refused to go away, something that got worse, not better. He couldn't recall a single time when he'd been unable to put a woman out of his mind at will. This one refused to be put.

Still damp from the shower, Cody rummaged through his closet for something clean to wear. Jeans? Or something a little dressier, in case she agreed to go out with him? Not too dressy, though, in case she got the wrong idea.

Hell, he was worse than a kid on his first date!

In white boxers and black wool socks, he paused in front of the mirror to frown at the battered visage that scowled back at him. Forty-three. Where had all the years gone? More to the point, what did he have to show for them?

Answers rose in his mind like curls of acrid smoke. An ex-wife he hadn't been able to hang on to and a son who'd managed to grow almost to manhood without much help from him.

The business, of course. From a one-man consulting firm in Atlanta, CMS, Inc. had grown to the point where he was turning down more jobs than he was bidding on, and now he was seriously considering going into debt to expand into manufacturing his own line of security equipment.

Anna had hated the years spent traipsing from one army post to another, living in enlisted men's quarters and even in the officers' quarters after he'd been commissioned. As soon as he could afford to, he'd busted his butt to find her the sort of house she wanted, but it hadn't helped much. They'd reached the point where they'd been unable to talk about anything. After a while, Cody hadn't even wanted to talk.

He'd clammed up whenever she'd started in on him about money, urging him to get out of the military and get into something more lucrative. They'd been over that ground a hundred times. The army had taken him off the streets and straightened him out. It had given him an education, and he owed the service something in exchange. Eric hadn't suffered from traveling around. Cody had made certain of that. It had been the relationship between Cody and Anna that had come close to ruining the boy, and that was why Cody had finally given in to Anna's demands and left the army.

Someone once said it took two to make an argument. That someone had never met Anna. She'd wanted to live in Atlanta, he'd moved there to start his business. He'd gone into hock to buy her the house she wanted, but Anna hadn't been satisfied. She'd been a compulsive spender, and in desperation, Cody had finally made an appointment for both of them with a counselor. The day before they were due to see him, she'd flown to Hawaii with Eric, charging the tickets to CMS, the fledgling company he'd been trying to get started.

He'd let her go. When she'd come back, she'd taken the boy directly to her parents. Cody respected his in-laws. He'd known that the stability of their home was the best thing for Eric at the time, and so he hadn't gone after them. He'd figured that sooner or later, Anna would grow up and things would get better between them.

They never had. After two years he'd agreed to a divorce, and because Anna had not put up too stiff a battle on visitation rights, he'd bent over backward to be fair in the property division. She'd had it all, every damned cent he could scrape up. She would have gutted the company, but even Anna had known better than to kill the goose that laid the golden eggs.

Then she'd married Jack Wright. A large-scale developer, Wright was a decent enough sort—rich as Croesus, but still hustling. He seemed to be genuinely fond of the boy, and Anna was happy for perhaps the first time in her life. It had been a good move as far as she was concerned, and Cody wished her well. Only after that, anything he could offer his son had paled in comparison.

Eric was more man than boy now, and Cody wanted to believe that the values he'd tried to instill in him as a child hadn't been completely compromised by his new life-style. But how could he know? A father couldn't own a son. A man could care until he ached with caring, but in the long run, there was nothing to do except let go. The bond either held or it broke. He might never even know.

So a phase of his life was over. What now? Who did he turn to in the night when the emptiness threatened to get to him, when the thought of his own mortality scared the hell out of him?

Cody uttered a sound of disgust. What he did was he thought damned hard before getting himself mixed up in another no-win situation, that's what he did! Thank God he'd instinctively covered himself there by telling Val up front that he wasn't looking for any sort of commitment.

In which case, why was he moping around here, wallowing in self-pity when there was a good-looking woman upstairs who was probably at loose ends? They could go out to dinner, or they could stay home and work on whatever crazy decorating scheme she'd cooked up while he'd been gone. Either option beat hell out of lying around feeling sorry for himself.

"Valentine Scott," he murmured, savoring the taste of her name on his tongue. She was as different from Anna as night from day. In fact, she was in a class by herself. Like fine porcelain, or the most fragile crystal.

Looking down at his large, callused hands, Cody shook his head. Somehow, he found it hard to picture those hands on something so delicate, so fine. Gray hair, a twice-broken nose, lines around his eyes from too many years of squinting into the pitch-black night or into a blazing sun. He didn't kid himself that he was the answer to any woman's prayer.

So what the devil, if she had something better to do, no big deal—he could handle it.

Quickly, Cody pulled on his best pair of slacks. He located a shirt that was new enough not to have lost any buttons. He was a fair hand in the kitchen, but his mending was something else. Pouring a splash of light cologne on his hands, he slapped the sides of his neck, whistling tunelessly under his breath.

Okay, so after three days of seeing her face come between him and every damned thing he tried to do, it was time he put her into perspective. So he'd skipped out on a promise. He hadn't done it deliberately. Things had come up at the last minute, and he'd had to move fast.

If she held it against him, that was just tough. There were other women in the world.

It occurred to Cody that he hadn't heard a sound from overhead in the past ten or fifteen minutes. What if she'd gone out? What if she already had a date? What if she simply shut the door in his face?

Letting himself out of the apartment, he took the steps two at a time.

Paint spattered and barefooted, Val answered the door, the hollow feeling in her bones warning her in advance. It was Cody. She'd known he was back, known by that sixth sense that seemed to clock his presence like radar.

"Cody? Hi," she said calmly, as if her heart hadn't shifted into overdrive. "Don't tell me the sound of my paintbrush is keeping you awake."

"Hello, Valentine, I had to go out of town on business and I couldn't get in touch before I left," he said in a rush. She was unfastening the chain; that was a good sign. "I was hoping you hadn't had dinner yet. I had lunch at a concession truck, and I could do with something a little more..." His voice trailed off as his gaze tangled with her luminous brown eyes.

Val, an unaccustomed flush of color showing beneath the spray of white spatters on the side of her face, struggled to keep her smile from spreading all over her face. "I don't believe I've ever dined in a concession truck. What's the menu like?"

Cody stood, feet braced apart, thumbs hooked in his hip pockets as a guard against reaching out to touch what he wanted desperately to touch. "One dines *at*, not *in*, a concession truck. As for the menu, I expect a chemical analysis would read like the FDA's most-wanted list. How've you been?'' He'd almost forgotten those wonderful highlights in her hair. Each strand seemed to carry its own halo.

"Fine. And you?''

"I've been fine, too. It's hot as blazes in Atlanta. I tried to call you at work before I left town, but your line was busy and my flight was boarding." He'd known scores of pretty women. This was the first one he'd ever known who could wear white paint on a shiny face and still manage to look incredibly lovely.

"You mean I backed you into a corner and you had to leave town to get out of helping me paint," Val teased. Acutely conscious of her uncombed hair, the makeup she'd never got around to putting on and the way her yellow slacks bagged out in the seat and at the knees, she swung the door wide. Her bare feet were spattered with paint, too.

"Glad to see you're keeping your chain up.''

"I forgot it only once, Cody. Believe me, I don't make a habit of it."

"Well, don't. The security in this old place is a farce.''

"So why don't you sell them a system?" Val filled her hungry eyes with the hard length of his body, the fascinating arrangement of his rough-cut features.

"What, and have them raise my rent? Besides, what have I got that anyone would want to steal?''

"Same here." Val indicated the stack of packages on the sofa and the jungle of potted plants clearly visible through the bathroom door. "I've plundered my budget for months to come for enough white enamel to do the window trim, some white curtains and tons of greenery. Do you have any idea how expensive houseplants are? My rugs will just have to wait.''

"From the looks of things, you've been working hard. I think you've earned that steak dinner tonight, don't you?" Cody found himself wanting to touch her, to wipe away the perspiration that beaded her temples. The sight of those damp patches under her arms and between the shoulder blades on her shirt stirred a powerful hunger in his loins. He managed to fight it to a draw.

"I still have one window to go. I suppose it could wait until later, but I couldn't go anywhere like this."

"You look wonderful." He truly meant it.

"I'm filthy," Val said with a laugh. She'd started painting as soon as she'd got back from Raymond's Variety, stopping only for a big glass of iced tea at noon.

"Are you washable?" Giving in to temptation, Cody touched one of the speckles on her cheek.

"With a lot of soaking and some scrubbing with a stiff brush. Now that you mention it, though, I am starved. Can you wait a few minutes? I'll hurry."

"Or I could help," he offered hopefully. Something in her face warned him, and he rushed to add, "By washing paintbrushes and closing up your can, I mean."

"Put a newspaper over the can before you step on the lid so it won't splatter. Fifteen minutes, all right?"

"You got it." Pink and yellow, she lighted up the dismal room like a tall, slender candle, Cody mused, his gaze following her as she moved toward the bedroom.

Adjusting the water temperature, Val ran through a mental inventory of the dresses hanging in her closet and found them all lamentably wanting. She'd hemmed and refurbished enough outfits to wear to work, but suddenly nothing seemed quite right. They all seemed so tired. Just as she was tired—tired of packing and unpacking the same old things year after year. Maybe there was something to be said for buying less expensive things and changing them more often, especially now that she was through traveling and settled for good.

In the end, she chose a pair of white sharkskin slacks and an emerald silk shirt she'd bought in New Bond Street during the few months they'd lived in London. The slacks were too loose, but with pleats pinned into the waistband and hidden by a yellow suede cummerbund, they hung well enough.

A scant eighteen minutes later, she presented herself in the living room, feeling unreasonably self-conscious.

Cody unfolded himself from her dark green chair, his eyes glowing as they moved slowly over the supple length of her.

"Will I do?" Val asked hesitantly. How many times had she asked that question in the past eighteen years? How many times had she been told that her hair was not right, or her makeup too obvious? How many times had she allowed her husband to humiliate her before she'd finally learned that the more critical he'd been of her, the more guilty his own conscience had been.

"Lady, anything I could say would be an understatement. You look beautiful, but I'm afraid I've forgotten all the proper ways of saying so."

To her dismay, Val felt a distinct prickling under her eyelids. The lack of food was telling on her. "I don't think there's an improper way of telling a woman she looks beautiful," her reply came softly. "Thank you."

Neither of them spoke while she collected her purse and a yellow cotton cardigan. Cody held the door and checked the lock as automatically as he would his own.

"You have a choice of seafood or steak. Or, if you're really in a rush, there's always burgers and fries."

Val laughed, suddenly exhilarated by the promising caress of the soft summer air. "Maybe I should warn you, Cody, I wasn't kidding when I said my budget's shot for the month. If I'm buying, hamburgers and fries will be lovely. If you're buying, the seafood sounds interesting."

Cody tucked her arm under his and steered her toward the tenants' parking lot. "At least you're honest," he observed wryly.

"Oh, at the very least," Val assured him.

Cody was silent for several moments while he negotiated the two block distance of Lakesboro's modest business district. "Seafood it is, then," he declared. He signaled a right turn, then changed it to left at the corner of the second block. He'd had every intention of driving to Charlotte to an excellent French restaurant where the rainbow trout was grilled in herb butter until it melted in your mouth. He knew damned well that in spite of her present circumstances, Valentine Scott was accustomed to the best. It stood out in the way she talked, the way she dressed, in a hundred subtle things he'd noticed about her.

Instead, acting on an impulse that he didn't even try to understand, he headed for the local fish camp, one of those family-type places where the tablecloths were paper, the food was fried and the choice of beverages limited to presweetened iced tea or coffee.

Two hours later, Valentine leaned back against the scarred wooden bench and closed her eyes. "Cody, if you *ever* do this to me again, I'll never forgive you. I just finished taking in my whole wardrobe, and now I'm going to have to let everything out again."

Cody's grin was slow and satisfied. "The staff's probably on the phone right now alerting every all-you-can-eat place in four counties, warning them against you."

"Well, I was hungry."

"Yeah, I noticed," he said lazily.

A boy of about five wandered past and gave them a curious look. He had a dab of red on one cheek, and Val resisted the urge to take him on her lap and wipe his face. Cody greeted the child with grave politeness, and he grinned shyly and darted away.

"Was that blood or catsup on his cheek?" Cody asked. "At that age, you can never be sure."

Val glanced at the table on the other side of the barnlike room where the child was tugging at a woman's skirt. "Probably catsup. You don't happen to know them, do you? The woman looks familiar, but I can't tell from here."

"I've seen her around town." Cody dismissed the thin woman who had turned and was staring at them while the child tugged at her skirt. "Think you can make it as far as the car?"

Val groaned. "If you're embarrassed to be seen with such a glutton, why don't you go on ahead? I'll stop by the ladies' room and follow you out after a discreet interval."

She was peering into the mirror to touch up her lipstick when the woman came through the door and paused behind her.

"It's Beetle Whichard, isn't it? I forgot your married name."

Val's gaze took in the tired face, the badly permed black hair and the faint look of resentment. "Tricia?" she hazarded. "I almost didn't recognize you." Hardly a tactful observation, since Tricia Rice—now Tricia Canfield—had been the most beautiful girl in school.

She'd been queen of everything from May to homecoming, and everyone had expected her to take Hollywood by storm.

Instead, she'd eloped right after graduation. Seven months later, her daughter Melanie had been born.

"Was that your little boy who came by our table? He's darling. That was just catsup on his cheek, wasn't it?" It seemed to Val that some of the resentment seemed to fade from the thin face then. Perhaps she'd only imagined it.

"Yeah, it's catsup. He's at the stage where he won't sit still long enough to get his face and hands wiped."

"I didn't know you had a little boy." Had Suzie mentioned it? She hadn't really paid much attention.

"He's Melanie's. They're staying with me while Melanie gets her nursing degree."

"Your *grandson*? Tricia, I can't believe it!"

"Oh, you can believe it, all right. *Some* of us weren't lucky enough to get to travel all over the world. *Some* of us," she said with a disdainful shrug, "had to make do with what's right here at home. I saw you in the store today. You should have waited," she went on with a smile as brittle as broken glass. "Everything's going on sale next week. Raymond's is closing down for good."

"Tricia, I'm so sorry," Val murmured sincerely.

"Oh, don't worry about me. I can take care of myself. God knows, I've been doing it long enough."

Chapter Five

With his hand branding her back through the silk of her shirt, Cody ushered Val up the rubber-treaded stairway, took the key from her fingers and unlocked her door. Neither of them made a move to enter. Cody didn't ask to come in, and Val told herself she was glad. It was as if a mutually considered decision had been reached.

"It's been a tough weekend," he said obliquely.

"Me, too," Val agreed, not wanting the evening to end, yet knowing that it must. If he came inside with her now, she couldn't be held accountable for her actions, not when all in the world she wanted to do was to fall into his arms and explore the boundaries of this strange intoxication that had been growing since the moment he'd appeared at her door.

"Have I made up for not following through on my promise?" With a quizzical smile, Cody braced himself on the wall with one hand. He didn't touch her, and Val shifted her purse and her sweater restlessly from hand to hand until finally he took them from her, looped the strap of her gray bag over the doorknob and hung the sweater from it.

"Your promise?" she echoed, staring blindly at a subtle pattern on his white shirt. It dawned on her gradually what she was seeing was the shadow of his chest hair, and she jerked her gaze away.

"I promised to help you paint your windows."

"You can make up for it by helping me hang curtains when I've finished painting the other one. Then there's the kitchen..." His breath warmed her hair, and Val knotted her fingers behind her back. The scent of his cologne stirred her senses, whispering silently of oakmoss and leather and sandalwood.

Cody's eyes touched on her mouth, fell to her breasts, which were showing definite signs of agitation, and then returned to her lips. He didn't say a word.

Distracted, Val tried to focus her mind on the mundane matter of interior decoration. "The cabinets wouldn't let me paint the—I mean, the super won't let me paint the cabinets," she blurted. "Satin varnish—something in pine, and maybe wallpaper everywhere else. How—how are you at wallpapering?"

"Willing," he murmured equably. "But not very able. I come unglued and so does the paper."

"I can't picture you draped in wallpaper. Maybe... I can find a pattern that goes well with your... coloring...." Val's voice tapered off as her mind ceased functioning. Neither of them spoke. Neither of them moved. Val wondered if he could hear the sound of her heartbeat.

"I suppose I'd better be going," Cody said reluctantly after an eternity. "It really has been a tough weekend."

As far as Val was concerned, he could have been speaking in Swahili for all the relation his words bore to the chaotic feelings that were sweeping through her.

It was with a feeling of inevitability that she lifted her face. Cody completed the ritual, closing the distance between them. "Ah, Valentine," he whispered almost despairingly as his mouth came down gently on her parted lips. Then there was no more talking, no more thinking, only a rare magic that seemed to cocoon them in its shimmering spell.

At first it was only a brushing of lips, as tentative as the wings of a butterfly. Standing before him, her hands still knotted behind her back, Val felt the force of him wash over her—the controlled strength, the gentleness, the sheer masculine magnetism.

Gentleness began to give way to passion, strength quickly outstripped control, and two tense bodies strained together, softness to hardness, bowing to arching. Val felt the heavy drumming of her heart echoed in Cody's breast. She knew a single moment of panic at the sheer power this man held over her, but it was quickly gone.

Cody explored the secrets of her mouth, even as his hands began to explore the secrets of her body. The tips of his fingers followed the shallow valley of her spine until it flowed out onto the plane of her lower back, then slid the smooth fabric of her slacks over a scrap of nylon and a band of satiny skin. He pressed her to him, telling her silently of his growing need.

One large palm slid up to capture her breast, and Val's heart fluttered wildly when she felt her sensitive flesh grow taut with a corresponding need. Her arms tightened around him, her hands sliding over the supple strength of his back.

"You're beginning to haunt my dreams, do you know that?" Cody whispered, smiling down at her through eyes that glittered like dark agates. He shaped the curve of her jawline with thumb and forefinger, his touch as delicate as if he were handling an infinitely fragile treasure.

Val covered his hands with hers. Restlessly, greedily, she touched his face, letting her fingers trail down the sides of his powerful neck and curve out onto his shoulders. She couldn't get enough of the feel of him, the warm, solid strength of his sinewy body. Her hands slipped up his sides to burrow under his arms, and she felt the swelling of his chest as he inhaled sharply.

"God, the touch of your hands drives me crazy. I want them all over me...please." He pressed her tightly against him, soft belly to hardening loins, chest to throbbing breast, groaning softly as he buried his face in her hair.

Deep in the very core of her being, Val felt something cold and heavy begin to give way. She knew a feeling of release, as if the ice of a hundred winters had finally succumbed to the warmth of a new season.

But sudden thaws could be dangerous, she reminded herself. The waters that flowed beneath the ice were treacherous—they could rise swiftly to flood levels, sweeping away the unwary. Dare she allow herself to melt so quickly? To trust so completely?

No, not yet. Maybe never. "Cody, please," she whispered miserably, hating what she had to do.

Instantly, his arms fell. He stepped back, and Val knew a moment of acute disappointment. He didn't have to give up *that* readily.

"Is this your definition of friendship, Cody? You must have a more liberal dictionary than I do." She struggled to regain the ground she'd lost, hiding behind the flimsy shield of banter.

Raking a hand across the back of his neck, Cody countered with a suggestion. "Maybe we could write our own dictionary."

Oh, Lord, it wasn't going to work. With that brindled hair of his flopping over his forehead, it was all Val could do to keep her hands to herself. How could she convince him she didn't want to make love with him when she couldn't convince her own body?

She could run away and then spend the rest of her life hiding. Or she could confess her weakness and throw herself on his mercy. Val made a snap decision. She'd lay it on the line, put him on his honor, so to speak. If the man had a shred of common decency, he couldn't very well take advantage of her after that, could he?

"Cody, you're not playing fair. You must know I'm attracted to you—I'm obviously not very good at hiding it. If you pressed for a—an affair, I'd probably give in, too, because I haven't learned yet how to deal with this situation."

She paused, giving him a chance to say something. To say *anything*. Instead, he continued to regard her with that maddening look of detached interest she'd noticed in him before. Val gritted her teeth and wondered how any mature, reasonably intelligent woman could get herself into such an awkward position.

Ignoring the heat that rose up to stain her throat, she forged ahead. "Look, I just don't think I could handle an affair with you, that's all. Regardless of what you say, I'm not willing to take the risk. If you don't care for plain speaking, then I'm sorry, but I happen to hate subterfuge." Without waiting now for him to respond, she hurried on. "Maybe I'm overreacting, but I happen to be feeling extremely insecure right now, because I'm living a lie at work. It was the only way I knew to get a job that would pay a living wage, and now that I've started the damned charade, I'm stuck with it."

She was babbling, a sure sign that she was coming apart at the seams. Valentine Scott *never* babbled. Her unflappable poise was one of her greatest assets, according to her late husband.

Well, Valentine Scott had evidently entered a new phase. She was just going to have to do the best she could with the few assets that remained in her possession, one of which was the courage not to duck the issue confronting her. Hiding her head wouldn't make it go away. The best way, the *only* way, to deal with the situation was to bring it out into the open.

"Well?" she challenged when he continued to study her as if she were some new and mildly interesting form of insect life.

"Clue me in, will you? Are we discussing the fact that you can't type, or the fact that we're two adults who live under the same roof, and who would like very much to make love to each other? Somewhere along the line I seem to have missed a beat."

Val leaned over, backside against the wall, and braced her palms on her knees. Feet together, she stared down at the tips of her pumps, wondering how she could have regressed so far, so fast.

"Look, this is as embarrassing for me as it is for you." Without glancing up, she continued to address her gray wing-tipped pumps. "Maybe I didn't put things too well, but that doesn't change matters." Steeling herself, she faced him unflinchingly. "It might sound crazy to you, Cody, but it makes perfect sense to me. Did you see the mother wren trying to teach her babies to fly in the dogwood tree out front?"

"Dogwood," Cody muttered sagely. "I'm trying to follow this, honey, I really am, but you're not making it easy for me." In spite of the look of perplexity on his face, his voice held a note of tender concern that was almost her undoing. The last thing she needed at this point was tenderness and concern!

"All I'm trying to say is that I fell out of my nest without so much as a pinfeather to my name, and I've *got* to learn to fly before I hit the ground. The ground's coming up too fast, Cody. My age, my training—or lack of it—these things don't help, you know. The very last thing I need now is a false sense of security."

The door between them yawned open in silent mockery. A few moments ago, their entering together could have had but one outcome. At least that particular danger had been dealt with, Val thought tiredly. There was nothing like making a fool of oneself to defuse a sexually explosive situation.

Bracing one elbow in the palm of his hand, Cody stoked his jaw thoughtfully. "I'm keeping you from learning to fly by giving you a false sense of security, is that what you're trying to tell me?"

"You could put it that way," Val said with a sigh. Emotional exhaustion piled onto physical exhaustion, and she sagged. "Look, let's just be neighbors, Cody. We borrow cups of sugar from each other, pass the time of day if we happen to run into each other in the lobby, but that's as far as it goes, agreed?"

With a sweeping glance that took in her slender, wilting form, Cody nodded. "For now," he agreed. "But keep in mind two things, honey—any sugar that passes between us will be freely given. Not borrowed, not stolen." He smiled then, and it was as if the sun had suddenly peeped over the horizon. "And you still owe me an explanation when you're feeling a little more coherent."

All of which left Val feeling more insecure than ever. There was a subtle threat in there somewhere, but at the moment she was too tired to argue. "Well... Just as long as I've made my position clear," she temporized.

Cody laughed softly. "Go to bed, honey. We'll hash it out another time."

Hash it out another time? Val repeated the words silently a moment later as she leaned against the inside of her door, listening to his footsteps descend the stairs. But wasn't that what they'd just done—hashed it out, as he so poetically put it?

Sniffing the fumes from the freshly painted window, she wrinkled her nose and wandered through her gloomy living room, snapping on lights as she went. To protect them from fumes and spatters, she had put Ollie in the bathroom with the jungle of plants she'd bought at the farmers' market. There was hardly room for her to squeeze through to the lavatory.

"We'll get you guys out of here just as soon as I've painted the other window," she promised, reaching for her cleansing cream.

Why did everything have to be so complicated? The muscles at the back of her neck were as hard as spring steel. She was growing distinctly uneasy about her job; what if she wasn't cut out to be a secretary?

She couldn't unload her worries on Grace, not as long as her cousin was determined to marry her off to that widowered orthopedic shoe manufacturer. As if that weren't bad enough, she couldn't even unwind in her own apartment because, like an idiot, she'd let herself be talked into this bizarre decorator's nightmare.

Either Robin had a macabre sense of humor or he was out to drive her mad. Wynn was probably behind the whole conspiracy, else why had he hired her?

Oh, great, Valentine, bring on the old paranoia! Of course, her car had been deliberately sabotaged so that she'd have to walk to work, which meant that the gray van she'd been seeing all over town wasn't really a building contractor's van, but a surveillance crew. CIA, Interpol, *polizia*...

Peering into the mirror, Val examined a fresh wisp of gray in the fine hair at her temples. "On top of everything else, you had to go and get yourself involved with Cody Macheris." She sighed. "Great. Oh, that's just marvelous, Valentine!"

Women were supposed to be the stronger sex, according to an article she'd read somewhere. They were supposed to be able to deal more efficiently with stress and cope more efficiently with business and personal relationships. So why was she feeling more alone and frightened and inadequate with every passing day? Why this demeaning urge to hurl herself into Cody's strong, sheltering arms and let him take care of her?

Was it a lover she wanted or a crutch? How could she be sure?

Grace Whichard sank her teeth into a second fried drumstick, munching as she studied her younger cousin speculatively. Only when she'd polished the bone to her satisfaction did she speak her mind.

"All right, missy, you're looking about as pert as last week's boiled dinner. What's wrong? Job? I told you you'd never get away with it. Believe me, there's a darned sight more to being a secretary than most folks realize. Didn't I run Horace McGuffy's office for twenty-seven years?"

"I'm doing all right. Wynn seems satisfied."

"Hmmph! Men. Give some of 'em a pretty face, and—"

"Oh, good Lord, Grace, it's nothing like that and you know it. Wynn's wife is one of the loveliest women I know. And one of the happiest."

"Just goes to show you, when a woman's been married as long as you were, she's better off having a man to look after her."

"How would you know?" Val broke in, stung into uncharacteristic tactlessness.

"I know a darned sight more than I get credit for," Grace snapped back.

"But a darned sight less than you think you do." Val regretted the words the minute they were uttered. Her nerves were strung up like a fiddle, but that was no reason to take it out on someone else. "Grace, I'm sorry."

"Me, too. We both know I enjoy meddling. You're still hurting, aren't you, honey? You told me you'd already left Albert when that awful business happened, and I guess I just thought you were all over it."

Val had felt such a deep need to share some of the horror of what she'd been through that she'd unburdened herself as far as she'd dared. She'd told Grace about Albert's unfaithfulness. Not the extent of it, nor the brutal way in which he'd bragged about it just before she'd left him, but enough so that her cousin wouldn't keep making those embarrassing references to her bereavement.

Because she hadn't felt bereaved. She'd come to terms with the loss of her husband a lot more quickly than she had with Albert's corruption and the breakdown of her marriage. She was still working on the latter, but it was all tied up with her worth as a person, as a woman.

"Oh, all right," she said now, "so I'm not the world's greatest secretary. Give me time. I'm up to moderately fast with shocking errors or moderately slow with minor typos."

"Must be a real comfort to your boss," Grace said dryly. "Well, if the strain gets too much for you, Charles is still asking about you. We play Scrabble a lot, and he was wondering just last night if there were any new men in your life."

The paper napkin disintegrated in Val's fingers. "What did you tell him?"

Grace shoved her scarlet-rimmed bifocals up into curly gray hair. "What could I tell him? You certainly haven't been spending your spare time with me." If there was a note of censure in the words, Val ignored it. "For all I know, you could be seeing a dozen men, but believe me, you're making a mistake if you pass up a solid catch like Charles for some flash in the pan."

"If he's such a great catch, why don't you grab him yourself?"

"Too set in my ways to want a man underfoot now, but I don't mind telling you, the day Charles Reedy moved into the old Pritchette place next door and told me he was all alone in the world but for those two girls of his, I said to myself, 'now there's a good man just waiting for the right woman to come along.'" She bobbed her head several times, endangering her glasses, and Val waited for them to slide off. "Thought about introducing him to Tricia Canfield, but they'd never have hit it off. Turned sour, poor girl. Can't say I blame her. Rotten luck. First that scamp she married, then that daughter of hers. Oh, is that lemon chess pie? Honey, you shouldn't have!"

Over pie and coffee they reminisced, with Grace doing most of the talking and Val content to listen. If now and then her mind tended to stray, Grace was evidently none the wiser. By the time the older woman stirred herself to leave, Val was feeling considerably more relaxed.

Actually, it had been an unexpected treat. She'd planned to wait until her apartment looked more presentable before inviting her cousin to visit, but Grace had driven to town for Sunday dinner with Lucy and ended up inviting herself to supper with Valentine.

Before Val had finished putting away the dishes, the phone rang. Her mind immediately flew to Cody. Patting her hair, she dashed into the living room and snatched it up on the third ring.

"Valentine? Lucy MacIntire. Grace mentioned something that set me to thinking," the older woman said without preamble. "You speak several languages, don't you?"

"Why...yes, as a matter of fact, I do," Val admitted, wondering if her linguistic abilities had been all Grace had divulged. In her years abroad, she'd forgotten Lakesboro's biggest industry: gossip. It was the feminine equivalent of sitting around talking about going fishing. "French, some German, Spanish. I can get by in a few others in a pinch."

"How'd you like to earn a little extra money?"

How would I like to go on breathing? Val asked herself, gazing around at the miserable sofa, the pathetic old chair and the naked floors. "I don't know enough to teach any of them," she said cautiously.

"Nobody asked you to teach. More 'n' more I get asked about translating for some of the businesses over in Statesville. They're commencing to get downright international these days."

"Who usually translates for them?" Val asked, allowing herself to feel a certain cautious elation at the prospect of picking up a few extra dollars.

"Language teachers, mostly, but school's out. Most of 'em gone for the summer. In my day, they taught Latin in all the schools, but things are different now. Anyhow, Grace mentioned your name. If you're interested, stop by to see me next week. 'Bye."

Val was left with a click and a dial tone. She smiled bemusedly. Miss Lucy hadn't changed at all since her days of teaching Sunday school at Riverside Methodist. The fact that Val had won a perfect attendance pin had had more to do with her fear of Miss Lucy's sharp tongue than any great religious fervor.

The following day, her purse was stolen.

It was her own fault for being so careless, but that didn't make it any easier to take. "Cody, I just turned my back for a minute, a single minute," Val exclaimed to the man who'd been waiting when she'd finally got home.

"All right, from the beginning," he said patiently after the super had let them into her apartment. "You were on your way home, and you stopped by Suzie's and—"

"And halfway home, one of my bags started leaking. I should have gone back for another bag, but you know how it is—I was in a hurry, and there was the usual going-home crowd," she explained tiredly.

"Yeah, all two dozen of them," Cody supplied, heading for the kitchen to fill the coffee maker.

"Do you want to listen, or do you want to make snide remarks?" She was feeling utterly drained, not up to dealing with Cody's idea of wit.

"Sorry, honey. How many measures for four cups?"

"Four," she said shortly. "Anyhow, someone bumped my arm, and the damned sack broke open and dill pickle juice went all down my skirt, my purse, and even into my shoes! I started wiping with a scarf, and I sat the rest of my things down on the hood of a car that was parked at the curb, and the next thing I knew, my purse was missing. Not the bag with the feta cheese and the dill pickles, just my purse."

The homey sound of a gurgling coffee maker filled the room, at odds with the stark indigo walls and the carnivorous looking plants grouped into one corner.

"And then you called the sheriff."

Val shook her head.

"You went by the sheriff's office," Cody prompted.

"No, I did *not* call the sheriff and I did *not* go by his office," Val declared. "I went back to Suzie's to see if maybe I'd left my purse there. I thought I'd had it. I could have sworn I had it with me, but you never know."

"*Then* you reported it to the sheriff."

"Look, for your information, I had exactly thirteen dollars, an international driver's license, one lipstick and my keys. No credit cards, no valuables. Whoever risked snatching the thing in broad daylight is in for a major disappointment.''

"Dammit, Valentine, you don't just let something like that go without reporting it," Cody said, slamming two mugs onto the counter.

"I do," she retorted calmly. Not that she had any intention of dragging up her past, but she'd had quite enough of law enforcement agencies to last her a lifetime. She even had, now that she came to think of it, a number scribbled on a scrap of paper tucked away under a shoebox on her closet shelf. It had been given to her by an intelligence agent in case she ever thought of something she'd forgotten to tell him. Or found herself in a situation that made her uneasy.

A panic number, Meekins had called it. He'd been her constant shadow for so long, a combination interrogator, bodyguard and mother hen. She never wanted to see his flat, homely face again as long as she lived.

"Drink this," Cody growled, shoving a mug of steaming coffee into her hands. "Val, you can't stay here tonight. I'll have your locks changed first thing tomorrow, and as for your car—"

"Don't worry about my car. If they can move it, they can have it."

His smile was a little grim, but it warmed her nevertheless. Wrapping her hands around the pottery mug, she realized for the first time that she was shivering.

"Look, honey, it's routine in a case like this. Someone out there has a set of your keys."

"I've still got a safety chain."

"And whoever has your keys probably has a pair of bolt cutters. We'll swap, okay? You take my bed, I'll take yours. If he comes looking for a soft touch, he'll get slightly more than he bargained for."

"Oh, good heavens, if you're going to be stubborn about it, I'll call Grace," Val grumbled. She didn't want to call Grace. Besides, what good would a call do? She had no way of getting to Sherrill Ford, and no way of getting back to town in time for work tomorrow.

Cody lifted her feet and sat down beside her on the sofa, carefully leaving enough space between them to keep from alarming her. She was covering beautifully, but she was in a bad way. Over thirteen bucks? He rather thought not. There must have been something else in that bag, something of value to someone. Why else would she be pale and trembling, and too upset even to go to the sheriff? It didn't add up.

"Look, Val, there are clean sheets on my bed, my cleaning woman was in today, so you can just grab a gown and a toothbrush and settle in. I'll pick up something to eat for both of us, but if you don't feel like company, just say so. I'll understand."

Like hell he would, Cody thought. There was already too much he didn't understand, not the least of which was the way he reacted whenever he was around her. Against all odds, he found himself wanting to cup her face in the palm of his hands and breathe color back into those pale, fragile cheeks.

"Oh, Cody," Val protested with an unsuccessful attempt to laugh. "Don't be so nice to me. I'll—I'll probably end up crying all over your nice white shirt." She lifted the mug with unsteady hands and then shuddered as she sampled the bitter brew. "God, you make strong coffee!"

"You needed it. So go ahead and cry—what's a shirt between friends?" He was more touched than he dared admit at the small crack in her painfully brittle armor.

A little desperately, Val made another attempt to change the subject. "Why do you always wear white shirts? You were wearing one the first time I ever saw you, remember?"

"Yeah, I probably was. If you must know, I've been told that my taste in shirts is pretty bad, so I tend to play it safe."

For a moment, Val almost forgot her own problems. "Who would have told you that, even if it was true?"

"My ex-wife," Cody replied dryly. "I was wearing a uniform when I met Anna. She liked uniforms, but once I started wearing civvies, she wasn't too impressed. Anna put a lot of stock in appearances—the more something cost, the better she liked it. I'd have worn silk and cashmere uniforms if she'd had her way." He chuckled, shaking his head ruefully. "It was just one of a hundred things we disagreed about, but that's water under the bridge."

No longer quite so cold now, Val placed her mug on the coffee table and examined the creamy gabardine shirt Cody wore with his flawlessly cut tan slacks. His gleaming cordovans were of excellent quality, conservative, but comfortable looking. "Did your wife choose the things you're wearing now?"

"Nope. I've been buying my own clothes for years now, believe it or not." He grinned modestly, and Val felt a swell of emotion so powerful that it actually hurt. "It's easy once you get the hang of it. You just go to a good clothier and throw yourself on his mercy. Once in a while I might get a bum steer, but what the hell, Anna's not around to rub my nose in it, thank God. As long as I'm comfortable, I don't care much what I have on."

At least he hadn't until recently, Cody added silently.

"My late husband was a firm believer in dressing for effect," Val said quietly. "He spent a fortune on his back, much more than I ever did, and I bought nice clothes." She shrugged. "It all seems so irrelevant, doesn't it?"

Cody nodded in silent assent. Stretching his legs, he leaned back against the inhospitable cold plastic. "In other words, clothes don't make the man, is that what you're saying?"

"If they did, I might still be married to Albert Scott." She shivered.

Cupping her knees with her hands, Val stared at her whitened knuckles until Cody's hand covered hers. He studied her averted profile for several moments, and then said gently, "Valentine, level with me. What's going on around here? Are you all right?"

Chapter Six

Val lifted her head abruptly and stared at him. "Of course I'm all right! Or as all right as anyone can be when they've just had their purse snatched."

"Feeling nervous?"

"No, I'm feeling angry... and *violated*!" Strangely enough, she felt more indignant than anything else. The other thing—the bombing—had been far too violent and terrible in its consequences to be taken personally. It had been more like a sudden, devastating storm, even after she'd learned that it had been directed at Albert, either in an attempt to frighten him into compliance, or as an object lesson to anyone else who thought he could break out of the arms-smuggling chain and go it alone.

Stealing her purse was personal. She'd bought that gray calf bag at Selfridges for her thirty-sixth birthday gift to herself, and it had been with her through the past two horrendous years.

"Then will you please go and collect your nightie and whatever else you need while I report this business to the sheriff?" Cody went on before she could interrupt him. "Look, Valentine, if some creep is running around hitting on women, Craddock needs to know about it. Maybe the next woman won't get off so easy. Maybe the punk will decide to take more than her money."

Val swallowed hard, feeling shame wash over her. "You're right, of course, I just wasn't thinking. Call from here, Cody, and then if I need to add anything, I can get it over with."

"You'll probably have to go by the sheriff's office sometime tomorrow, but that's no problem, is it? Joe Craddock's a pretty good guy—knows his business, sticks to the point. He's not the type to throw his weight around, election year or not."

In the end, it was surprisingly painless. Craddock knew who she was, although Val didn't remember him. "Tell Miss Grace I said hello, will you? We still miss her around these parts since she moved over to Sherrill Ford."

Val, clutching her pajamas, a short robe and her toilet case, agreed to pass on his regards. Hanging up the phone, she sighed and turned a challenging look on Cody. "All right, I've done my duty as a citizen. Are you satisfied? *Now* may I go somewhere and indulge in a quiet bout of hysterics?"

Cody's expression was above suspicion as he ushered her downstairs to his apartment. All the same, Val decided that she'd have her dinner alone tonight, and then she'd go right to bed. Also alone. And if he didn't understand why she couldn't trust herself in his company after a day like today, then she'd spell it out for him.

Only the issue never arose. Half an hour later, Cody rapped on the door of his own apartment, waiting for her to open it instead of simply letting himself inside. Val appreciated his tactfulness. She was more shaken than she'd realized.

"Brought you some dinner from Suzie's. She sends her sympathy and an extra big hunk of chocolate cheesecake to cheer you up."

"How on earth did Suzie know?"

Patiently, Cody explained. "You went back to see if you'd left your purse at the deli, remember?"

Val hunched her shoulders, hands clasped in her lap as she sought a semblance of composure. "I've been trying to put the whole rotten episode out of my mind. Looks as if I succeeded, doesn't it?" Her smile wouldn't have convinced even the most casual onlooker, and Cody was hardly that.

"You also succeeded in forgetting the local grapevine. At least a dozen people saw what happened, but nobody actually saw who bumped into you or who made off with your bag. By now, half the town's convinced there's an international crime ring operating right here in Lakesboro."

Val's smile quivered at the edges and fell away. She wrapped her arms around her body and stared at a worn place in the bronze carpet. Cody might laugh about it, but the past was still too recent and too raw for Val to share the joke.

After one long, discerning look, Cody took her shoulders in a firm grip. "Hey, little Valentine, cheer up. It's over now. You're home safe."

"I *hate* things like this," she said intensely, turning her head so as not to be seduced by the false promise of security he seemed to be offering by his very kindness.

"I've got just the medicine for you," Cody went on. He brushed her hair behind her ear and then tilted her chin until she could avoid his eyes no longer.

With every cell of her body alive to his virile appeal, Val waited almost in relief for the inevitable proposition. It was bound to happen. At least tonight she had a passable excuse not to want to sleep alone.

"When's the last time you went cane-pole fishing?"

"Wha-a-at?" she crowed disbelievingly.

"You know, the poor man's meditation? You take a scruffy old wooden boat and about a three-horse outboard, find a quiet cove and drop anchor. And then you bait a hook and dangle it over the side and wait. If you're lucky, they won't rise to your bait right away. That means you can lie back with your eyelids at half mast and stare at your cork until the whole world disappears. Best thing in the world to put your problems into perspective."

Val stared at him in openmouthed wonder until, with a gentle nudge, he lifted her chin. "How about it, hmm? If you think you can hang in there until Saturday morning, I'll reserve us a boat at the marina."

To Val's amazement, she discovered that the idea had enormous appeal. Small-time muggers, CIA types, sheriffs—they could all go take a flying leap. Valentine was going fishing.

Val provided a portable snack, Cody a carton of red wigglers and an ice chest filled with drinks. The cane poles came with the rented boat, he told her, and Val was thoroughly delighted with the whole prospect. Out on the main body of Lake Norman, sleek pleasure craft of all types could be seen taking advantage of the flawless weather. There were scores of wind surfers and water skiers, a few powerful cruisers and even an authentic Chinese junk.

"Watch how you toss your gear aboard, lady," Cody warned, stowing Val's new straw purse and the picnic basket before helping her into the battered old wooden skiff. "Don't scratch the teak. I had to pay extra for the use of this baby—genuine wood, not an inch of fiberglass on her."

Val examined the scruffy looking boat, with its peeling green paint and makeshift appointments. "This isn't the same boat Bogart and Hepburn used in *The African Queen*, is it?" she asked guilelessly. "No, on second thought, theirs was a later model." As she settled herself on the middle seat, it occurred to her that the shorts might have been a mistake. The sky was completely cloudless and her thighs were still parchment pale.

"Another crack like that and next time I'll get us one of those flashy bass boats with the sequined finish and the wall-to-wall carpet."

"And a thousand-horsepowered engine so we can hurry and get to a nice, relaxed fishing spot," Val added, eyes dancing as she watched him crank the outboard.

It caught after only a dozen or so tries, and Cody guided the dilapidated skiff away from the marina. Val allowed her gaze to wander admiringly over his hard, fit body in the ancient khakis and a threadbare white shirt. It was obvious from the skill with which he maneuvered their lumbering craft past the gently dancing row of gleaming hulls that he knew precisely what he was doing and where he was going.

Which was more than Val could say. Relaxing, she began to soak up the breeze-cooled sunshine, her eyes lingering on the tanned and capable hand at the tiller. She no longer bothered to hide from herself the fact that she wanted to feel those hands on her body, guiding her with the same sure touch.

Did all women look at strange men and wonder what they'd be like in bed, or was this recent aberration peculiar to her? She'd never slept with any man except Albert. From the very beginning, the physical part of their marriage had been a disappointment to her. She'd blamed it on her lack of experience at first, but things hadn't improved much as Albert's impatience had gradually turned into boredom.

Sleeping in Cody's bed, she'd hugged his pillow to her, wanting him there beside her with a fierce heat that was shocking to recall under the noonday sun. If she had a grain of common sense, she'd have thought of some excuse not to come along. A day alone together in a small boat? Just the two of them? Val shook her head in disbelief. Nothing like playing with fire.

Behind a pair of oversized sunglasses, her eyes lingered on the heavy musculature of Cody's chest before moving downward over a hard, flat stomach. He was sprawled in the stern of the boat, one arm resting along the tiller, one foot propped against the ice chest. The worn khakis hugged his sinewy thighs with a faithfulness that made her stir restlessly, and as her imagination caught fire, Val felt a rush of heat steal over her entire body, rising last of all to her cheeks. Abruptly, she jerked her gaze away.

"Getting too much sun?" Cody inquired solicitously.

"Sun," she repeated. Thank God for sunglasses. He might suspect, but he couldn't actually know. "I brought along some sun screen. I think." Grateful for something to do, she fumbled inside her colorful straw bag, finally coming up with the protective lotion.

"Want some?" she offered after slathering a layer over her legs, her arms and last of all, her burning face. "Not that you look as if you need it."

"Afraid my hide's too tough to benefit from cosmetics at this late date, but thanks anyway." He cut the motor, using momentum to guide them into a secluded cove off the main body of the lake. "This place suit you?"

"You're the captain. Everything's changed so much since the last time I was here."

"Nice to know you respect my authority." His grin was a dare she refused to accept. "If the bluegills bother us too much, we'll up anchor and move on, okay?"

"I thought the whole object of this outing was to catch fish," Val teased, helping herself to a cold drink and opening one for him.

"The whole object of this outing," Cody reminded her, lowering an anchor in the form of a bucket of cement with a line attached, "is to give you a chance to unwind enough to gain a little perspective on your problems."

Despite the weathered lines around his sparkling eyes and the gray that shone in his hair, there was something so essentially boyish about his smile that Val had to force herself to remember which problems she was supposed to be putting into perspective. Unfortunately, Cody didn't help. Her body reacted to his presence the way a compass needle reacted to a chunk of iron.

"I warn you, if I unwind much more, I'll fall apart," she admitted after stifling her third yawn.

"What's the matter, did you have trouble sleeping in my bed?"

She glance up at him quickly, wondering if he could possibly have heard her twisting and turning until all hours. "The bed's great, but I'm used to my own mattress."

"Mattress? I thought that thing was a hammock," Cody observed, rubbing his back with a wry grimace.

"I happen to like sleeping on a swaybacked mattress. It—it's snug," Val fabricated. Now she *was* embarrassed. She had a dreadful mattress, so cheap that it was already hollowed out to fit her narrow body. Cody was a large man, accustomed to the solid support of a firm, king-sized bed.

"I can think of a couple of things that might have improved it," he said slyly.

"Such as a sheet of plywood? Don't think I haven't considered it."

"That wasn't exactly what I had in mind," Cody replied. He leaned forward and retrieved the carton of worms from the shade of her seat, and Val watched the play of muscles in his back. In contrast to the white shirt, his arms gleamed like polished bronze. "Would you rather meditate on a red cork or a green one?"

"You're the guru. Which one is going to catch more fish?"

"Probably the green."

"I'll take the red," she said promptly.

He flashed her a wicked smile and then deliberately baited her hook with an enticing tangle of wigglers. "Lazybones," he scolded. "Did I forget to mention rule number one? He who catches the most fish is exempt from dressing them."

Val offered him her best tea-at-the-embassy smile. "Rule number two: she who dresses fish is exempt from cooking and dishwashing." She removed most of the worms from her hook and dropped them back into the bait box. "I'll bait my own from now on, thanks just the same."

The rules agreed upon, they both settled down to an un-fishing competition. Val tossed her line shoreward, while Cody cast his into deeper waters. She watched as nibble by nibble, her bait was stolen by the small fry who clung to the shelter of the bank. When her cork no longer bobbed, she sighed in contentment and closed her eyes, and if Cody noticed, he was gentleman enough not to mention it.

In no time at all the gentle motion of the lapping water, plus the heat of the sun, proved an irresistible soporific. Bent into an awkward position, Val shielded her head under the shade of an overhanging honey locust tree, leaving her legs to the mercy of the sun.

"Why not toss the life cushions into the bottom of the boat and stretch out?"

She opened one eye. "Don't tempt me. It's not the company, Cody, honestly." She yawned again.

"No problem. We came out here to unwind, remember? With no bait, you're not going to catch anything but forty winks anyway, so you might as well do it in comfort."

"You noticed."

"Yeah," he said with that the same gruff gentleness that always got through her guard. "I noticed. Tell you what, I'll catch us about three apiece, you clean 'em, and I'll do the rest. How's that for a fair division of labor?"

"Frankly, I'm too sleepy right now to worry about a fair division of anything. Just let me doze for five minutes, all right?"

Cody could easily have joined her if there'd been room. Instead, he watched as she wriggled herself into a comfortable position on the kapok cushions. As much as he needed the break, she needed it far more. He was glad she'd come along willingly. There was something hypnotically soothing about watching a bobbing cork; a few hours of it could drain away a hell of a lot of accumulated tension.

Eyes narrowed against the glare of reflected sunlight from the water just outside their shady cove, he studied the woman at his feet. Something was really bugging her, something a damned sight more than the loss of a few bucks. That business in the park with the backfiring convertible for instance. That had hardly been a normal reaction.

When he'd first started out in the security business, even after years of similar work for the military, he'd had a lot to learn and some tough adjustments to make. One of the things he'd learned early was never to discount instinct. Especially a woman's instinct. Women were naturals when it came to subliminal observations.

Which still didn't give him a clue as to what was bothering Val, and that in itself was bothering him. That and the fact that she hadn't wanted to report the incident to Craddock.

Cody's eyes strayed over the pale pink thighs beneath him, followed the rising line of her hip until it dipped abruptly into a small waist. As to what else was bothering him, he didn't have to search far. Even sprawled in a heap in the bottom of the boat, she was the most graceful thing he'd ever seen. And utterly defenseless.

He hauled in a fighting bluegill and deftly removed the hook, his usual pleasure completely missing as his mind lingered on the woman asleep at his feet. She was getting to be an obsession with him. He wanted to sleep with her. Damn it, he *needed* to sleep with her, if only so he could get her out of his system!

Then what? What if she wouldn't budge? She'd said she wasn't open to a casual affair, but what else could he offer a woman like Valentine Scott. She needed permanence, not just a brief fling with some burned-out bum who already had one strike against him.

He felt another tug on his line. The cork ducked under, bobbed to the surface and then took off again. Automatically, Cody set the hook, but he'd long since lost his enthusiasm for the game of fishing. It hardly seemed a fair match.

True to her word, Val dressed the fish, a bit surprised to discover that she still retained the knack after all these years. Proudly, she turned them over to Cody, who'd insisted that if he was to do the cooking, it would have to be on his own turf.

Val rinsed the fish scales from herself, the sink, the wall and various utensils. "That's it for me," she announced smugly. "While you do your thing, I'll run upstairs and shower. By the way, I like mine extra crispy, please, with slaw and baked potato on the side."

Cody made a swatting motion at her backside. "You'll eat what I cook and like it. Did I tell you how to dress fish?"

"You did," she returned promptly.

"Only when you tried to scale them with my Swiss filet knife," he said self-righteously.

"Pick-y, pick-y! See you in half an hour. Remember, extra crispy."

"Hey, that's no fair," Val cried some forty-five minutes later when, showered, shampooed and dressed in an ice-blue linen blouse and her white slacks, she stood in Cody's kitchen doorway.

"What's not fair about it?" Shower-damp himself, Cody stood on his handkerchief-sized patio, presiding over the charcoal grilling of several ambiguous foil packets.

"You were supposed to fry those fish. That's the way God intended bluegills to be cooked."

"The first thing a bachelor learns is how to avoid KP and still satisfy the inner man. Want to pour the iced tea? These things are ready."

Paper plates and napkins, and pint jars to drink from. Val spared a thought for the many twelve-course dinners she'd endured at the homes of the various dignitaries abroad and decided that this was much more her style. After all, she'd grown up in a town where lunch was called dinner and dinner was called supper, and "brunch" was a self-conscious term one read about in glossy magazines.

"Still want yours extra crispy?" Cody teased later. He'd enjoyed his share of the plump little bream, seasoned and stuffed with onions and crumbs, wrapped in a slice of bacon, and cooked in their own succulent juices over a bed of coals. But more than that, he'd enjoyed Val's enjoyment. After the first suspicious taste, she'd been an enthusiastic convert, putting away her share, as well as a large baked potato and two broiled tomatoes. It occurred to him that Anna would have refused to allow herself to enjoy such plebeian fare, especially once she'd made up her mind not to.

Dammit, he wasn't comparing Val to Anna! That hadn't been his intention at all, it was just that...

"Cody? Why the frown? If the thought of having to wash the silver and these pint jars is getting you down, I might be persuaded to—"

"No way, honey. When I make a deal, it stays made. Go relax now while I douse the coals, and then I'll bring on dessert. Brie and and '82 Duplin Magnolia, all right?"

"After all that, I won't be able to waddle, much less get myself back upstairs," Val said with a groan.

Cody's eyebrows danced wickedly. "As to that, my hospitality knows no bounds."

Wandering about his living room a few moments later, Val reexamined the contents of Cody's bookshelf. She'd noticed before that the books were mostly technical, with a few spy thrillers thrown in. There were several photos, all of Eric, but at different ages. Picking up the one on his desk, she angled it toward the light and studied it closely. Sixteen or seventeen, she guessed, with a strong resemblance to his father. They shared a certain directness of gaze, as well as a striking similarity around the mouth. In Cody, the chiseled upper lip and the fuller bottom one had a look of control that amounted to sternness; in the boy, the same feature registered either vulnerability or sullenness...or a touch of both.

"He graduated from high school this year. Only seventeen, too," Cody said quietly from the doorway.

Startled, Val dropped the photo and then righted it again, embarrassed at being caught snooping. "Sorry, I didn't mean to pry."

"Val," he said impatiently, "quit being so damned defensive, will you? Haven't we gotten past that stage yet? You stayed here last night, you even slept in my bed. Don't tell me you didn't look around while you were here, because I'd hate to think you were that uninterested in me."

"He—he's very much like you."

Cody placed the cheese board on a table, returned to the kitchen and emerged a moment later with two glasses and a North Carolina wine, the vapors still curling from the green-throated bottle. "I wonder," he said, in answer to her observation. "To tell the truth, I feel like I hardly even know him. He's lived in Florida for the past five years. Whenever I've gone down to visit him, he's either in school, or too wrapped up in other activities to spend much time with his old man. Every time I see him he's grown another six inches."

Val carved herself a slice of the soft cheese, smeared it on a cracker and then laid it down again. "How old was he when it happened?"

"The divorce, you mean? Eleven. God knows, it couldn't have come as any great surprise. Anna and I—" He cradled the bowl of his wineglass in his palms as if it were a snifter. "Honey, you don't want to listen to this," he said abruptly.

Curling her feet under her on the sofa, Val leaned forward. "Only if you want to tell me, Cody. I really don't want to pry. Sometimes things are too close, too...too painful to share with someone else."

"Hmm." Cody kept his response carefully noncommittal. He was quite certain that Val was referring to her own situation rather than his, and he discovered that at this moment, it wasn't his own problems with Eric that concerned him.

Good Lord, what kind of a man did that make him?

As if sensing his shifting interest, Val began to draw a protective mantle around her. "Cody, this has been lovely," she said, reluctantly getting to her feet, "but I think I'd better go upstairs. I took on some translating for Lucy, and she's expecting it by Monday."

"Hmm," Cody murmured again. Something was stirring inside him, something he wasn't yet ready to face. "Don't forget to lock up," he reminded her. He'd had deadbolt locks installed on her door, but short of bars, there wasn't much he could do about the windows. She'd drawn the line at an alarm system.

Moving toward the door, Val half hoped he'd call her back. She wanted to stay, wanted it badly enough to know that she really should go. "Well . . . Good night, Cody."

No response. With her hand on the knob, she made the mistake of looking over her shoulder. "Cody, what is it? What's wrong?" He was looking at her as if she were his last chance for salvation. Any hope of remaining uninvolved drained away as their eyes met.

"Cody, if you—if you want me to stay, just say so." What was the matter? Had she said something—done something?

The sharp edge of discovery began to dull, leaving Cody caught between wonder and despair. What else could it be? he asked himself with bitter amusement. Crazy or not, he had fallen head over heels in love with her. He hadn't the least idea what to do about it.

One thing was certain: if she came any closer . . . if she touched him . . . he thought he'd go up in flames.

What he needed was time. He needed to back off and study this whole situation objectively. He wasn't ready for it, and he'd lay odds that she wasn't either.

"Cody, are you all right?"

"It's nothing, I—" *Don't look at me that way,* he pleaded silently, filling his eyes with her patrician loveliness, his soul with something that went far deeper.

Unconsciously, Val opened her arms in a gesture as old as time.

"Ah, Valentine," Cody groaned, "why didn't you leave when you had the chance?" Two quick strides and he caught her to him, kissing her with a force born of anguish and need and desire. There was no thought of her fragility now. What Cody needed was the strength of her, and it was there, just as he'd known it would be—a strength to meet his weakness, a weakness to draw forth his strength.

"Valentine, I want to make love with you," he whispered into the sensitive shell of her ear. She was molded to his body, the elegant length of her legs a match for his own muscular ones.

What little control Cody had left was quickly lost as they swayed together, holding each other tightly. The fine-boned softness of her aroused in him a need so fierce it took his breath away. Cody groaned as one hand moved down over the slope of her buttocks.

"We shouldn't," Val protested breathlessly, but the words meant nothing. She was caught up in a storm of passion, far past the reach of reason.

"For God's sake, love, we're not children any longer. Let's not waste what we've found."

He swept her up in his arms, her long legs dangling, and the look in his face was both tender and regretful.

"You deserve to be courted, darling, but I'm afraid courtliness was never my strong suit."

Laughter brimmed her voice, laughter that could easily have turned into tears, as Val fought to contain an overflow of emotion. "I'm more worried about the strength of your back than the strength of your suit."

"This is no time to be cracking jokes, woman!"

Val laughed aloud. "Wasn't laughing at each other's jokes included in the articles of our friendship?"

"I'm about to propose an amendment." His face taut with a new kind of tension, Cody managed to smile as he eased her down onto the bed.

Val reached up to touch his lips with a trembling finger, her eyes lambent under heavy lids. "I'll vote we undertake a serious study of your amendment... starting now."

Cody refused to allow her to participate in her own disrobing. After tossing his shirt aside, he knelt beside her to concentrate on the handful of covered buttons that traversed the front of her handkerchief linen blouse. "There's one," he muttered, laying bare a slice of her midriff. Bending over, he tasted her flesh, bringing forth a shuddering gasp.

"There's two more," he declared, saluting the expanse of skin thus revealed.

Eyes shut tightly, Val willed him to get on with his task. Pressures suddenly clamored to be released, pressures that had been building since the first time she'd seen him at the airport, his lean, muscular build enhanced by the fit of his clothes as well as that deceptively lazy stride of his. She felt like a volcano about to erupt.

Take 4 Books
–plus two Gifts–
FREE

And preview exciting new Silhouette Special Edition novels every month—as soon as they're published!

Silhouette Special Edition®

Yes...Get 4 Silhouette Special Edition novels (a $10.00 value), a Folding Umbrella & Mystery Gift FREE!

SLIP AWAY FOR AWHILE ... Let Silhouette Special Edition novels draw you into a world of love and romance. You'll know the allure, the enchantment, and the power of romance. Romance *is* alive, well and flourishing in these moving love stories that let you escape to exotic places with sensitive heroines and captivating men.

EVERY BOOK AN ORIGINAL ... Every Silhouette Special Edition novel is a full-length story, never before in print, superbly written to give you more of what you want from romance. Start with 4 new Silhouette Special Edition novels—a $10.00 gift from us to you—along with a Free Folding Umbrella and Mystery Gift, with no obligation to buy another book now or ever.

YOUR FAVORITE AUTHORS ... Let your favorite authors—such as Linda Howard, Jeanne Stephens, Nora Roberts, Kathleen Eagle, Carole Halston and others—take you to a whole other world.

ROMANCE-FILLED READING ... Each month you'll receive novels created especially for you. They'll take you to a world you have always imagined, where you will live and breathe the emotions of love and know the satisfaction of love triumphant.

NO OBLIGATION ... Each month we'll send you 6 brand-new Silhouette Special Edition novels as soon as they are published, without obligation. If not enchanted, simply return them within 15 days and owe nothing. Or keep them, and pay just $11.70 (a $15.00 value) for all six books. And there's never an additional charge for shipping or handling.

SPECIAL EXTRAS FOR HOME SUBSCRIBERS ONLY ... When you take advantage of this offer and become a home subscriber, we'll also send you the Silhouette Books Newsletter FREE with each book shipment. Every informative issue features news about upcoming titles, interviews with your favorite authors, even their favorite recipes.

So send in the postpaid card today, and take your fantasies further than they've ever been. The trip will do you good!

CLIP AND MAIL THIS POSTPAID CARD TODAY!

NO POSTAGE NECESSARY IF MAILED IN THE UNITED STATES

BUSINESS REPLY MAIL

FIRST CLASS PERMIT NO. 194 CLIFTON, N.J.

Postage will be paid by addressee

Silhouette Books
120 Brighton Road
P.O. Box 5084
Clifton, NJ 07015-9956

Take your fantasies further than ever. Get 4 Silhouette Special Edition novels (a $10.00 value) plus a Folding Umbrella and Mystery Gift FREE!

Then preview future novels for 15 days— FREE and without obligation. Details inside.
Your happy endings begin right here.

Silhouette Special Edition ®

Silhouette Books, 120 Brighton Rd., P.O. Box 5084, Clifton, NJ 07015-9956

☐ YES! Please send me my four Silhouette Special Edition novels along with my FREE Folding Umbrella and Mystery Gift, as explained in this insert. I understand that I am under no obligation to purchase any books.

NAME _____
(please print)

ADDRESS _____

CITY _____ STATE _____ ZIP _____

Terms and prices subject to change.
Your enrollment is subject to acceptance by Silhouette Books.

Silhouette Special Edition is a registered trademark.

CTS066

At last her blouse lay open. Her arms falling limply at her sides, Val allowed Cody to lift first one shoulder and then the other in order to remove it altogether.

"Now, as to this scrap of lace you're hiding behind—" His hands curved over the peaks of her breasts, bringing them to rigid points under the transparent covering. "It's a nice bit of engineering—protects the property without obstructing the view." His lips moved over the textured surface until he found what he was seeking, and then, using tongue and teeth, he quickly brought her to a state of utter helplessness.

"Cody, please," Val panted.

"Please stop?" He lifted his head and gazed at her through a dense thicket of sun-tipped lashes. "Or please go on?"

With a gasp of helpless laughter, she pounded his shoulder. "Please go on!"

"Anything to oblige a lady." He reached for the button at her waistband, and Val shifted her hips impatiently.

A moment later, molten desire surged through her as she watched his eyes move over her body. She made no effort to hide herself, although she'd never in her life made love in a lighted room. One hand strayed to her breast, and she murmured, "I'm not very..."

The rest of the statement was lost as Cody, having quickly shed the rest of his clothes, came down beside her. "You *are* very," he stressed. "Very, very beautiful, very, very desirable, and very—" He kissed first one breast and then the other. *Very loved.*

He couldn't bring himself to say it aloud. The words burned like fire inside him, but they lodged in his throat. Instead, Cody covered her mouth with a kiss that held all the love, all the doubts, all the hidden fears of a middle-aged man with a failed marriage behind him.

It was the textures of him that drove Val out of her mind. The roughness of body hair over satiny skin, the hardness of muscles that quivered under the bonds of constraint. As his tongue played games with her own, alternately aggressive and seductive, Val felt the blossom of sweat spring from the pores on his back. She was acutely aware of the hard, heated thrust of him against her body, and she twisted helplessly in an effort to press herself against him, torn between the need for swift fulfillment and the desire to prolong this incredibly sweet compulsion.

Cody refused to free her from bondage. Moving slowly down her body, he paid homage to each small breast, caressing with the gentle rasp of his tongue, tugging gently with his lips until she was a shuddering mass of helpless need.

"Now, please, Cody... *help me*," Val whimpered.

Instead, he buried his face in the softness of her belly, trailing a chain of exploratory kisses along her waist. He discovered a hundred unkissed places on her body and proceeded to drive her wild. The sides of her waist, the small of her back, the backs of her knees... even the soles of her feet.

"Cody, you're killing me," she wailed.

At last he moved over her, blocking out the world as if nothing outside the reach of their body heat existed. With one exquisitely slow thrust he brought her to the edge, but then, denying the inevitable until they were both all but destroyed by the sweet inferno, he began to stroke her breasts once more, whispering her name as if it were a talisman.

Val twisted against him instinctively, lifting herself in a desperate drive to put an end to the sweet torture. Cody's hands slipped under her hips, felt their way to her knees and lifted them higher, until he felt her long, cool legs embracing his body.

Then, deliberately pacing his strokes until the last possible moment, he brought her home.

For an instant, she lost consciousness as waves of unbearable pleasure swept over her. Clinging, they remained perfectly still until the echoes of ecstasy had throbbed into ever diminishing circles, fading at last like the ripples on still waters.

Chapter Seven

Sometime during the night, Cody awakened with Val in his arms. Memory flooded his senses and his body grew taut with need once more, but he didn't awaken her. He brushed his lips against her hair. For a long time he simply held her, eyes open to the darkness. He had an uneasy feeling that he'd just made a very grave mistake.

It wasn't the first time he'd awakened to find himself in bed with a woman. It was the first time it had been a real problem, though. Mostly, the others had been strangers; there'd been no feeling at all other than a mild disgust and a sense of disappointment that had left him feeling old and tired. Funny how being intimate could make a man feel more alone than ever.

Val stirred, her hair tickled his chin, and with a touch as light as the brush of a moth's wing, he smoothed it back from her sleeping face. There was an endearing spray of fine gray hair at her temples that she didn't bother to try to cover. Cody touched it, wondering what made this woman unique in his experience. It had never been this good before, not ever.

God, if what he suspected was true, if he was in love with her, what was he going to do? Could he handle something like that? It was scary enough at any age, but with his record at forty-three, starting over took more than guts—it took sheer blind faith.

What if he'd been wrong? He'd been celibate for a long time now. Could be just a case of the old hormones tricking him into action. Lust. Physical attraction.

Valentine Scott. He didn't even know her middle name. He didn't know what she ate for breakfast, or if she liked old movies or football or opera on a rainy Saturday afternoon. She was a stranger, Cody argued with himself.

But she didn't look like a stranger, he argued back. Didn't feel like a stranger. What did he know about her? How could a man fall in love with a woman he didn't even know?

She'd grown up in Lakesboro, and she had a cousin named Grace who used to live around the corner from Lucy McIntire. She could dress fish and bait her own hook, and it just so happened that she looked like a million dollars in anything she happened to put on.

And sometimes she was afraid.

What was she afraid of? What caused the shadows that came and went in those big brown eyes of hers?

The phrase "still waters" came to mind, and Cody drew in a deep breath. For perhaps the first time, he knew what it meant. She was not unlike the lake, itself. More than thirty-thousand acres of impounded waters, with whole communities buried beneath the surface. Sea gulls, regattas, water skiers, fishermen—they all skimmed the surface, but did they ever give a thought to what lay beneath their playground? The drowned churches and farms and schoolhouses, the lives that had been lived out in a place where the sun would never again shine?

Oh, hell, he was at it again. In the small hours of the night, his mind had a tendency to angle off down some pretty strange roads.

But dammit, he had no business risking involvement at this point in his life. He had the wreck of one marriage behind him, not to mention a son who took priority over all else. He'd be a fool to get mixed up with another woman just because she had great legs, a vulnerable look about her and a droll sense of humor. One more mistake might finish him off. If he was smart, he'd avoid the risk by putting as much distance as he could between Valentine and himself while he still had his wits about him.

The smell of coffee woke her up, and Val allowed the memory of the past few hours to trickle through her consciousness before she even opened her eyes. Oh, Lord, she'd really done it. The very last thing she needed, the very thing she'd vowed to steer clear of...

Where was her brain? Where was her sense of self-preservation?

"Coffee's making," Cody announced from the kitchen. Was it her imagination, or was that the sound of regret she heard in his voice?

Well, he didn't regret it anymore than she did, Val told herself. She could practically feel the armor plates clanging back into place as cautiously, she touched her feet to the floor. She hadn't a stitch of clothing on, and suddenly the room felt cold. Cold in the middle of June, with a cranky old air conditioner that should have been replaced a hundred years ago.

Funny, she hadn't noticed how very masculine Cody's bedroom was. One chair, a single chest and a bed. No accessories, no pictures on the wall—only the basics, and those all in shades of brown. As though he were afraid to trust his own taste. Anna had really done a job on him, and Val could have killed her for it!

"Be there in a minute," she called, darting across to the chair where Cody had draped her blouse and slacks. Her neatly folded underthings looked totally alien, like a tea rose puddle on the leather-covered chair. For some reason, the sight of her intimate garments in these stark, unfamiliar surroundings made her feel slightly debauched.

This sort of thing happened all the time, she reminded herself, annoyed at her puritanical, small-town reaction.

But not to her. She could argue all she wanted that both she and Cody were of age and unattached, but it didn't do any good. She'd been a virgin when she'd married, and she'd taken her vows seriously. Thirty-eight years of conditioning wasn't something that could be overcome in a single night.

Moving swiftly, she splashed cold water on her face and shaped a resolution in her mind. The sooner she made her position clear to Cody, the better for all concerned. After that, she'd do her best to put the whole thing out of her mind.

Several minutes later she presented herself in the kitchen, a closed look on her rather pale face. "Cody,

I've been thinking," she began firmly, when he interrupted her.

"Val, I know this is rotten timing, but I've got to get to Atlanta before noon, and since I don't like to leave my car in the airport parking lot, I've got a ride coming by any minute now. I've made coffee. Help yourself to anything else I have, and if you want to go ahead with your painting and varnishing, feel free to bunk here. I dropped a spare set of keys into your purse." The words came out in a rush as Cody continued to cram things into a bulging attaché case. One swift glance at Val's stunned expression and he began to swear softly, just under his breath. Striding into the living room, he began slamming desk drawers.

Waiting just long enough to catch her breath, Val followed him. "You're leaving *now*?" she asked, ashamed of the dismay she couldn't quite conceal.

"Look, I'm really sorry about this, Val," he said brusquely, hoping to God she wasn't going to make a scene. He called himself every name in the book and invented a few more, but he knew he was doing the right thing.

It wasn't that he wanted to go off and leave her now. This was business! If he wanted to close the Centry-Ward deal, he needed to be on the spot Monday morning, and it would take hours of concentrated effort to recheck every single figure. How much work would he get done if he stayed here?

"Car keys are on the ring, too. You're welcome to drive mine while yours is in the shop."

Val hovered in the doorway, her blazing eyes accusing him of every crime short of murder as she struggled with disappointment and frustration. He hadn't even given her a chance to reject him before he'd rejected *her!* "No thanks," she said shortly. "Until I either get mine fixed or buy another one, I'll walk."

"If you decide to look around for something else, I'll be glad to help you when I get back."

"Cody, this may come as a surprise to you," Val said with a coolness that pleased her enormously, "but I'm perfectly capable of choosing my own car." She had no intention of shopping for a car, now or later. Unless she happened to come into an unexpected fortune, she'd make do with the lemon she already owned.

"Well, don't forget, mine is yours if you need it," he reminded her. "Believe me, I don't make that offer to just anyone." He met her eyes with a wary look. "Val, about what happened—"

"What happened? Oh. You mean last night. Cody, I do hope you're not going to try and make something out of that." She managed a disparaging shrug. "It happened, that's all. It certainly didn't—"

"Mean anything?" he supplied.

Val nodded. "I was going to tell you, only you didn't give me a chance," she said. "I really don't think we'd better see each other again, Cody. Frankly, I find that I'm a little too susceptible." She smiled with disarming candor. A master stroke, Valentine, she congratulated herself. Just enough truth to be believable. "There's really too much going on in my life at the moment, and I simply don't have time for you. You *do* understand, don't you, Cody? It's nothing personal."

Cody's gaze hardened. It struck Val that he suddenly looked enormously tired. "Of course I understand, honey. This way's probably best all round." He nodded thoughtfully, as though the idea were brand new to him. "Frankly, I'm relieved. I've had a lot on my mind lately—business and personal matters. You're a very attractive woman, Valentine Scott. I don't need to tell you what you do to me, do I?''

She took the cue. "Whatever it is, I'll promise not to do it to you if you'll promise not to do it to me. Look, I've really got to run. I have all that translating to do, and then I want to finish some odds and ends in the living room so that I can get started on the kitchen." Her smile glittered with suspect brilliance as she let herself out the door.

Nothing like going down with all flags flying, she told herself as she rushed up the stairs to her own apartment. She had a miserable feeling that she was going to do a lot more hurting before she'd be able to get Cody Macheris out of her system. Might as well get on with the pain. Wouldn't it be lovely if she could simply push a button and switch off all feeling?

Twenty minutes later, Cody was pounding on her door. "Val! Hey, open up, will you?''

Wet hair clinging to her head, Val clutched her tailored silk robe around her and opened the door, leaving the chain fastened. "Cody, it's Sunday morning! People are still trying to sleep," she whispered, exasperated. How was she ever going to get him out of her system if he refused to get out of her life?

"Sorry," he said in a stage whisper. "I forgot it was still so early. Look, my ride to the airport just fell through, and I was wondering if you had anything planned for this morning.''

Which was how Val found herself a half hour later driving Cody's powerful car south on Interstate 77, her hair still damp and her mood fluctuating between elation and resentment.

"Honey, I—" Cody began, when she interrupted him.

"I'm not your honey. I know it's a southernism, and it doesn't mean a thing, but I'd rather you didn't call me that."

From the passenger side, Cody studied the clean lines of her profile, tilted now to a distinctly imperious angle. "I'm not a southerner," he reminded her gently. "Except by adoption."

Meaning *what*? Val asked herself rancorously. She downshifted and passed a tractor trailer, her lips tightening in irritation. At least she had the satisfaction of knowing that she was an excellent driver. She'd been tempted to refuse when Cody had told her that his ride had fallen through at the last minute and that he had to catch a certain flight, as he was being met on the other end.

"Valentine, I really appreciate this," he said quietly. "Under the circumstances, I wouldn't have blamed you if you'd slammed the door in my face."

"Believe me, I was tempted," she admitted, thawing so far as to allow a slight smile to break through. Lately she'd found herself reacting more like an adolescent than a woman of thirty-eight, but she did draw the line at door-slamming.

For the next dozen or so miles, Cody remained silent. It wasn't an uncomfortable silence. In fact, as far as Val could tell, he was perfectly at ease. Something told her, though, that given the need, he could spring into action at a moment's notice. More than once she'd caught glimpses of the Cody who had worn a green beret.

They reached Douglas Airport with minutes to spare, and Val barely brought the heavy car to a halt before Cody was grabbing his luggage from the back seat. "Don't get out," he commanded.

"I wasn't!" Val snapped, resenting the fact that he hadn't wanted her to.

Then with a rough curse, he yanked open the door and leaned inside to plant a swift, hard kiss on her mouth. Her lips had parted in surprise when the door opened, and they remained parted, the taste of him lingering on her tongue as she stared after his retreating figure.

The airport again. That easy motion that had caught her attention the first time she'd ever seen him, the slight swing of his shoulders counterpointed by the lean economy of his hip action.

He waved off the redcap who would have checked his single bag and turned back to where she'd pulled crookedly into a parking slot. "I'll see you when I get back, all right?" he yelled across the concrete. Then, quite deliberately, he added, "Honey."

Val had a great deal of emotional energy to burn off before she could even think about going back to her apartment. Thanks to her troublesome car, it had been weeks since she'd been back to Sherrill Ford. Besides, it was a great day to be out, the skies a brilliant Carolina blue, the tall, straight pines swaying in a light southwesterly breeze. On the spur of the moment, she decided to take the long way home, going by Grace's and then driving up past Long Island to cross the river at Buffalo Shoal Bridge.

There was very little traffic, and the sheer bliss of driving such a beautifully engineered piece of machinery almost convinced her that she could outrun her problems.

Val liked to drive. She'd always done the driving, with Albert as often as not in the back seat asleep. He was subject to motion sickness, and it was the only way he could get by in passable comfort. He'd always insisted on leasing the heaviest car available for the smoothest ride, and after the first few months of sheer terror, Val had come to enjoy the long hours of solitary driving.

She'd grown adept at getting them from border to border, through customs, through the occasional spot check. Once she'd even barreled through a band of armed ruffians who had attempted to stop her. She hadn't slowed down until she'd reached the outskirts of town, and then she'd had to pry her fingers, one by one, from the steering wheel of the Mercedes.

Now she wriggled luxuriantly on the sheepskin-covered bucket seat. Reaching out, she switched on the radio. It was tuned to WFMX, and Val laughed aloud as a nasal baritone held forth on the sorrows of a divorced man. For someone with his cosmopolitan background, Cody had developed some very unlikely tastes. Country music, fish camps, cane-pole fishing. Surely he hadn't picked those up in Chicago, New York or Stuttgart.

It occurred to her to wonder that both of them, after living in so many different cities in different parts of the world, had both ended up here in a sleepy three-stoplight town in North Carolina.

It took only a moment to see that Grace wasn't home. Before Val even switched off the engine, she could tell that the front door was closed behind the screen. She shrugged. It had been a pleasant drive anyway, and not all that far out of the way. Furthermore, she didn't feel in the least bit guilty at having taken the liberty of using Cody's car. Well . . . perhaps a *little* bit guilty.

From the corner of her eye, Val saw someone step out on the porch of the square brick house next door, and she shifted into reverse and carefully began backing down the graveled driveway.

"Valentine?" Charles Reedy called as he hurried across his own impeccably kept lawn. Ninety degrees, and he was wearing a suit. He must have just come from church.

"Oh, good morning, Charles." With a feeling of dismay, Val forced a smile, pretending she'd just now noticed the sandy-haired man who'd sucked in his stomach to sidle through the camellia hedge. "I was passing by and thought I'd say hello to Grace. I really can't stop."

"Isn't that a new car?" Charles's rather colorless eyes took in the elegant length of the European model 928-B and returned to her with a speculative look, and Val gave in to the devil's prompting.

"Just test driving it, Charles. I really don't need all this power for local driving, but it's hard to resist the quality. Besides, who knows when I might decide to take off again? Give Grace my love, will you? Sorry I missed her."

"But Valentine, if—"

She revved the engine, and with a casual wave, left him standing there staring after her.

That should fix his wagon, Val though maliciously as she turned off Sherrill Ford Road and headed north. Not only would he get the message that he couldn't afford her, this should convince him that she was thoroughly unreliable. With two daughters in private school, he'd hardly welcome a wife with a taste for expensive cars, would he? Especially one who was apt to take off on the spur of the moment.

Val managed to stave off most of the hurting until late that night. She had painted all she could paint, hung the loosely woven curtains over the badly placed windows, and then shifted and reshifted her exotic array of shrubbery, striving for the best possible effect. As long as she'd been able to fill the hours with scraping paint off windowpanes and hammering up curtain rod brackets with the heel of her shoe, she'd been all right.

Cody's car was back in it's allotted place in the parking lot, his key ring pinned to the lining of her purse for safekeeping. She'd have left it in his apartment on his desk, but she didn't want to go down there. She needed no more reminders of what she was so desperately trying to forget.

"Of all the stupid things to do," she muttered aloud, uncertain whether she was addressing herself or Cody.

Cody stayed away, and after the second day, Val gave up hoping he'd call and concentrated on trying to forget him. Robin started her week off by talking about going back to school to study interior design. She panicked, of course, and by the time she'd gotten over that particular threat, she'd managed to lose an entire file folder. Luckily, it was only their personnel file. Considering the size of Wynn's staff, it was hardly a major loss if it never turned up again. Goodness knows, with all the people who'd trooped through her office lately— contractors, clients, telephone repairmen, and some poor man who'd insisted that Flowers, Inc. was a florist shop—it was a wonder she hadn't lost her head!

At least her typing was improving, Val consoled herself. It was beginning to look as if the translating she was doing for Lucy might work into something more substantial than she'd thought, too. There was a great deal more industry in the area than there had been eighteen years ago, which meant imports and exports, not to mention foreign branches to be dealt with. With a little ingenuity and a lot of effort, her years abroad just might pay off yet.

Val uttered a sound of disgust. So why, with her professional life finally on the move, did she have to go and ruin her *personal* life? It wasn't as if she didn't know better. Good Lord, if any woman had reason to be cautious, she did. Hadn't she wasted half her life on a man who hadn't been worth a single minute of it?

Val was only now realizing how very badly she'd been used all those years. Chauffeur, valet, maid...social secretary, travel agent, not to mention a convincing cover for a man who led a double life.

Oh, she'd been used, all right, but she'd gained an education in the process. She'd even learned, she recalled with bleak amusement, to play honeymoon bridge with a humorless intelligence agent who'd been half convinced that she was a part of the whole ugly business.

Meekins had been her shadow. He'd been a part of the furniture in the hospital room while Val, still suffering from her own injuries, had maintained a silent vigil by Albert's bed.

Thousands of miles from home, she'd been surrounded by strangers, and terrified of them all. Someone had shaved off Albert's mustache, so that even he had looked like a stranger.

But then he had been a stranger. She'd had to keep reminding herself of that. Val had tried to feel sympathy, but the best she'd been able to do was a vague feeling of regret.

Meekins had seldom left her side. Had he really believed that Albert would suddenly regain consciousness and confide in her? It would have been laughable if it hadn't been so tragic.

"Oh, God, Valentine, just stop it!" Jumping up, she began to move about the room. Whenever she started thinking about it, she began to feel confined, inse-cure... as if she were somehow still threatened. She'd simply have to train herself not to think of the past.

Which left the present and the future. Which left Cody, damn his hide! With his gentle hands and his soft words and his wonderful, loving body. *Cody, why couldn't you have let me alone?"*

On Wednesday morning Val located the missing file. She'd evidently gathered it up with a stack of trade pe-riodicals and shoved it onto the bookcase. Now all she had to do was replace every item she'd removed from the bookcase, and then check to make sure she hadn't lost another file when she'd removed everything to search the filing cabinet.

On Wednesday afternoon, she copied thirty-seven pages of an article Wynn had written for *Southern Liv-ing* magazine without first resetting the copier con-trols. Every page was reduced to an illegible hundred-and-twenty-percent smaller. She was supposed to have copied and mailed it on Tuesday, but Tuesday had been one of those lost days. She'd forgotten all about it.

Val's chin wobbled twice before she got herself in hand, and then she reset the controls and switched on the machine. The minute it was done, she asked Robin to cover for her while she express mailed it to Atlanta at her own expense.

On the way back to the office, she stopped by the hardware store and bought a can of varnish for her cabinets. Something told her she was going to need to stay occupied until she was tired enough to drop.

It began to rain just as she left the store and, cursing her luck, she ran the last two blocks to the office, bursting through the door to see Robin perched on her desk. He grinned and indicated the inch of slip that showed beneath her skirt. "What's this I see before me, a lace-edged Valentine?"

It was a slubbed rayon skirt; the tag read "dry clean only." Now she knew why. "Robin?" Val smiled sweetly. "Thanks for covering for me. Drop dead!"

That night Val scrubbed her cabinets inside and out. She waited for the phone to ring and told herself she wouldn't have answered it even if it had. The hell with Cody, anyway! Just thinking about him made her feel positively lecherous. He would have to go and stir up all those old coals. What was she supposed to do with them *now*?

It rained all the next day. Her varnish would stay sticky forever, at this rate, but she'd had to do something—she was wound up like a coiled spring. "Like a woman possessed," she told herself, and then she laughed. "Oh, yes, a woman very *much* possessed." Unfortunately, she wanted nothing so much as to be possessed again. By the same man.

The phone remained stubbornly silent. In a sudden panic in case it wasn't working properly, Val laid her sticky brush on the lid of the varnish can and dialed Grace's number. Not until she heard the sleepy response on the other end did it occur to her to glance at the clock.

"Are you out of your mind?" her irate cousin grumbled. "Charlie said you came by last Sunday morning driving a fancy new car. Valentine, sometimes I wonder which side of the family you took after. The Whichards never had much money, but at least they always had good sense."

"Don't forget Great-uncle Alph and his solar-powered submarine. Grace, I'm sorry," Val repented. "I had no idea it was so late. I've been working on my kitchen ever since I got home from work, and I just forgot."

"What's this about a new car?"

"It's not mine, it belongs to a—a friend."

"Hmmph. Must be a good friend, if he lets you drive his fancy car. Charlie said it cost a pretty penny."

Val didn't want to discuss Cody or the cost of the car he'd bought in Germany and had modified there. "Oh, so it's Charlie now, is it? Is there something you're not telling me, Grace?"

"Oh, for pity's sake, the man's my neighbor, that's all! I told you it's you he's interested in, but would you even go out to dinner with the man? Oh, no, not you. Independent as a hog on ice, aren't you?"

There was more in the same vein, but Val wasn't listening. At the mention of the word *dinner* her stomach rolled over.

"Grace, I've got to go open some windows. These varnish fumes are beginning to get to me."

"It's raining—at least it is on this side of the lake."

It was raining on that side, as well, Val saw when she opened her window to draw in a deep breath of fresh air. The instructions had mentioned something about a well-ventilated room, but how could she ventilate a kitchen that didn't even have a window?

Her bedroom was little better. Catching sight of Ollie's bowl on the small table in the living room, Val wondered if fish could smell. Ollie was much more sensitive than the average goldfish, she was certain of that. With the way her luck had been running, she'd find herself in trouble with the Fish and Game Commission.

Her stomach churned ominously, and Val wondered what her lungs were being forced to endure. If she opened the windows, the humidity might affect the curing of the varnish. "Oh, heavens, can't I manage to accomplish a single thing without fouling up?" she wailed, yanking her pajamas off the back of the bathroom door and cramming a few toilet articles into the pockets of her robe.

"Just for tonight," she promised herself as she hooked the straw purse over her shoulder, carefully lifted the fishbowl and let herself out of the apartment. What difference would one more night make? Cody had said he'd be away for several days. If he'd offered her the use of his car, he could hardly begrudge her the use of his bed, especially as he'd insisted on giving her a set of keys.

Her stomach felt better before she'd even let herself inside. By the time she'd settled Ollie for the night, she was ready to drop, the past few nights having caught up with her.

After staring at the same set of figures for what seemed hours, Cody gave up trying to make sense of them and closed the folder. He slapped his shirt pocket, automatically reaching for a cigarette to soothe his raw nerves. What had happened to that steel-trap brain he'd prided himself on possessing? He'd almost blown the whole deal that first day, simply because at a crucial point in the negotiations, he'd lost his whole damned train of thought.

If he bought out Centry-Ward, he`was more or less tying himself down for at least another year. What if Val decided to pull up stakes and look for work somewhere else? CMS was portable enough. It could stand pat on its record and function as a consulting firm almost anywhere in the Southeast if he had to go after her.

But Centry-Ward was already in trouble. If he bought it and then left it to go chasing after a woman, it might not survive. He'd planned on personally overseeing every single phase of operations for at least the first six months. Regardless of all other considerations, the real story was right here in the books. These figures would tell him whether he was going to be able to pull the company out of a dive.

Centry-Ward had first come under his personal scrutiny when their quality control had started going sour. It had always been a reliable concern in the past, one whose products he'd come to depend on. He'd come to Atlanta to find out what the hell was wrong, and walked into the middle of a family battle.

It hadn't taken long to figure out that the main problem involved a fundamental difference in business philosophy between the conservative older Wardner brother and the daredevil younger one. It had taken about a week for Cody to realize that they weren't going to be able to resolve it.

He'd talked to his accountant, gone over their books, his books, their books again, and then considered the matter from every conceivable angle. If he waited any longer to make his move, there might not be anything left to salvage.

From all he'd been able to see, it was worth the gamble. His accountant urged caution, but then, what accountant worth his salt didn't? In the long run, it was up to him, and he was guided more by instinct than intellect. Only time would tell if he'd saddled himself with nothing but a whopping tax write-off.

One thing was certain: this was no time for his personal life to start getting complicated. So why couldn't he seem to convince himself of that? At the most inopportune times he found himself wanting to talk over some aspect of the deal with Valentine, to share his worries with her.

And at night . . .

The nights were worst of all. No matter how many hours he worked, no matter how tired his brain was, it was never too tired to summon up a distracting image of the way she'd looked in his bed, her small white breasts rising up to meet his lips, those long legs of hers sort of drawn up like she was eager, but half afraid, too. A surprising degree of physical discomfort went along with those visions.

At his age!

Chapter Eight

Embracing a thick down pillow, Val was deeply asleep when the overhead light flared on. She flung an arm over her eyes and struggled to throw off the threads of a confusing dream. Cody had been there. She'd been running with typical nightmare slowness, either toward him or away from him, she couldn't remember. Now for some reason she found herself in Cody's bed, alone. The faint, clean scent of his body tugged at her senses, and she opened her eyes.

The sound of a profane oath brought her upright as remembrance flooded back. The varnish...the fumes...

Her mouth was cottony dry. "Who—" She tried to speak, but the muscles of her throat refused to cooperate; the whisper died away even as her eyes blinked to focus on the strange man who stood just inside the door.

Tall, blond and deeply tanned, he was wearing
grubby white ducks and a rugby shirt. She'd never seen
him before in her life—and yet even with the harsh glare
that distorted his features into a frightening mask, there
was something oddly familiar about him.

"Crap! I might have known he'd have some tramp in
his bed." The intruder made no attempt to hide his disgust.

Illogically, Val felt her confidence begin to return. If
his voice was any indication, her intruder wasn't as old
as she'd first thought. He might even be the boy who'd
snatched her purse—Lakesboro's one-man crime wave.
She hadn't been hurt that time; if she kept her head, she
might just manage to talk her way out of this situation.

"The stereo's built-in, but if you want the television,
take it." *Forgive me, Cody, but I'm no heroine.* "The
owner of this apartment never keeps any money
around, and I don't even belong here, so if—"

"Damned right you don't belong here! Where's my
dad?"

His dad?

"Eric?" she croaked. Clutching the sheet and bedspread under her chin, Val squinted against the painful
glare at the boy who confronted her so belligerently, feet
apart, arms crossed over his chest. To Val, her mind still
tangled in the threads of a fast-fading dream, he looked
both threatening and endearing.

"How the hell do you know my name? Who the hell
are you, anyway? What the hell are you doing here?
Where's my old man?"

"Don't you mean where *the hell* is your old man?"
Val asked dryly. "You passed up a perfectly good opportunity to throw in a swearword, Eric."

"Dammit, don't you—"

Tossing aside the covers, Val stood up, looking as regal as her five feet eight inches would allow when it was clad in rumpled cotton pajamas. "No," she interrupted firmly. "Don't *you*! Don't you presume to judge me, don't you try to frighten me, and for heaven's sake, stop swearing at me! Of course I know who you are, Eric." At least she did now that she was fully awake, and he'd moved from under the distorting glare of an overhead light. "Your father has pictures of you all over the apartment."

"Where is he?" Slowly, the arms uncrossed, but the thumbs caught in his belt loops and stayed there, elbows thrust slightly forward. Val's vocabulary of body language was limited to a few basics. Did this new pose indicate bravado or something more threatening?

"Your father is in Atlanta," she said calmly, more sure of herself now that she knew the identity of her unexpected caller. "A business trip. I have his number at the hotel if you'd like to call him."

He looked as if she'd struck him in the face, and Val felt her heart begin to soften. Oh, Lord, how very defenseless the young were. "I'm sorry you missed him, Eric," she added softly. "I'm sure he didn't know you were coming. How did you get in, anyway?"

"Keep your damned sorry!" the boy snarled. Unfortunately, his voice still had the slightest tendency to break under stress. Shoulders that would one day equal his father's in breadth lifted and fell in a gesture of defeat. "Dad gave me a key the last time he was in Lauderdale. In case I ever needed him, he said!" He uttered a bark of raw laughter and then released another stream of profanity, and Val's newfound sympathy withered on the vine.

What *was* it with men and their swearing? Did they think it made them more masculine, for goodness' sake? More invincible? Or was it an alternative to showing some other, less acceptable emotion?

"Look, I'll change the bed and you can have it," she said. "I came down here to give my lungs a break from the paint fumes, but if you're going to continue to assault my ears . . ."

"Oh, hell, I don't care." It was a hollow protest. The boy was obviously dead tired and sick with disappointment.

Had he driven all the way up from Florida just to see Cody? Somehow, Val told herself as she deftly stripped the bed and smoothed fresh sheets across the king-sized mattress, she didn't think he'd appreciate her concern.

By the time she'd completed the chore, Eric had disappeared. She heard the refrigerator door open and shut and wondered if he'd found enough to satisfy his hunger. "Your father's at the Hyatt on Peachtree if you want to let him know you're here," she called out.

A moment later, with Ollie's bowl balanced on one hip, she opened the door to the lobby. The chances of meeting another tenant were slim at this hour; she'd risk her reputation rather than hang around long enough to change out of her pajamas. "I'm leaving now, Eric. My apartment's the one over this one if you need anything." After waiting a moment for the response that never came, she shrugged and closed the door behind her.

Eric's throat tightened with disappointment. So what was he supposed to do now? Hell, his old man had a right to his woman—this one had class, even if she was pretty old. But why now? And why did he have to be *gone*? When a guy needed to talk, he needed eyeball to eyeball, dammit, not just another phone call with his mother listening in on the extension!

He dug a tablespoon into a jar of peanut butter and then sucked on it absently as he figured his next move. He'd bummed a ride as far as Columbia with a trucker who called himself King Vernon the First. Vern had treated him to a steak and shake for dinner and then got him a ride on a chicken truck headed for North Wilksboro, which had dropped him off at the Troutman exit out on I-77. He'd had to walk the rest of the way, and he was wiped out.

By the time he'd hit Lakesboro, he'd been worried sick that his mother would have got the wind up and called Cody, who'd be waiting up to land on him with both feet the minute he walked through the door.

So now what? He could call the hotel and get his father out of bed, or he could hang around here and wait. One thing for sure—he wouldn't answer the phone. The minute Jack discovered that he wasn't out on *The Great Escape* with Tuck Taylor, he'd know where to look for him. Any why. His mother would pitch a fit and want to call out the National Guard to find her precious baby boy and bring him back home.

Eric knew how his mother's mind worked. She was determined to ruin the rest of his life by making him into a carbon copy of Jack Wright. They'd had a big blowup last spring. Eric had agreed to hit the books and quit spending so much time with Tuck, and his folks had agreed to get off his case about taking tennis and golf lessons at the club.

He'd done his level best to play it their way ever since, knowing that if he could just hang in there long enough to get out of high school, he'd have it made. Even when his old man had come down for a visit, he hadn't said a word. Oh geez, he'd wanted to! It wasn't as if he couldn't trust him, but it hadn't been worth the risk, not with graduation so close.

He'd leveled with Jack from the first about two things. He refused to go to any more deb balls, and he had no intention of wasting the next two years at that cubic prep school Jack was always harping about. He hadn't mentioned his real plans. The last time Cody had come down, Eric had made himself scarce rather than risk blowing the whole thing before he was finished with school. Dammit, when he made a deal, it stayed made, but school was over now. It was a new game.

He'd picked up his grades on Friday, but he hadn't hung around for the festivities. He'd lay it all out and see what Cody thought. Not that it would change anything. With or without approval, he had his future mapped out. He was going to work with Tuck and gradually buy shares of the boat, and when Tuck's arthritis finally got so bad he couldn't hack it out there any more, he'd manage the business end and Eric would run the charters. One day Eric would own a whole fleet of charter boats.

Eric had already peeled off his shirt and was ready to crash when he heard the noise from directly overhead. It sounded as if something had hit the floor, and then someone had yelled.

He had no trouble finding the right place. Once at the head of the stairs, the sound of a woman's voice led him directly to the open door.

"Oh, no, oh, no," Val wailed, staring with stricken eyes at the mess that surrounded her.

"Ge-*eez*! What's going on up here?" Eric stepped cautiously inside the room, staring at the uprooted plants, the trail of stuffing that spilled across the floor from the scattered sofa cushions and the wrecked chair. Grimacing, he looked down at his bare feet, lifting first one and then the other as he felt the wetness. It was then that he saw the feeble flap of the goldfish. "Hey, poor little fellow, what happened to you?" He knelt, dodging a shard of glass, and managed to slip the mottled Japanese fantail into the palm of his hand. Looking curiously at Val, he spoke. "Don't move, lady, there's a lot of broken glass. I'll be right back as soon as I find a place to park Jaws here."

Val couldn't have moved if her life had depended on it. Still caught up in the nightmare that had enveloped her the moment she'd opened her door and switched on the light, she stared at the ruins around her. Suddenly, the chair and the sofa she'd hated so much were terribly dear to her. She knelt, hardly feeling the slivers of Ollie's bowl, and began cramming the stuffing back into a split pillow.

Eric reappeared with the bottom part of her glass coffee maker. Ollie drifted somewhere between the four- and the six-cup mark. "This okay for now, lady? Boy, somebody's sure got it in for you. Any ideas?"

Numbly, Val shook her head, still mechanically stuffing the fiber filling back into the cushion. Eric leaned down and grasped her wrists, and she stared down at the prominent knuckles on his man-boy hands. "Lady, I told you to stand still. Now look, you've gone and cut yourself."

"It's Val," she said. "Valentine Scott."

"Sure, Val—uh, Ms. Scott, Like I was saying, you shouldn't touch this mess until we get the cops here." Oh boy, oh boy, I would have to walk in on something like this, Eric thought tiredly. Just his luck to get mixed up in a housebreaking when he was doing his damnedest to keep a low profile until he had his old man lined up solidly behind him.

He let go a succinct oath and then he straightened and began prowling the littered room. After only two turns, he came back to where Val still stood. "Look, for what it's worth," he burst out impatiently, "I'm sorry again, but if you'd just stop staring at me like that, maybe I could think of what to do next! It's not every day a guy runs away from home and walks in on a robbery! I mean, how's it going to look? What's my old man going to say?"

"Eric, kindly sit down somewhere and be still for a minute, will you? You can't think, I can't think— somebody has to think!"

"I guess we have to call the cops," he said morosely. "Geez, I wish my old man was here."

Val did, too. She'd never wished for anything so much in all her life. "My purse was stolen last week," she said, plucking at the fibers that stuck to her hand. They must have been wet. She hadn't noticed.

"Are you rich or something?"

"Do I look rich or something?" She regretted the sarcasm immediately. The boy was obviously trying to be helpful.

"Sort of," he said, shrugging. "Jack says you can never tell. These days, what with kidnappings and all, smart people don't flash it around any more."

"Well, I'm not, and I wasn't even before my purse got stolen, so I wish to goodness whoever is doing this would just stop it!" Tears threatened, and she fought them back. The poor child was shaken enough without having an hysterical woman on his hands. "I'll call Joe Craddock and report this," she said. "Look, Eric, you don't have to stay if you'd rather not."

To his credit, Eric stuck by her while the sheriff and one of his deputies went over her apartment. Val explained his presence by telling the law enforcement officers that he was visiting his father, who'd had to leave town for a few days on unexpected business.

The inspection took slightly more than two hours, and Val hung on by sheer determination alone until the door finally closed behind the heavyset sheriff. Eric had stayed by her side all through the ordeal, touching her occasionally in an awkward gesture of reassurance. There was so much of Cody in him that Val felt like crying on his shoulder and comforting him in her arms at the same time.

"It's four-ten," the boy said after glancing at the elaborate gold watch his mother had given him for graduation. He'd asked for a stainless-steel diver's model, for all the good it had done him. "I think we'd better call Dad, don't you?"

With all her heart, Val wanted to agree, but where was the logic in disturbing Cody over something that didn't even concern him? Especially after the way they'd parted. "No, I really don't think so, Eric. It was my apartment that was broken into, not your father's."

"But you two have something going. Don't you think he'd want to know?"

"We don't have anything going, as you put it, except that we're friends and neighbors."

"And sometimes you hop into his sack, right?" Eric regretted the words the minute they left his mouth, but what the hell, it was the truth, wasn't it? But middle-aged women like Val probably liked to dress it up with a few frilly words.

Meeting those direct eyes, so like Cody's, but lighter, younger, Val refused to deny the crude accusation. "That's none of your business, Eric. My relationship with your father has nothing to do with any of this." She gestured to the chaos around her. "I'm not in the habit of bothering him with my personal problems, and anyway, nothing was taken. It was obviously all a mistake."

"Some mistake," Eric snorted.

"You asked if I had money," she reminded him. "I do happen to wear good clothes because good clothes last, and at one time in my life, I could afford them. Probably someone just assumed—" She broke off, staring unseeingly at the slit arms of the ugly green chair. What was it Meekins had said when he'd forced that phone number on her?

Your first impulse will to be to throw this number away. Don't do it. If things start happening, things you can't explain, just pick up the phone and dial through. Someone will be with you within a matter of hours.

If Cody had been here, it would have been different, Val thought distractedly. But he wasn't. Val had that awful hollow feeling in the pit of her stomach that things weren't as simple as they appeared on the surface.

And Cody's son, through no fault of his own, was involved.

"Eric, go home. Please," she pleaded. "I'm dead tired. All I want to do is sleep until noon, and then wake up and start in on this mess."

"I don't think you ought to stay here."

Val flung out her arms impatiently. "For goodness' sake, why not? My visitor, whoever he was, certainly isn't going to come back! What more could he do?"

The boy had his father's stubborn chin. He didn't say a word. He didn't have to.

"I'm not afraid, Eric," Val lied. She was growing more afraid by the minute. She wanted him to go so that she could call Meekins.

"Either you come down to Dad's place, or I'll stay up here with you. I don't much like the way it smells up here, though."

One the verge of collapse, Val ran a hand through her wildly tousled hair. "Neither do I," she admitted, laughing tiredly. "That's why I left the windows cracked open when I went downstairs." Craddock had quickly spotted the open windows and identified one as the point of entry. "Look, go on back downstairs. I'll close up here and get some clothes and be down in five minutes, all right?"

"Okay," Eric agreed reluctantly. "But if anything happens, just stomp on the floor."

After what seemed an interminable wait, but was probably no more than two minutes, Val was put through to Meekins. He sounded sleepy. Before she'd even finished explaining that it was probably just a false alarm, she could practically hear the cells of his brain clicking over with that maddening precision. The man was a robot in a three-piece suit, about as bloodless as a turnip. But at the moment, the cold efficiency she remembered all too well was oddly comforting.

"Nothing was taken?" he pressed.

"Thirteen dollars and some odd change. Plus a darned expensive gray calf purse."

"I doubt that this person has a leather fetish," Meekins retorted dryly, with the first hint of humor she'd ever glimpsed in him. "What about from your apartment. Anything missing there?"

"My few pieces of jewelry are still here. There were two tens stuck under the edge of the phone to remind me to go by the office and pay my phone bill. They're still there."

"Tell me about any new people in your life."

"Now? Mr. Meekins, I haven't been home in almost twenty years. Everybody in town is new to me."

"Give it a shot."

"Well...there's my boss. I understand he moved here from Charlotte seventeen years ago. Robin Chatham, his assistant, wasn't even out of grade school the last time I was home, but I remember his family."

"Any attentive men?"

"No," she said too quickly. "Well, yes, but..."

"How well do you know them?"

"Mr. Meekins, that's none of your business!" Val said indignantly.

"Don't be dense, Mrs. Scott. You're not playing party games with a bunch of kids now. Your husband made off with close to a million dollars and then tried to make it look like he'd been double-crossed. They made an example of him. If they think you know anything at all about the money or the people he was dealing with, they won't politely ask your cooperation. I want you to promise me that you won't trust anyone. Not *anyone*, is that clear? Any stranger who tries to get close to you is automatically suspect, and I mean that!"

A shudder passed through Val as she huddled on the cushionless sofa and stared at the ruins of her partially redecorated living room. "There's really no one like that. And besides, how could anyone think I'm hiding all that money? Mr. Meekins, I hardly make enough to pay my rent, and I live in a thirty-year-old apartment house. I drive a seven-year-old car that smokes like a chimney and supports a major oil company single-handedly, all my clothes are years out of date, and I—"

Meekins sliced through her protests. "You're not dealing with fools, Valentine. How's your security for the rest of the night?"

Thinking gratefully of the boy downstairs, she reassured him on that score. "Will you...send someone?"

"I'll be there as soon as I can make it."

"Where are you?" She had visions of his booking a transatlantic flight to New York and then having to make his way from there to Charlotte-Douglas.

"I'm in Virginia. Keep the coffee warm."

It was the one of the longest nights Valentine had ever spent in her life. As she huddled on Cody's leather sofa, the king-sized quilted bedspread that Eric insisted she take trailing halfway across the floor, the terrible realism of her waking nightmare began to prey on her mind.

They'd followed her. The obscene animals who had murdered Albert and had badly injured her were now after her in earnest. And she'd done nothing! She *knew* nothing—she *had* nothing. But how could she protect herself from such rabid vermin?

Strangers, Meekins had said. Beware all strangers asking questions. For some reason, Suzie Pauley popped into her head...plump, brown-haired Suzie with her innocent questions about Albert and what had happened.

"Oh, for God's sake, Val, you, might as well suspect Grace!"

Val made a deliberate effort to organize her thoughts. Wynn Flowers? Of course not, she scoffed. Wynn hadn't even asked all the questions he should have asked before hiring her. Otherwise, she thought with a bleak shaft of humor, neither of them would be in the fix they were in at the office. If she was a failure as a secretary, then he was a failure as a boss.

Robin thought it was hilarious, watching her scramble through the files trying to remember whether she'd filed the specifications for a line of custom-designed ceiling chandeliers under specs, lighting, chandelier, or the name of the designer.

Robin? No, not Robin. He was too zany, too obvious, and in spite of a wicked sense of humor, much too nice.

Which left...

No. She refused to consider it. All the same, her relentless mind kept throwing up small details. Denver, Atlanta, Nam, Stuttgart, New York. A man who claimed to have lived in so many places would be difficult to trace to any one. And he had asked questions. He'd shown an interest in her from the very first. But no more of an interest than she'd showed in him.

Maybe that was all part of the plan, her exhausted mind whispered beguilingly. Disarm her first by making her fall in love, and then pry the information from her. Only it wouldn't work because she didn't know anything. She didn't have the money, she didn't know any names, wasn't privy to any mysterious numbers that would lead to a secret fortune stashed away in some Swiss bank account.

So what now? Why had Cody run off the way he had? How convenient that he should suddenly have a business trip to make.

But of course... He'd gone to report his progress, her tortured brain supplied. To report that he'd successfully seduced her and ask what he was supposed to do next.

But then, if Cody was in Atlanta, who had broken into her apartment? And who had stolen her purse? It couldn't have been Cody. She'd have known instinctively if he'd been anywhere around.

A partner. What did thay call them, henchmen? What was a hench?

"Oh, Lord, I'm losing my grip," Val whispered into the first gray light of dawn.

By the time Eric shook her by the shoulder some hours later, Valentine was sleeping as if she'd been drugged. "Hey, Val, wake up. Your cousin's here to see you."

Groaning, she sat up, wiping sleep from her eyes. "Grace? Oh, no, Craddock must have called, and now she'll insist . . ."

"He doesn't look like any 'Grace' to me. I made him wait outside."

He? Her cousin? She only had one close cousin. The Whichards had been a diminishing strain, and her mother's family, the Stevenses, consisted only of a distant cousin in Kodiak, and another one who was a tax assessor somewhere in the eastern part of the state.

Val rubbed her eyes again, clearing her vision and a portion of her mind. "Give me ten minutes, will you? I don't suppose Cody has any instant coffee . . ."

"I made a pot. If you like Dad's, mine is probably too weak, but I'll bring you a cup anyway."

She folded the bedspread and made herself as presentable as she could under the circumstances. By the time Eric returned with her coffee and a stale cinnamon bun, she'd already figured out the identity of her so-called cousin.

It would be Meekins, of course, and she didn't even know his first name. He probably didn't have one, she thought as she braced herself to face that flat, granite-like visage.

Eric ushered the visitor in from the hallway and moved around to hover protectively just behind her, and Val fought down a ridiculous urge to giggle.

"Hi, Cous," Meekins greeted, looking completely ludicrous in a wildly colorful shirt and a pair of flapping bell bottom jeans. Didn't he know that no one wore bell bottoms anymore? "Surprised to see old Freddie, aren't you? I had to ask your neighbor upstairs where you were, and then cool my heels until young Macheris here agreed to let me in. What's up?"

Oh, Lord, he was going to be breezy, Val thought as she allowed herself to be embraced by the middle-aged agent. She didn't think she could face a breezy Meekins, and certainly not after a night like the one just past. Of course, he wouldn't be here if it weren't for what had happened last night, she reminded herself. The urge to giggle had completely left her by now.

"Have you had breakfast...Freddie?" She almost choked on the name. People like Meekins didn't have names, they had numbers. He smelled faintly of mouthwash. She'd never been close enough to him before to smell anything.

"Coffee. Why don't we go up to your place and fry an egg for old times' sake? How's good old Grace getting along? I'll have to run over to Sherrill Ford to see her before I leave."

He'd done his homework, Val gave him full marks for that. She only wished he wouldn't try quite so hard. If there was one thing she wasn't in the mood for this morning, it was a jovial G-man.

They finally managed to escape Eric's protective curiosity when Val suggested he try to reach his father before Cody got tied up for the day with business.

"Sorry about the cousin thing," Meekins said quietly once he'd closed the door behind them. "Your place is clean—I went over it while I waited for your watchdog to stop growling."

"He's a nice boy, and he was giving me time to wake up." Val led the way to the kitchen, where she began putting away the contents of her cabinets. "Clean" was hardly the term she'd have used to describe her apartment, especially after her messy intruders had sampled the contents of every canister she owned. At least the varnish had dried.

While she cleared away some of the mess, Meekins cooked half a dozen slices of bacon, four eggs and a stack of whole wheat toast. Under any other circumstances, she might have been amused at the domestic side he was revealing.

"D'you mind?" he asked belatedly, opening the refrigerator door to help himself to her fig preserves.

Val shook her head. Telling herself she couldn't eat a bite, she began nibbling on a slice of bacon, and then reached for a piece of toast.

"I checked out Craddock. He's okay. One of his deputies was picked up on a misdemeanor in Norfolk eight years ago, but he's been clean since then. Anything missing?"

"Not as far as I could tell. I almost wish they'd messed up my walls. My renters' insurance might have covered a new paint job."

"If you'd had wallpaper, they might have stripped it for you. They were after something small, a list of names or numbers or the key to a deposit box, probably. Ring a bell?"

"My God, you don't think I really had anything like that, do you?" Had she been wrong all this time in thinking she'd been cleared of all suspicion? "The only list I had in my purse was a shopping list. Meekins, I—"

"Freddie," he corrected, his mouth full of bacon and eggs. "It happens to be my real name, in case you're wondering. Who's the kid?"

"The son of a friend of mine," she shot back. "He just got here last night from Florida, so if you're thinking—"

"I'm not. Who's the friend?"

Val looked away. She didn't want to discuss Cody with this hard-eyed man. Not until she'd settled a few things in her own mind. Not even then. "He's in Atlanta. He couldn't have done it."

"What are you covering, Valentine?" Fred Meekins persisted.

"I'm not covering a thing! I just know Cody couldn't have done anything wrong, that's all, and I don't like your suspicious mind."

"I'm paid to be suspicious. I'm very good at what I do, and if he's clean, he has nothing to be afraid of."

She laughed, a harsh sound that made her throat hurt. "Can you guarantee that? *I* had nothing to be afraid of. I've never done anything wrong, at least not knowingly. That didn't protect *me* from violence."

"We live in an imperfect world."

"Oh, keep your damned platitudes to yourself!" Val launched herself up from the kitchen table, realizing for the first time that she was still wearing her pajamas and robe. "Whatever you have to do here, do it quickly and leave me alone. I'm going to get showered and dressed, and then I'm going to work, and I'd just as soon you weren't here when I got back."

Meekins stood, too, looking not nearly as ludicrous as he should have looked in the lurid Hawaiian shirt and the unfashionable jeans. His eyes were small, his cheekbones high, and his face looked as though it had been retreaded more than once.

"I'll spell it out for you, Valentine, and I could get in trouble for this, so listen hard. You're bait. Do you understand? You're a nice, juicy chunk of bait, and I'm the hook. I've been sitting by the phone practically ever since you hit the States, waiting for something like this to happen, and if that makes me a bastard, that's good. Nice people don't last long in my line of work. Here's another platitude for your collection: it takes one to know one."

"You mean it takes a thief to catch a thief," she shot back, chaffing her arms. The coldness she felt in her bones would take more than a hot shower to relieve.

"If you want to put it that way." He shrugged, sat down and went on with his breakfast. "You're a nice lady. You had a rotten break, and you didn't deserve it. It happens. My job is to cut the odds so that it doesn't happen too often."

Icy fingers curled tightly into fists, and Val stared at him. "So I'm to risk my life so that you can be a hero and catch the criminals who murdered my husband?"

Meekins looked up blandly, blotted his lips on a napkin and said, "I've been less than an hour away ever since you got back to the States. I don't think your life is in any real danger, but there's always the chance."

"And you'll take it, right?"

"Not willingly. Like I said, I play the odds. I'm not out to avenge your husband's death, because quite frankly, I think he deserved what he got. My aim is to shut off a specific pipeline of illegal arms. This one particular organization is small, but it's efficient because of a couple of men like your husband, men in positions of trust who went sour because they didn't feel appreciated, didn't get promoted fast enough or paid what they thought they were worth."

He reached for the coffeepot and held it questioningly over her cup, but Val didn't even notice. He was right, of course. Albert had complained bitterly for years that people in his position did all the donkey work and then, while the horns tooted and the flags waved, a few political figureheads stepped before the cameras and claimed all the glory.

"We've been trying to get an in for a long time." Meekin's small eyes were flat and opaque as they filed away every nuance of expression that flickered across her face. "We knew Scott had done them a few favors, but he only went on the payroll, as close as we can figure, about four and a half years ago. Just his luck that it turned out to be the same old story: little dog runs all the risks, big dog gets the bone. When he tried to do something about it, they paid him off, and you got hurt in the process."

He turned away, ramming his hands into his hip pockets as he stared at the crooked calendar beside her refrigerator. Val waited, knowing he wasn't finished yet.

"So now I've got to risk getting you hurt again to protect a few hundred thousand poor fools who don't know who the hell's fighting over what. All they know is that when the fighting starts—and it always does—they're caught in the middle.''

"You're all heart, Meekins." Val knew she was being unfair, but she couldn't help it. She had to strike out at someone, at something, and Meekins was the nearest target. If only Cody was here! She needed him. She *wanted* him.

Val stood under the shower as long as she dared. Then she dressed quickly, hearing the low murmur of Meekin's voice on the phone in the next room. She was going to be late, but somehow, it didn't seem important. Wynn had told her she'd be driving out to a building site with him and a client one day this week to take notes. In case he decided to go today, she wore her most comfortable shoes and a paisley skirt in a blend of earthy colors that wouldn't show mud stains.

Anything would be better than trying to concentrate on estimates and computer-printed excuses for items like the custom-made bathtub units that were shipped three times from a factory in Tennessee and still hadn't arrived. She had an idea that her efficiency was going to plunge to new depths today. "I'll be paying a visit to cousin Grace this morning," Meekins informed her when she was ready to leave.

Hand on the door, Val halted, wondering if she could simply leave the country again. Grace was going to get all riled up and want her to move back to Sherrill Ford for her own safety, and Val wasn't sure she had the energy to hold out any longer.

"I wish you didn't have to do that," she said with a sigh. What on earth would Grace make of Fred Meekins? There was a peculiar bulge under one arm of his palm-tree-and-flamingo shirt, and Val envisioned buttons flying in all directions if he had to get to his gun in a hurry. Oh, Lord, if she was in serious trouble, why did she have to have this Mickey Mouse agent on her case?

"How much does she know?" her Mickey Mouse agent asked.

"Mostly what was in the local papers. She thinks it was just a random terrorist thing. I wrote her from the hospital to tell her that I was all right, and after I got home I told her that Albert and I had been separated for several months when it happened." Val breathed in deeply and stood her tallest, bracing herself for whatever came next. She knew she looked pale. She *felt* pale.

If granite could soften, the look on Fred Meekin's tough face did. "She'll have to know who I am and why I'm claiming to be a cousin. By the way, I'm from Virginia, on my way to Florida for some sport fishing. Just stopped off here for old times' sake."

"Claiming kinship in a small place like this is risky. Everybody knows everybody else."

"You just finished telling me that you didn't know anybody, and you grew up here. I'm one of those black sheep types. Every family's got a few. It was the best I could come up with at short notice."

"Where'd you get the costume?"

Meekins looked down at his shirt and jeans. "Costume? You mean these? They're mine. I don't sleep in three-piece suits, you know."

Her shoulders lost some of their military stiffness as Val actually smiled. Her smile quickly faded as he went on to say, "Okay, suppose you give me a list of all the people you've spent more than an hour with in the past three weeks."

"Now?"

"Now."

Val glanced at her watch, decided that she was already so late another few minutes wouldn't matter and closed the door. "I see Suzie Pauley almost every day, but I've known her forever. There's Lucy McIntire, but she used to live around the corner from Grace. My boss and his assistant, and I've already told you about both of them. In fact," she added dryly, "you've probably already checked them out." Meekin's nod confirmed it.

Then there was Cody. Always, it came back to Cody. Something in her face must have given her away, because she saw a sudden look of interest flicker in Meekin's eyes.

"Tell me about him," he commanded.

Resentment flared, and as swiftly died. As if she'd ever had any choice. Meekins would have ferreted it out one way or another, and then he'd have accused her of obstructing justice and been more suspicious than ever.

"You mean Cody Macheris," she said flatly.

"What's your relationship with him?"

Val leaned over, staring down at her feet. "He lives downstairs. Eric is his son. Cody and I are...good friends."

He nodded, interpreting the phrase as she'd known he would. He didn't ask her anything more, and yet Val was certain that before an hour had passed, he'd know everything there was to know about Cody Macheris.

"Is that it?" she demanded bitterly. "May I go to work now?"

Meekins nodded almost absently, and as Val closed the door behind her, she tried to close her mind to the ruins all around her. Her apartment, her past...

Her future?

Chapter Nine

Wynn was ranting about the lost bathtubs, and Val got out the file again. She gave up all hope of escaping the office because from the looks of that sky, by mid-afternoon it would be raining again. Pity. She'd have welcomed a chance to clamber over the red hills overlooking the Catawba River while Wynn and his client argued over the best use of the terrain. Wynn had earned himself a reputation for giving his clients precisely what they wanted. It hadn't taken Val long to realize that instead, he saw to it that his clients wanted precisely what he deemed appropriate for their personalities, their financial and social positions, and more importantly, their particular chunk of real estate.

Val made a deliberate effort to close her mind to everything outside the plush suite of paneled offices. The problems here were ones she could handle—for the most part. By noon she'd even managed to get a line on the misshipped tub units, plus a guarantee of delivery within the week.

"Headache?" Her employer inquired, swinging by her polished cherry desk as he returned from an extended lunch. He nodded to the neat stack of correspondence she had typed, and then, when she looked up at him questioningly, he pointed out the fact that she'd consistently assigned her own zip code to each addressee.

"Oh, Lord, I couldn't have done anything so stupid," Val moaned.

"Go home and take a couple of aspirin."

"But the bills—I was going to finish paying those today."

"Don't even *look* at my checkbook until you've cleared up whatever's been bugging you lately. Between you and my accountant, the IRS'll make crow bait outta my carcass. Go home, Valentine, and that's an order." He replaced the stub of a cigar in his mouth and turned away.

Hesitating, Val fought down the urge to tell him that home was the very last place she wanted to be. "But Wynn—"

"What's the matter, car still on the blink? If you leave now, maybe you can make it before the bottom falls out. Quit worrying—Robin'll catch the phone."

Val would be the first to admit that she needed to get away before she committed an even more serious blunder, but her apartment held little attraction. If there'd been a movie within walking distance she'd have sat through it, no matter what it was, for the few hours of oblivion it offered.

"I'll just redo these letters first, and—"

"Go," Wynn commanded, pointing a stubby finger toward the brass and glass door. "You wear a raincoat today? No? You're nuts. Take my umbrella in case you get caught short."

So she was nuts. So what else was new? The sky was slate-gray. Over toward the Blue Ridge Mountains, lightning flashed sporadically as a gust of wind revealed the chalky undersides of the leaves. She'd gone less than half a block when the first big drops machine-gunned down on her shoulders.

Wynn's umbrella was a large one, but by the time she'd opened it, her blouse was a transparent gray film glued to her body, and her shoes were squelching with every step. At least they were her oldest. The same couldn't be said for the soft paisley skirt that clung damply to her thighs.

"Damn, damn, *damn*," she muttered, struggling as the wind threatened to turn the umbrella wrongside out. If she'd been smart, she'd have called Meekins and had him collect her. He owed her something for that gargantuan breakfast he'd consumed. Who'd have thought a secret agent could put away so much food? He probably stored it up, she thought irritably, the way a bear stored food against hibernation, never knowing when he'd have to go underground.

Val had only a hazy idea what the term implied, nor did she care to find out. Unlike her cousin Grace, who adored gory cops-and-robbers thrillers, Val had never been much of a mystery buff. After all that had happened to her—was still happening, for that matter—she'd stick to reading cookbooks and poetry.

The sidewalk was quickly littered with wet, torn leaves. It gave off that distinctive wet-pavement smell, and Val sniffed appreciatively as she dodged puddles and attempted to focus her mind on her most pressing problems. The trouble was, there were just too many of them.

Logical or not, at this point, her career problems took precedence over all others. She might worry about some real or imagined threat to her life in the small hours of the morning, when her imagination was inflamed by a lack of sleep, but in the cold light of day, those worries tended to fade into oblivion. Wet clothes and shoes— those were real. The job that paid her rent was real; terrorists and housebreakers and purse snatchers were not.

As for Cody, she hadn't quite made up her mind which world he belonged to, the real or the imaginary.

Val was almost home when she glanced up to see her green chair sitting half on the sidewalk, half on the patch of grass that fronted the apartment building. With its sodden arms trailing cottony stuffing, it looked both ludicrous and touching.

Eric appeared in the doorway with an armload of sofa cushions, and Val hurried forward. "Eric, would you mind telling me what's going on?"

Peering at her over the top of his burden, the tall youth stepped aside, turning to block the door open with one foot. "Gee, Val, you weren't supposed to be here yet. Hey, watch that step-down, guys!"

There was no mistaking the straining, white-clad shoulders that backed out through the front door. Nor the colorful shirt at the other end of her ruptured sofa.

"You're early," Eric accused. "We were going to get it all hauled away before you got back. I swept the place out and Fred got your fish a new bowl so we could make coffee. We turned your mattress so the slit was on the bottom, but I don't think it's much good anymore."

Was there anything more pathetic than old furniture exposed to the elements? The sound that emerged from Val's throat could have passed for laughter, but when her chin began to quiver and her nose got that burny feeling, she knew she was on the verge of doing something gauche.

"Oh, please, I don't need this," she protested, shaking her head from side to side. There was no end to this farcical nightmare.

With a turtlelike reaction that was purely involuntary, Val slid her thumb up the handle of the big, black umbrella and collapsed it silken folds about her head, covering her face and shoulders completely. Thus shrouded, she stood helplessly by like a blind wet witch in a pointed hat while the three of them manhandled her belongings into the battered old van that waited at the curb.

"Val? You all right?" It was Cody's voice, Cody's hand cupping her elbow. What other hand could scorch her skin right through her clothing?

"Just go away," she pleaded. "Please! When I open my eyes, you'll all be gone and none of this will be happening."

"We were going to have it all cleared away before you got home so you wouldn't have to do it. My watch must have stopped. Val, would you please uncover your face? I can't talk to an umbrella."

Cody tugged at the umbrella shaft, but Val held on tightly. She was feeling more idiotic by the minute, but what could she do? If there was anything more embarrassing than *doing* something so silly, it was having to *undo* it.

"What am I supposed to sit on?" she demanded, finally lifting the smothering folds only to find that the metal hinges had caught in her hair.

"Keep on the way you're going and you won't want to sit," Cody threatened. "You and Eric—I don't know which one of you is worse!" He tried to wrestle the umbrella from her hands, and she winced.

"Stop pulling, darn it, my hair's all tangled in the spokes!"

With the rain steadily drenching them both, Val waited impatiently while Cody reached under the umbrella and freed her hair from the tiny hinges. For once, he was not noticeably gentle.

"Now get in here out of the rain and stop acting like a five-year-old," he barked, grabbing her elbow as she massaged her stinging scalp. Fred and Eric were moving around the cab of the van.

"Where are they going with my furniture?" Val exclaimed, trying once more to escape as Cody herded her in out of the rain.

He blocked her with ease. His arms went around her, and Val's protests died on her lips. He was doing it to her again! How could she be expected to deal with a brand-new crisis situation with Cody on the scene to short circuit every cell in her brain?

"The stuff's beyond repair. Eric's going to haul it off—and technically speaking, it's not yours anyhow, it's the property of Country Club Apartments. I warned 'em about the lack of security when I first moved in. Since they didn't do anything about it, they've agreed to replace the things that were ruined."

"You mean I'm stuck with another green chair and another brown plastic couch?" Val wailed.

"Not necessarily. You pick, they pay, all right?"

Grudgingly, Val admitted the fairness of the arrangement. It occurred to her to wonder if it had been quite so easy, but with the warmth of Cody's hands on her shoulders melting every shred of her resistance, she found that furniture was the least of her worries.

"C'mon, let's get you inside," he said gruffly. Ignoring her halfhearted protests, he ushered her into his own apartment instead of allowing her to go upstairs. "We've only got a few minutes, hardly enough time to settle anything. It'll have to wait, I'm afraid."

Once inside, Val moved abruptly away from the circle of his arms and began prowling nervously. "What'll have to wait?" Try as she might, she couldn't seem to pin her mind to the myriad problems confronting her, not with Cody glowering at her like an eagle about to pounce.

Finding herself beside his desk, she began nervously dog-earing the pages of the phone book; the closer he came, the faster her fingers crimped.

He halted no more than a foot away and said, "Val, look at me."

Val didn't want to look at him. She was no fool, in spite of every appearance to the contrary. Once she looked into his eyes, she'd sink without a trace.

"Valentine..." Cody's vibrant voice shimmered on the air between them, and her chin jutted in determined resistance.

"Why don't you just leave me alone?" she said through clenched teeth.

"Good God, do you think I haven't *tried*?" His voice rose, arms lifting in a gesture of impatience. "Why the hell do you think I took off in such a hurry? Why do you think I couldn't stay away?"

Val groaned, feeling as helpless as one of the leaves that had been beat to the ground by the driving rain. Everything was moving too fast, nothing made sense anymore—least of all her feelings toward this maddening man.

Should she warn him that he was probably at the head of Meekin's list of suspects? No, Meekins was supposed to be her cousin. Besides, he'd probably cleared Cody immediately, otherwise would the three of them have been hauling her furniture out together? Perhaps.

They continued to eye each other warily, with Val torn between wanting to dump her suspicions on his capable shoulders and wanting to run from him. The trouble was, nothing was ever quite what it seemed. She *hated* duplicity!

What did she really know about Cody Macheris? Only what he'd told her, and that could have been a pack of lies. As for Meekins, the thought process of a secret agent remained a mystery to her. For all she knew he was trying to trap Cody, using Val for bait. Hadn't he as good as admitted that that's all she was?

Val's spine stiffened abruptly, and she turned away just as Cody reached out to take her in his arms. Dammit, she was sick and tired of being *used*! "Look, just leave me alone, will you?"

"Valentine, I wish I knew what the devil was going on around here. You seem to attract trouble like a magnet—first your purse, and now this." Arms crossed over his chest, Cody watched her with a look of growing wariness. "I've missed you," he added gently when it became obvious that she wasn't going to enlighten him.

"You've missed me? I haven't been anywhere. *You're* the one who could hardly wait to get away." Her voice sounded about as firm as if she'd just staggered off a giant roller coaster.

"Lady, I was scared stiff of you, and what you were doing to me."

Suddenly it seemed as if the very air rushed from the room, leaving Val starved for oxygen. She spun around to stare at him, and then, desperately fighting against the urge to surrender, turned to stare out the window. "When did you get back?" she asked with a commendable semblance of poise.

"Not long before you showed up."

"How did you meet Meekins?" Catching her gaffe, she tried to recover. "My cousin Fred, that is."

"Valentine, please don't lie, not to me. If that guy's your cousin, he's my grandmother."

Val swallowed the brittle laugh before it could emerge. "I'm not sure just what kin that makes us, are you?"

Lunging forward, Cody reached for her. He yanked her around to face him, fingers biting into her arms, and glared down into her stark white face. "Will you just tell me what the bloody hell is going on around here? For God's sake, Valentine—"

Val wrenched her arms from his grasp. "Stop it! Just stop it, Cody. I'm sick and tired of men barging into my life, yelling and swearing and wrecking everything!"

"*Wrecking* everything! Is that what I've done to you?" His eyes narrowed. "Did you have something going with that so-called cousin of yours? Don't tell me that hard-nosed bastard turns you on, because I refuse to believe it!"

Nerves stretched beyond bearing, Val flung back her hand and would have struck him if Cody hadn't caught her wrist.

Narrowed glittering eyes bore into wide, brimming ones. Somewhere deep inside her, a blind and craven creature urged her to throw herself into his arms and shut out the rest of the world. Val hardened herself against giving in to her own weakness. How could she trust any man when her world kept falling apart? She had lived with one man for almost eighteen years, only to discover that she'd never even known him. This had all the earmarks of another such disaster.

The silent battle continued as Cody held her wrist away from her body. Val refused to demean herself by struggling further. If she'd had a thread of dignity left, it was lost now, in that last reckless act.

"Don't you think you're being pretty childish?" Cody's quiet words were at odds with the look he sent her. His eyes fell to her agitated breast under the wet, translucent blouse, then swept downward to take in the skirt that clung damply to her hips and thighs.

Instinctively, Val fell back on a manner that had carried her through some of the worst times. "I beg your pardon, but I happen to bruise rather easily. Would you please let go of my wrist before you crush it?"

Cody dropped it instantly, the shamefaced look gone so quickly she thought she must have imagined it. "Then act your age," he grumbled. "And don't play the grand duchess with me, lady, because I'm not in the best of moods."

"But then, you never were," she replied coolly. As the tug of war between Cody's powerful temper and Val's brittle pride continued, Val drew in a deep, steadying breath and willed herself to hang on. If she blew up again, it would be all over. He'd have won whatever it was he wanted to win, and she'd have lost far more than her self-respect.

"Val, there's something you're not telling me. That hard case passing himself off as your cousin has cop written all over him. I'm giving you fair warning, lady—I intend to find out what's going on. You can lie all you want to, but in the end, it won't do you a damned bit of good."

A feeling not unlike nausea swept over her then. Suddenly, the room seemed to darken, and Val clutched the corner of the desk for support. If Cody noticed her sudden weakness, it didn't show in the grim set of his features as he went on to issue a warning. "I know what I want. And I know exactly how to go about getting it."

Val had never thought she'd be so glad to hear Fred Meekin's gravelly voice. He called through the door, and while she struggled for composure, Cody moved silently to let him in.

"Sorry, the latch must have caught when I shut it," Cody apologized unconvincingly. "Eric get off all right?"

Before answering, Fred swept the room with a practised eye that struck Val as comically at odds with his unprofessional appearance. "Yeah, he thinks he's taking the stuff to the county dump. Craddock'll have it impounded before it hits the ground."

Cody scowled. "Then why the runaround?"

"The kid's clean. The less he knows, the better. Craddock's already gone over it for prints, but in case anything comes up..." Meekin's hard, flat eyes sized up the man who'd come barging onto the scene while the furniture was being removed from the apartment upstairs. "Nice kid. You and your wife must be proud of him."

"My ex-wife," Cody corrected softly, the words falling into a chasm of silence that lapped around the three people in the room.

He resisted the urge to throttle the creep. He'd dealt with too many of the breed not to recognize a smart-ass cop when he smelled one. Whomever Meekins was working for, it sure as hell wasn't local. He'd lay odds this guy wasn't out of Raleigh, either, which left either the feds or some private interest. Whoever he was, he was playing a cagey game, deliberately blowing his own cover this way.

Cody made a silent commitment to keep him off Val's back until he was in a better position to protect her.

"Yeah, sure," Meekins muttered, as both men continued to size each other up.

Val looked from one man to the other as she breathed in a measure of control. At that moment, she hated them both with equal fervor. Not content to shatter her fragile peace, they were squaring off against each other like a couple of feral dogs.

Well, she refused to be a part of it. Let them fight it out between them. "I'm leaving," she announced. "Fred, there's no hotel around here. Why don't you see if Cody will lend you his sofa? I'd offer you mine, but—" Shrugging tiredly, she let herself out, leaving the pair of them staring after her. She'd had, quite literally, all she could stomach.

Despite the persistent thunderstorms that seemed to hover in the area, Sherrill Ford was a haven of peacefulness after what Val had left behind. Not even Charles and his obsequious attentions could have spoiled her relief in having escaped from under the noses of her two watchdogs. Fortunately, Charles was away on a business trip.

She'd hated to leave without seeing Eric, but luckily, he'd driven up in the van while she was waiting outside for Grace.

"Hey, what's wrong? What's going on?" he'd demanded, swinging down from the cab with a worried frown on his good-looking face.

"Oh, I, uh, Eric, I was afraid I'd miss you, and I wanted to thank you for—well, for being there."

He'd shifted his weight awkwardly, glancing up at her window and then back again. "Heck, I didn't do anything. Hey, look, you wanna come on back inside? I've got to tell Fred about this jerk at the dump who—"

"You go ahead, Eric, I'll be right with you. I just needed to catch a breath of air."

He'd given her a look that would one day mature into the kind of look that had hooked her on Cody that first time. The smile had lagged only a second or two behind. "Yeah, I think I know what you mean. Val...you know, Dad comes down pretty hard sometimes, but he doesn't mean anything by it. I guess he takes things more seriously than some guys do." He'd reached out to touch her arm, and Val had almost crumpled right then and there.

"Oh, Eric..." The tears had been totally unexpected, but they'd served to convince him.

"Look, you take your time and then come on back inside. I'll make you some coffee. None of that bilge Dad makes, either. That stuff'll strip paint."

She'd laughed, albeit a bit unsteadily. Clasping his hand in both of hers, she'd said, "Oh, Eric, what a wonderful friend you are. Give me a minute to pull myself together, will you? And don't tell Cody or Fred I'm out here. They both think I need a baby-sitter."

He'd left her then, his angular shoulders swinging around just inside the door for one last try. "You're sure, now?"

"I'm sure, Eric. But thank you." She knew full well he'd be watching her from the nearest window. She'd almost decided she might as well go back inside and take her chances when Grace pulled up to the curb.

She'd dashed out, not looking back, and flung herself inside the car. "Thank goodness! Let's get out of here. I'll explain later, just *go!*"

Grace had driven the whole distance without once mentioning Val's desperate phone call. If her expression hinted that she suspected her younger cousin had finally buckled under the strain, she'd been tactful enough to withhold all questions.

Now, as Val washed and her cousin dried, Grace said, "Your old room's still made up, Valentine, but the minute this rain lets up, you need to open the windows. Been thinking about having central air put in. There's been a contractor over at Charles's lately—I think he's planning to enlarge the girls' rooms. I might see if they do installations."

Val only sighed. She'd done far too much sighing since they'd arrived at the tall frame house with its overgrown shrubbery, well-tended vegetable garden and tall shade trees. Grace had walked out and left supper on the stove when Val had called, and they hadn't bothered to reheat the baked chicken or the home-grown string beans and fresh Silver Queen corn.

"I'm not going to ask what it is you're running away from, Valentine, but I need to know if you're planning to go in to work in the morning. With one car between the pair of us..."

"Oh, Lord," Val said, rinsing the dishcloth, "I'd better call Wynn. He sent me home early with a headache, and then one thing led to another."

"Go out on the porch and settle your supper," Grace ordered. "I'll call Wynn and fix everything up, don't you worry about a thing."

Val was only too glad to escape to the hypnotic comfort of the squeaky old porch swing. She'd spent long hours there when she'd first come back home, not unmindful of the symbolic retreat to fetal security. Once more she was taking the coward's way out, letting Grace run interference for her with Wynn. Somehow, she'd make it up to her, she vowed. Somehow...

By all rights, Wynn should fire her on the spot. He might just do it, too, Val acknowledged with a surprising degree of relief.

At least she'd be better off than the last time she'd gone job hunting. Then she'd still been frightened, half-sick, and dangerously near the end of her funds. She had her health back now. Furthermore, she'd gained considerable confidence in her abilities. She might be temperamentally unsuited to be a secretary, but she'd proved to herself that at thirty-eight, she was still capable of learning new skills.

Val smiled in the darkness, one foot tucked under her, the other one pushing lethargically against the gray-painted porch floor. It occurred to her that there was something essentially safe and sane about a front porch swing. Rolling her neck to relieve muscles stiff from an accumulation of inner tension, she inhaled deeply. The scent of corn tassels, cabbages and rich, damp earth filled her lungs. As if on cue, a chorus of tree frogs tuned up, almost succeeding in blocking out the questions that tumbled about in her mind.

Maybe she should move back here with Grace, after all. There were far worse ways to live.

But what about a job?

I could always take in sewing, she mused, shifting the patchwork pillow to a more comfortable position.

Yeah, some seamstress you'd be—some of your hems are still held up with masking tape and pins.

So all right, maybe she'd tackle Statesville again. Or make grape leaf pickles to sell at the county fair. There was always the translating thing. If she could talk Lucy into expanding her small operation, perhaps even on a partnership basis... It was something Val would enjoy exploring further, but it would have to wait.

Meanwhile, what about Cody? Could she actually be in love with a man she could suspect of...? Of whatever it was she'd suspected him of? Good Lord, she wasn't even certain what that was, which only showed how little she was equipped to deal with the situation she found herself involved in.

Staring unseeingly at a glimmer of light that shone through the trees between Grace's house and that of her neighbor, Val made an attempt to organize her thoughts. Someone thought she knew something she didn't—or suspected she *had* something she didn't. That someone had traced her to Lakesboro and was now trying to find whatever it was they thought she had.

But she didn't *have* anything.

Next problem: what happened when they discovered that she didn't have whatever they were looking for? Would they try to pick her brain for whatever bits of information Albert might or might not have imparted before he died? How could she convince them that she didn't know anything? How did one go about picking a brain?

"Oh, Lord, I don't want to know," she whispered, stilling the motion of the swing as tension crept over her once more.

Cody? Surely not Cody. Cody had taken her fishing. He'd made love to her. They'd laughed, and talked, and spent hours together saying little of any importance. It had been the feeling of integrity and strength she'd sensed in him that had first attracted her. Well...that had *secondly* attracted her, Val corrected, a mental image of his intense masculinity swimming before her eyes.

Ironically, that same strength, both physical and emotional, had also been the reason she was afraid of letting him get too close to her. She'd tried so desperately to establish her own identity and stand on her own two feet. It would have been fatally easy to lean on those powerful shoulders and let Cody solve her problems.

She'd been no closer to coming to terms with her relationship with Cody when everything had started coming apart. Her nice, orderly existence had developed cracks that had widened until she'd had no choice but to run away.

How could she stay and fight when she didn't know who or what the enemy was?

Meekins had implied that her life might be in danger. Val was far more concerned about her heart, but things were happening so swiftly that she couldn't think clearly, much less intelligently. Running had been her only choice under the circumstances. The question was, had she run far enough?

Through the lace-curtained window, the jangle of the telephone broke through her troubled thoughts.

"Want to get that?" Grace called out from the kitchen.

"You answer. If it's for me, I'm not here."

"I'm not going to start lying, not when I'm this near meetin' my maker," Grace snapped. Val could hear her soft-soled slippers marching across the room toward the phone. Before she could pick it up, it shrilled again.

"Let it ring—please, Grace. Maybe they'll think we aren't here."

Grace's ample figure filled the doorway, arms akimbo as she peered through the screen door. "That's lying just as sure as sayin' the words, missy. You're in some kind of trouble, don't think I don't know it. Who're you running from?"

"I told you about my apartment," Val reminded her. "If you'd had your purse stolen and your house broken into, wouldn't you be nervous?"

"Town's getting too big," the older woman said with a snort of derision. "All those water skiers and plastic sailboats. You can't tell me that they're not out there doing things they've got no business doing in some of those boats . . . drinking, fooling around."

"On water skis?" Val jeered. "It's when they start fooling around in my apartment that I get worried. I shouldn't have come here, Grace, it's not fair to you."

The phone stopped ringing. Both women listened to the intense silence for a moment, and then Val said, "Grace, you remember the man who came out here a day or so ago? His name was Fred Meekins and he—"

"I'm not senile yet. He was a federal agent pretending to be some sort of cousin so he'd have an excuse to sniff around and find out what's going on." She came outside and plopped down in one of the cane rockers. "You want to know what I think? I think it's somebody living on one of those fancy houseboats. I was telling Fred about this bootlegger I once knew who—''

Val sat up, planting both feet on the floor. "Grace, exactly how much did Meekins tell you, anyway?"

"Enough. At least he didn't take me for a fool, like some I could name. I saved all the newspapers, and after Fred left, I went upstairs and reread the whole kit 'n' kaboodle. Looks to me like Fred was right. Whoever bumped off that scoundrel you married thinks you were in cahoots with him."

Val was stunned. She didn't know why she should have been; Grace hadn't changed all that much from the days when, as secretary and office nurse to the town's only physician, she'd known all there was to know about every family in town.

"How long did—did Fred stay?" Somehow, she couldn't picture the two of them together, cozily exchanging theories on who was trying to blow Valentine to kingdom come.

"Oh, he stayed long enough to help me stake my tomatoes and pick the last of the pole beans. Then I fixed us a pitcher of iced tea and we sat out here on the front porch and talked things over. Fred's a lonely man, you know, Valentine. He never married, being's he was always traveling around at the drop of a hat. At least I have my home. Fred lives in a residential hotel in Arlington when he's not off gallivanting. Retires in a couple of years. Wonder what he'd make of Tricia Canfield?"

Horrified, Val cried, "Grace, you're unbelievable!"

The rocker creaked rhythmically, punctuated by the sound of slippered feet tapping the wooden floor. "Told him he was welcome to come for supper any time he wanted to take a break. If Tricia happened to be here at the same time, then who's to say what might happen?''

Val closed her eyes in silent supplication. "What did he say to that?''

"Oh, just that he'd be around for a while. Already got his sights set on a suspect, you mark my words. I don't mind telling you, Valentine, I'm glad you're out of that apartment. Not that I'm one to say I told you so,'' she add piously.

"Of course not,'' Val said quickly, stifling a smile.

"Reckon I'd better go in and call Wynn before he takes out his bridgework. Can't understand a word he says without it.''

Bridgework? Val marveled. She hadn't even suspected. Did anything escape those bifocaled eyes? "Grace, you shouldn't be saddled with my obligations. I'll call Wynn, and if he wants to let me go, then—''

"Oh, stop looking so down in the mouth. I told you you weren't cut out to be a secretary in the first place, didn't I? Happens I've been thinking about a solution. Of course, it's going to take some planning.''

"Grace,'' Val said warningly, "if this involves Charles Reedy, I'm going back to Lakesboro this minute.''

"Sit still. You're not going anywhere tonight, so just settle back and let me handle things. I didn't get to be this old without learning a thing or two, which is more 'n can be said of some folks I know.''

Chapter Ten

If someone had told Valentine that she'd be on a plane headed toward Tampa before the week was out, she'd have laughed and told them flatly that her traveling days were over. Yet here she was, bundled into the last seat available with only the clothes on her back and the few things she'd thrown together when she'd escaped to Sherrill Ford.

She didn't even know why! All she knew was that Fred had called sometime after she'd gone up to bed and talked to Grace for several minutes before Grace had called her to the phone.

"In case you thought you got away with something, you didn't. I figured you'd be better off with Grace."

"*You* figured!" Val had exclaimed.

"But now I'm sending you south for your health," he'd said, ignoring her indignation.

"If that's your idea of a joke, you'll notice I'm not laughing."

"You're booked on a nonstop out of Douglas at six-twenty-three tomorrow morning. Your ticket is at the counter, and your name is Mary Whitmore, by the way. As soon as you get into Tampa, pick up a courtesy phone and ask for any messages under that name."

"Who is this Mary Whitmore?" Val had asked.

"My grandmother, rest her soul. There'll be funds waiting for you there, in case you need anything, but you're not to go by your apartment on the way to the airport."

"But what—"

"There'll be a message or a ticket on the next flight out. You'll know what to do in either case."

"But, Fred—!"

"Grace will drive you. And Valentine...you can save your breath because she doesn't know anything."

A logjam of questions had prevented her from speaking for a moment. Not to mention fear, anger and a sense of frustration that had made her want to strike out at that flat, gravelly voice on the other end of the line.

Val had tried reasoning with herself; midnight phone calls and hurried flights were certainly nothing new in her life. Albert had often received such calls, and then they'd be off to another Third World country to lay the groundwork for a commission to come in and lay still more groundwork that was supposed to end up in industry and prosperity for all concerned.

Only there was nothing reasonable about the occurrences of the past few days.

"Valentine? Still there? Have you got that?" There'd been no sign of impatience in Meekins's voice, no sign of expression at all.

"Will you just tell me one thing?" she'd asked in desperation. "Just who are you? What's happening? Who do you answer to, anyway?"

"That's three things. Would it make you feel any happier if I said I answer to my conscience? Forget it, Mary. Just do as you're told."

This simply wasn't happening, she'd told herself. In a few hours, she'd wake up and get ready to go to work, and sometime during the day she'd remember snatches of a dream in which her life had been turned upside down again, and some strange man had called her in the middle of the night to tell her she had to get on another plane.

"Val? You still there?"

"What about Cody Macheris?"

"Forget about Macheris. He's got troubles of his own. You just go on down to Tampa and have yourself a nice little vacation on Uncle Sam's tab. One way or another, I'll be in touch shortly after you land."

He'd hung up then, leaving Val to lie awake the rest of the night wondering at what point she'd lost control of her whole life. This had gone far enough!

The flight was smooth, short and uneventful. Val had been prepared for anything, including a hijacking. Instead, she found herself entering Tampa's spacious international airport clutching her carryon and trying to remember what it was that she was supposed to do next.

As soon as the crowd thinned, she took an unobtrusive seat at a nearby gate and waited until she'd composed herself enough to search out a courtesy phone.

"Message for Mary Whitmore?" she inquired then, expecting at any moment to be clapped into irons for impersonating a grandmother.

"Yes, Mrs. Whitmore, you're booked into the Airport Hotel." She was given concise instructions on how to reach it from her concourse, and then told that there would be a message waiting for her at the reception desk.

"Thank you," Val said dazedly to the dead instrument.

Less than an hour later she was seated cross-legged in the middle of a queen-sized bed, staring at the large denomination bills that had cascaded from the envelope she'd just opened. Three, four... five hundred dollars? Goodness, how much was this suite costing her, anyway? And why a whole suite? Why not a single?

"Oh, Lord, I'm part of all that government waste I've been reading about." She could see the headlines now: RUNAWAY SECRETARY LIVING IN PALATIAL SUITE IN FLORIDA HOTEL AT TAXPAYERS' EXPENSE.

There was no note. The money couldn't be for meals, because Fred had told her to use room service rather than venture out. He'd also indicated that she'd be contacted. But by whom? Or what?

Val flopped onto her back and stared at the ceiling. "It's just plain crazy, that's all," she said aloud. Things like this happened in other parts of the world. They happened in countries where opposing factions struggled for power, where splinter groups sought instant fame through acts of violence. They happened in spy novels and adventure films—but they certainly didn't happen to secretaries in small southern towns. Hadn't she come running home from Cyprus just so that she could lead a nice, dull, safe life?

In an ill-conceived attempt to reassure herself that she was back home in the United States and not in one of those volatile spots that were apt to erupt at any given moment, Val ordered a cheeseburger all the way and a double order of French fries for lunch. The minute she hung up the phone, she regretted ordering the food. She wouldn't be able to eat a bite. Why hadn't she asked for something light? A salad, or fresh fruit?

She reached for the phone to change her order and quickly snatched back her hand. The surest way to arouse interest was to start making a nuisance of herself with the kitchen staff. Word would spread, and . . .

"Oh, God, I'm really getting paranoid," she said with a groan.

Somehow she managed to get through the rest of the day without gnawing her nails to the quick. She diligently ate her way through the complimentary fruit basket, watched two soap operas in horrified fascination and read every single headline and subhead in the local paper, including those in sports, about which she knew little and cared less.

By dinnertime, she was prowling like a caged lioness. She treated herself to a lavish bubble bath and shampoo, compliments of the hotel's amenities, and then looked over the room-service menu, ordering the most expensive five-course dinner she could contrive and topping it off with a bottle of excellent wine.

The minute the order was placed, she felt ashamed of herself. As penance, she switched on an aerobics class and put herself through the paces until she was ready to drop.

"I can't survive another day of this," she panted to her image in the bathroom mirror. So far she'd managed to keep her thoughts from plunging too deeply into her bizarre situation, but what about tonight? The time would come when she was physically too tired to stay up, yet not tired enough to sleep.

She sat through the HBO offering, which unfortunately, was a James Bond classic, and then switched to the news, hearing, if not absorbing, updates on the various world crises.

Where was Cody now? What had Fred meant when he'd said Cody was in trouble? *In* trouble, or *had* trouble? Was there a difference? Like a frantic guinea pig, her mind raced through the maze of possibilities, always returning to the same old place.

Cody Macheris. Brindle hair, worn features, teasing, inquisitive eyes. Val could no longer evade the truth. She loved him with a passion that had nothing to do with common sense or sound judgment. If he walked through that door right now, she'd open her arms, no questions asked.

It was the sound of laughter and noisy conversation just outside in the corridor that aroused her. Sleep hadn't come easily, but it had finally come, and Val resented being dragged from its warm security by a group of inconsiderate late-night arrivals.

Slowly she became aware of a weight across her body, and she plucked at the covers. She'd turned on the air conditioner full blast for the lulling noise, and then had to reach for the quilted bedspread in the night.

The weight moved. It tightened, drawing her against a warm mountain.

"I didn't want to wake you," a deep, familiar voice whispered sleepily. Val's heart expanded wildly and then froze.

"Honey, it's me."

"Cody? *Cody?*" She recognized his voice even as she recognized the distinct scent of his body, clean and masculine, like balsam fir.

"I got in late, and you looked so cute with nothing but your nose and one hand sticking out of the covers."

"What are you doing here? How did you get in?"

"With a key, how else? Did you think you rated all this space by yourself?"

His hands were doing lazy, wonderful things to her spine, and Val began to breath again. In fact she began to breathe quite rapidly. "Cody, I don't understand what's going on. Is it over? Have they caught whoever it was?"

His hand moved around to her front, sliding under her pajama shirt to find her breast. Instead of answering, he used his mouth to a much better purpose, and Val snuggled closer, her lips parting as he began to explore with hands and lips and tongue.

There was a dreamlike unreality about the whole situation, and Val was swiftly caught up in it. Trembling, she lay there in heated expectancy as Cody slowly unbuttoned her top and eased it over her shoulders. His fingers brushed the sides of her breasts, and she could see the faint gleam of his smile.

"Your dreams must have been something else, lady," he whispered into her ear. Drawing the small lobe into his mouth, he suckled gently for a moment. "You're awfully affectionate in your sleep, you know that?"

Was she? Val was in no position to deny it. His fingertips circled the hardened tips of her breasts, arousing a storm of sensation, and she wondered if he'd touched her this way while she'd been sleeping. In an unconscious gesture of supplication, she shifted herself on the pillow, lifting her breasts closer to his mouth.

"Oh, sweet Valentine, you break my heart," he groaned, propping himself on one elbow to gaze down at her. For a long moment, they stared at each other in the near-darkness. Val could feel his warm, sweet breath on her face, the burning palm of one hand on her waist.

"Cody, I—we need to talk." Reason flickered in and out of focus, finally losing out completely as he began to weave his magic spell over her body.

"Talk," he murmured. "I never felt less conversational in my life. Sweetheart, I'm stealing time. I'll have to clear out in the morning."

"Oh, no." The protest was all but inaudible, and she wrapped her legs around his as if to keep him there by physical strength alone.

"Eric has a problem at home, and we're right in the middle of sorting it out. I had every intention of playing by the rules, but I hadn't figured on how I'd feel, knowing you were so close. I had to touch you—I have to..."

His face descended, and she felt his lips on her breast. "We'll talk, love. One day we'll talk all you want, but for now, this will have to be enough." When his tongue began to rasp a circular pattern around the sensitive peak, she moaned softly. He was so incredibly dear—all her fantasies come alive. If she could have Cody's arms to hold her, Cody's lips, his hands and his body to ease this intolerable ache he created, talk could wait.

"You don't know how I've needed this," he said fervently as he trailed moist kisses up the side of her throat. On reaching the vulnerable softness under her chin, he nipped her with tender ferocity. Val shuddered as, hungrily, he devoured her, taking her chin between his teeth, moving on to nibble at her cheeks, to bathe her eyelids in kisses.

With impatient hands, he shoved her pajama pants down over her hips, dragging her against him. For the first time, she realized that he was completely naked. With the last barrier gone, he aligned her to him, and as if they'd done it a thousand times before, her toes pushed against the tops of his feet, her knees bumped cozily against his, and she felt the brush of his diamond-shaped pelt as it tickled her breasts. Something suspiciously like laughter vibrated deep within him as his hardened body nudged impatiently against her belly.

"Still want to talk?" he taunted.

Val shook her head, beyond speech. What a wild and wonderful force, this magic between a man and a woman that could transcend such madness. She slid her hand up his sides, brought them to his chest and found what she was seeking. He was hard everywhere! Hard and fierce and incredibly sweet, and she loved him so much it was a physical ache...loved him and needed him and wanted him.

"Tell me what you want me to do to you," he urged, holding her away so that he could watch her reaction.

At some time during the past few minutes, the heavy covers had been thrown to the floor. Val didn't remember whether she'd done it or he had. All she knew was that in spite of the frigid air pouring into the room, she was melting like chocolate under a blazing summer sun.

She felt like laughing. She felt like crying. After years of thinking of herself as lukewarm in matters pertaining to sex, Cody Macheris had managed to turn her into a woman she hardly recognized. The very first time they'd made love it had been beyond anything she'd ever experienced—and yet it had been so inevitable, so *right*.

She felt daring and desirable, a creature of her own fantasy, with a fantasy lover all her own. "I don't know," she said helplessly. Unfortunately, her fantasy was still circumscribed by the limits of her own experience.

Cody took her hands and brought them back up to his chest. Guiding her, he moved her palms over his small, taut nipples, back and forth, raking her fingers, through the bed of crisp, flat curls. Then he took her hands slowly down his body, lingering where he wanted her attention.

She gave it. Freely, lovingly, lavishly, she tested his powers of resistance and her own power to arouse, first with feathery fingertip caresses, then with the judicious use of her fingernails, and finally, irresistibly, with a series of lingering kisses that brought him to a state of near catatonia.

"Dear God in heaven, woman, what are you trying to do, cripple me for life?"

At the agonized tone of his voice, Val cringed, and he caught her in his arms, burying his face in her hair to croon soft love words. "Oh, no, love, you don't understand. Sweet, lovely, desirable Valentine, you're the most wonderful woman in the world, but I'm only human. Lord, sweetheart, don't you know what that does to a man?"

She shook her head, seeing her elusive fantasy waver and threaten to disappear. Cody levered himself to a sitting position, leaning against the headboard. His hands continued to caress her back until they slipped beneath her hips to lift her astride his thighs.

"Look at me," he said gruffly. "Lift your head and open your eyes, darling."

She did, gazing into those strangely colored irises that were neither brown nor blue nor gray. "I'm not a young man, love, and I've been under a lot of strain. The first time with us was unbelievably good. I thought if I could make this time even better for you, it might help my case." He laughed shakily. "I hadn't allowed for the effect you have on me."

"What case, Cody? I don't know what you're talking about." Val searched his face, impatient with the shadows that kept her from seeing his expression. "Cody?"

His breath came in deep, rasping gasps. "Next time, love, I'll make it up to you," he promised, shifting her so that her knees clasped his hips and her legs trailed along his thighs. Taking her lips in a kiss that spoke of need and want...and perhaps love, as well, he arched his hips to meet her.

It was like setting a torch to dry grass, a match to lightwood. Clinging to him, Val matched the furious pace of his mounting passion. All too soon she felt herself going over the top, heard as if from a distance the soft, wild cries that issued from her throat. Then she collapsed in his arms.

It had been, if possible, even more wonderful than the last time.

In spite of the feverish heat that bathed them both, Cody refused to release her. Somehow, they managed to work their way into a horizontal position without once breaking their embrace, and Cody grabbed a corner of the sheet and drew it up over them.

"Val, sweet Valentine, there's so much I need to tell you, but this is not the right time. I've got no business even being here with you, but I couldn't stay away." He kissed her eyebrows, smoothed the hair away from her face and captured one of her feet between both of his. Gently, he squeezed. "That's a hug," he whispered sleepily, and she hugged him back in like manner. She had just enough energy left for that, no more.

Someone had closed the draperies. Perhaps that was why Val slept so late. Slept until hunger prodded her awake, and then lay there, her eyes closed, and thought longingly of the five-course dinner she'd sent back practically untouched the night before.

Slowly her thoughts broadened to take in what had happened afterward, and she reached out to Cody. By not opening her eyes, she could prolong the night's magic, she told herself, sliding her hand across the rumpled sheets. Moments later, when she'd encountered nothing more than her pajama pants, she opened her eyes reluctantly.

"Cody?"

The bathroom door was hidden from this angle. He was probably shaving. Come to think of it, he'd had a bit of a stubble last night. Her skin was still slightly tender in spots.

"Cody, I'm hungry, what about you?"

He wasn't shaving. He wasn't in the bathroom, nor was he in the adjoining room. Val tried to convince herself that he'd only gone out to buy a morning paper, but in her heart she knew better. He was gone. No goodbye, no note.

Nothing.

By the time she'd ordered breakfast and was staring morosely at her yogurt and banana with wheat germ,

Val had almost managed to convince herself that she'd dreamed the whole thing.

Cody shaded his eyes and searched the milling crowd for a familiar face. He'd half expected Eric to meet the small commuter plane, but there'd been no definite arrangement. He hoped to hell the boy hadn't skipped town again.

His conscience nagged at him for the self-indulgence that had prevented his sticking by his son's side until they could settle the matter of Eric's immediate future. But when they'd arrived at Jack and Anna's Hillsboro Beach house, it was to find only the staff in residence. The Wrights had gone to Nassau for a few days.

Whatever Eric had been feeling—relief, hurt, disappointment—he'd tried to cover it with profanity. Cody had jerked him up short. Too short, probably, but then, he'd had his own problems.

"Y'know, this is great," Eric had cried, his voice rising emotionally. "This is really great! I go to visit you, and what do I find? Some strange female in your bed! I come home, and what do I get? Is Mom here? Oh, hell, no, she's off on a—"

"Knock it off, Eric." Cody had had years to learn to deal with guilt—he refused to accept it now. "Look, if you're old enough to take off when you feel like it without asking permission, then so's your mother."

"Well, hell, she could have hung around long enough to find out if I'd been hurt or something. I mean, for all she cared, I could have been kidnapped! It's been known to happen, you know, when a guy's as loaded as Jack is."

"She knew you were with me," Cody had said flatly. "Now, I suggest you go shower and change while I get a hotel room." He'd begun formulating the change in his plans the moment he'd learned that Jack and Anna were gone. "We'll have some dinner and then get a good night's sleep. I expect your mother will be back tomorrow. She probably thought we'd be getting in late tonight, or maybe even in the morning. I wasn't sure about schedules when I told her we were coming."

Eric had nurtured his hurt feelings a bit longer. He'd begged off from dinner, preferring to go down to the marina and hunt up his friend, Tuck Taylor. Cody had dropped him off there, but not before he'd admitted that he was flying to Tampa if he could snag a late flight. "But I'll be back before breakfast in the morning," he promised.

"Can't stay away from her, can you?" Eric had jeered.

"Who?" The jolt of adrenaline had hit him like a thunderbolt, and then the boy had laughed.

"Who, the man says! Your Valentine, that's who."

"What makes you think Val's in Tampa?"

"You do. You've got that wimpy look on your face. Man, you've really got it bad, haven't you?"

Cody had dropped his guard then. "Yeah, Eric, I've really got it bad. How do you feel about it?"

Eric had blinked twice and seemed to consider. "Well, I guess . . . I guess I sort of understand. I mean, it's not like you and Mom could ever—"

"No, son, it's not." Cody hadn't pretended to misunderstand. He'd waited for Eric's response, hardly aware that he was holding his breath.

"I like her, Dad. We get along pretty good, so if you've got something going for you there, I'd say . . . go for it!"

The air had rushed from Cody's lungs and a wide grin broke across his face. "Thanks. I'll be back here first thing in the morning and we'll work it out. I won't leave until we've got you squared away, okay?"

Val was frightened. By now, she was fairly certain Cody had actually been there. Her imagination simply wasn't up to such elaborate flights of fancy. But if he was in Tampa, then why all the mystery? Why the disappearing act? Could he be using her as an alibi? Oh, damn that movie she'd watched on television! It was poisoning her judgment.

Yet, things like that did happen. It was one of the most common alibis used these days, spending the night with a convenient girlfriend.

No, she refused to think like one of those highly expendable characters from a James Bond film, no matter what was going on around her. As long as she could convince herself that she wasn't actually a part of any of this madness, then perhaps she stood a chance of surviving it.

If *she* wasn't a part of it, she decided illogically, then *Cody* wasn't a part of it. A stress-related dream, that's all it could have been.

Without giving herself time to think, she dialed an outside line and then punched Cody's number. She counted the rings. On the seventeenth one, she hung up the phone.

Grace. Grace would know what was going on. Hadn't she talked at length to Meekins? Hadn't she driven her to the airport and seen her off with a promise to look after Ollie and Val's houseplants?

But again her call went unanswered. By now, fear had once more begun to curdle her judgment. Meekins? She didn't even know where he was. She might have tried to reach him through the panic number if she'd remembered to bring it with her. It was probably still under the shoe box on her closet shelf.

As unreasonable as it was, she told herself she wouldn't be in this fix if she hadn't lost her head and called him in the first place.

Impulsively, she dialed her number at work. She desperately needed to hear a familiar voice, if only to convince herself that she wasn't losing her mind. It was picked up on the first ring.

"Flowers, Inc., Mr. Flowers's secretary speaking."

Tricia. Val swallowed hard and slowly replaced the instrument in its cradle. She hadn't really needed that.

What she did need was to hear a friendly voice, needed it badly. For two cents, she'd dress and go out into the terminal just to be with other people. She wouldn't even need to talk to anyone, just to hear normal voices talking about normal matters. The unnatural strain of all this running and hiding was beginning to work on her nerves. Especially after what had happened during the night.

If it actually had.

In a compulsive gesture she didn't even try to understand, Val lifted the phone once more and dialed her own home number. While she listened to the series of tones that indicated that the call was being put through, she rationalized it by telling herself that Meekins would have to stay in her apartment unless he was commuting from Statesville. There was no other place in Lakesboro for him to stay.

"We are sorry," the mechanical voice announced with bright insincerity. "The number you have dialed is no longer in service."

Shaken to the soles of her feet, Val dialed again. And again. The third time she listened to the witless voice telling her in essence that she no longer existed, she slammed down the phone and glared at it.

"All right, you damned windup toy, we'll see whose number is in service and whose isn't."

Chapter Eleven

Without ever leaving the terminal building, Valentine was able to change her appearance enough so that even Grace would have passed right by her without giving her a second look. There were shops of all sorts to choose from, and she had five hundred dollars to spend.

With every carefully chosen purchase, she grew more cunning. By the time she was finished shopping, she was thinking like a fugitive from the law. It would never do to don her disguise and then check out; someone might remember that Mary Whitmore had changed drastically between checking in and checking out.

She stopped by registration on her way back from her shopping spree and explained that she'd just learned that she could get an earlier flight to Seattle. "I might as well check out now, while there's no waiting line. Then I can just dash up to my room and grab my bag."

The clerk's fingers danced across his computer keyboard. "That was a credit card, wasn't it? Mmm... Here we go, Mrs. Whitmore." He slid a pen and a statement across the desk. "If you'll just look this over and sign it, you can drop the key in our express checkout box on your way out."

The charge was under the name Mary Whitmore, the address Arlington, Virginia. Val felt her tenuous grasp on reality waver once more, and she tightened her grip on the ballpoint and scrawled an illegible squiggle across the bottom of the bill.

"Hope you enjoyed you stay, Mrs. Whitmore. I see Mr. Whitmore checked out early...hope everything was all right."

With a mechanical smile, Val turned away. All right, so she hadn't dreamed it; Cody had actually been there. Something about a problem with Eric. But how had he known where to find her? Had Meekins sent him? If so, why? Who else might turn up if she stayed long enough? The questions were beginning to pile up again, and Val discovered that there were a few answers she really didn't want to hear.

If Meekins had made those reservations expecting to share the suite with her, he was in for a rude awakening. She'd done all the waiting she was physically capable of doing. Another day like yesterday and she'd be suffering every stress-related symptom in the book; *two* more such days and she'd be cutting paper dolls!

The minute she was safely in her room again, Val began shedding her clothes. Valentine Scott wore classic styles in subdued colors, the genuine article, even if the famous designer labels had been carefully clipped.

Mary Whitmore preferred hot pink jeans with a carefully clashing tanktop under a colorful tentlike shirt. Her yellow espadrilles were laced over, not under, the legs of her jeans. Grandmother or not, any designer togs Mary wore were of the mass-produced variety, with the designer's name emblazoned in a prominent place.

"Face it, Valentine, you and friend Mary will never agree on the matter of taste," Val informed her mirror image. In the revealing glare of a fluorescent light, she studied her face with complete objectivity. The features were clear-cut, the bone structure, though delicate, quite pronounced. Not a lot could be done to hide the hollows under her cheekbones, but she could try. A little blusher along the tops, a lighter foundation below...

Val turned her head this way and that, examining the results of her handiwork. Not bad, not bad at all, she mused. Perhaps she should forget about Scott-McIntire Translation Services and look for a job in the cosmetic field.

Impulsively, she puffed out her cheeks, and then giggled at the grotesque effect. "Terrific, Valentine," she congratulated herself as she snipped the sales tag from a colorful scarf and arranged it to cover her hair. "At least you haven't lost your sense of humor."

But was it a sense of humor, she wondered as she reshaped her mouth with a brilliant pink lipstick that made her look sallow, or was it the hysterics she felt she truly owed herself?

Capping off the remarkable transition with a pair of fuchsia, outsized sunglasses, Val hurriedly stuffed her few belongings into the small carryon. By force of habit, she checked the room thoroughly for leftovers, and on impulse, rescued the toast and jelly from her breakfast tray and wrapped it in the plastic laundry bag supplied by the hotel. Recalling her uncharitable thoughts about Fred and the enormous breakfast he'd put away that first day, she had to smile.

With seven car-rental agencies to choose from, she couldn't decide whether to try the safety in numbers theory and go with the largest, or hope a smaller one might have a less efficient bookkeeping system. Either way, it was a calculated risk that, short of stealing a car, she had to take.

"Eeny, meeny, miny—"

Before she even got to "mo," another potential problem presented itself. Mary Whitmore had boarded a flight in Charlotte, deplaned in Tampa and checked in and out of the hotel. But renting a car required certain credentials, none of which Mary Whitmore happened to possess. Valentine Scott was going to have to rent a car under her own name.

Val shrugged. So be it. If they'd tracked her this far, they'd be looking for Mary Whitmore. Perhaps the switch would buy her a few hours' time.

Heavens, she was really getting into her role, wasn't she?

Thirty minutes later she was on her way north. She'd debated taking Route 41 instead of the much faster interstate. Speed won out. She could have flown, but this way she retained a certain degree of control. At any time along the way, she could change her mind about going home.

Cody leaned back in the linen-covered chair and stared up at the vaulted ceiling of Jack and Anna's spacious living room. Anna toyed with the cover of a jade music box on the cocktail table, while Jack helped himself to another gin and tonic and Eric stared out at the glassy swells of the Atlantic. The house sprawled across more than three hundred feet of beachfront property.

They had just returned from one of the smaller marinas, where Cody and Eric had spent the morning aboard Captain Tucker T. Taylor's charter boat, *The Great Escape.*

"The boat's sound," Cody acceded. "I liked Taylor. I've checked out his background and he has an excellent reputation, both personally and professionally. Retired Coast Guardsman, wife crewed for him until she died two years ago. No children."

Eric's expression went from anxious to pained. "Aw, Dad, did you have to throw your weight around? I *told* you he was okay."

Cody grinned at his son. He was tired, but not too tired to remember how acutely sensitive the young could be when their pride was at stake. "I was discreet," he assured him. "I've always encouraged you to think for yourself, son. Now that you've made your decision, I can't complain."

"Then it's okay?" the boy asked eagerly. "I can live aboard the boat and mate for Tuck and go to night school instead of going off to some dumb prep school?"

Cody had had exactly three hours' sleep out of the past thirty-six. He was getting too old for this sort of life. "Your mother and I agreed that as long as you maintain your grade average and check in here at least twice a week, you can give it a shot. If the grades drop, you'll have to move back here with Jack and your mother and curtail your fishing activities to weekends only. If they still don't pick up, we renegotiate the whole deal."

"Fair enough!" Eric exclaimed, his broad grin encompassing the three adults who smiled with varying degrees of enthusiasm.

"I still don't see why you prefer that tub of Taylor's to *The Wright Stuff*," Jack said ruefully, pride in his new sixty-four-foot luxury cruiser evident in every word.

"It isn't as if we hadn't offered to buy you a little runabout of your own," Anna reminded him.

"*The Great Escape* is no tub! She's one of the best charter boats anywhere. Every stick of her was custom designed and built by Rose Brothers, and she's got a pair of Johnson and Tower 671s that'll—"

Anna shuddered delicately. "Please, darling, spare us the gory details."

"I don't think your mother's interested in the specs, son, but you're right—she's solidly built. Next time you come up to see me, we'll drive down to Harker's Island and look around Rose Brothers's boatyard, if you're interested."

Cody, his pride in the son he'd helped raise tucked away to be savored in private, took his leave soon after that. The boy was made of good stuff. He was bright and he was determined. Anna called it stubborn. For the first time in years, Cody felt a certain freedom from responsibility.

Now to get on with something of equally pressing importance.

Back in his hotel room, Cody dialed information and got the number of the hotel in Tampa. He dialed again, and then figeted when he was put on hold. By the time the operator was able to take his call, he had snapped a pencil in two and was ready to snatch the frustratingly short cord out of the wall.

"Valentine Scott, please," he demanded, his mind spanning the distance of some two hundred and forty miles. God, he could have been there by now!

"I'm sorry, sir, we have no one by that name registered," the soft drawl informed him.

Cody's heart froze. When it resumed its proper function, he swore under his breath. "Would you ring Mary Whitmore's room?" That had been a bad slip. Now he knew why surgeons never operated on someone they loved.

The wait of mere seconds seemed an eternity. When the soft voice came back to inform him that Mary Whitmore had checked out, he hung up the phone without a word.

A mistake? Possibly. Between computer foul-ups and human error, such things did happen, but the inner gyroscope that had guided him through some pretty tight spots told him that this was no mistake. Valentine had left Tampa.

He felt like striking out blindly at whomever was responsible for keeping them apart. For days now he'd been running on a mixture of caffeine and adrenaline, and it was beginning to tell on him. He was starting to make stupid mistakes. Potentially dangerous mistakes.

Forcing himself to relax, Cody called on the analytical part of his brain for a systematic summary, and then began to plan his next move. He was well aware that the slightest mistake on his part could spell real danger for Valentine.

If she had checked out, there had to be a good reason. He'd pick the four best reasons he could come up with and then narrow it down to the two most likely. That should give him something to go on. That much he could do while en route to Tampa. Once he landed, he'd need to talk with the hotel staff, find out when she'd gone, who had seen her, which maid had done her room and when she'd done it.

It didn't help matters a few minutes later to find that he'd just missed a flight to Tampa. Rather than wait for the next commercial one, he hunted up the nearest charter. While the pilot filed his flight plan, Cody borrowed a phone.

"I can put someone on it from this end, or I can call in one of our people in St. Pete," Fred Meekins said after Cody had outlined the situation. "Frankly, I'd just as soon keep things cozy as long as we can handle it. I think we can. I ran a make on you before you ever showed up, you and everyone else in the building."

"I hope to hell you did," Cody bit off. "I'd hate to think you gave out that much information to anyone who showed an interest."

"Quite a record you've got there, fellow. You must have worked on some pretty high-level jobs, because you're cleared all the way to the pearly gates."

"Yeah, well how about checking all airlines to see if she booked a flight out. That's something I can't do while I'm crossing the peninsula."

"She might not be traveling alone," the agent reminded him.

Cody's knotted fist punished the edge of the borrowed desk. "You don't have to paint a picture."

"However she's traveling, alone or not, chances are she won't use her own name. Meanwhile, check out the hotel for anything you can learn. A few bucks in the right palms might net you something to go on."

"God, I've never felt so helpless in my life," Cody said harshly.

"Then maybe this isn't the time to tell you that your car's been located under sixteen feet of water."

"I hope to hell you're joking."

"Nope. They haven't brought her up yet, but the divers say she looks like something the sharks chewed up and spit out."

"Hell, it hasn't even been missing much more than twenty-four hours!"

"They did a good thorough job," the agent said almost admiringly. "Pity, too...she was a beauty. I don't think they were looking for anything this time. More likely they were just trying to scare the hell out of somebody. But why you?"

With a sinking feeling, Cody hung up the phone. He thought he knew why. Val had driven him to the airport in that car, and he'd encouraged her to use it, as he hadn't liked the idea of her being stranded somewhere when that piece of junk she drove broke down.

He left the charter office and loped across the sizzling concrete to where the small plane waited. He didn't give a damn about the car, he only wanted Val back in one piece! And if he didn't get some quick answers with a little polite bribery, he'd change his tactics. One of the prime requisites for his line of work was the ability to think like a crook. Trouble was, they came in all different shades of bad.

The professionals he could deal with. It was the amateurs that scared the hell out of him. He still wasn't quite sure what they were up against. Some of the best professionals recruited amateur talent. It was cheap and it was expendable.

Driving through the beautiful horse country of central Florida, Val deliberately avoided thinking about what lay ahead. If she was walking into another explosive situation, at least this time she should have more warning. Who would recognize her in this getup? Finding the pink jeans and the polyester shirt much too hot for Florida's sultry weather, she'd stopped in Gainesville and bought herself a pair of shorts, a colorful cotton skirt and several T-shirts. She'd never owned a T-shirt before.

The plump cheeks had been great in theory, only she hadn't figured on the devastating heat and humidity. Her cheeks had become jowls the first time she'd stopped at a rest stop to stretch her legs and ease the tension that collected at the back of her neck. When she'd checked her appearance in the rest room mirror, it was only to find that all her lovely camouflage had melted and run down her face.

By the time she pulled in for the night just outside Macon, Georgia, Val had managed to convince herself that the whole threat had been grossly exaggerated. Someone had swiped her purse. It was a very good purse, even though it had been practically empty. From that, they'd learned her address, and when she'd obligingly left a window open, they'd broken into her apartment, hoping that anyone who carried such an expensive purse would have expensive jewelry, as well. Perhaps they'd been frightened away before they'd discovered her single strand of good pearls and the few other things she'd kept.

Such things happened all the time, all over the country. Through her own stupidity, she'd become a crime statistic.

Val continued to rationalize as she put herself through a series of stretching exercises to work the kinks out of protesting muscles. She'd simply overreacted. If she hadn't panicked and called Meekins, this thing would never have been blown out of shape, but because of her previous experience, she'd lost her head. Poor Fred had had no choice; once he'd come charging onstage, he'd been obligated to do his thing.

Val left a call for five-thirty and proceeded to fall into a deep, dreamless sleep. She awoke refreshed, the events of the past few days already hazed over by time and distance. After an enormous breakfast at a nearby truck stop, she felt ready to tackle her most immediate problem: that of negotiating with Lucy to expand her business to accommodate a partner. The pearls and her wedding and engagement rings ought to bring enough to keep her afloat until the new services caught on.

It was late afternoon when Val first caught sight of the lake. With miles still to go, she felt the pressure begin to ease off. On an impulse she didn't bother examining too closely, she bypassed the turnoff to Lakesboro and headed toward the tall stacks of Marshall Steam Station, on her way to Sherrill Ford. No matter how euphoric she was feeling at the moment, she wasn't up to facing navy-blue walls and no furniture. Besides, Grace was probably worried sick by now.

Under the shadowy canopy of two enormous tulip poplars, the house was dark. There were no lights anywhere as far as Val could see, but still she had no misgivings.

Was this Sunday? She'd lost all sense of time over the past few days. If today was Wednesday, Grace would be at Prayer Meeting. If it was Sunday, she'd probably have gone to town for lunch with Lucy and ended up staying for supper. Their friendship went back more than forty years, and Val was counting on that relationship, if necessary, to help expedite her new career. In fact, she might even see if Grace would be interested in getting involved.

But not tonight, she decided, yawning widely. For several minutes, she simply sat there, enjoying the welcome feeling of being motionless. It had been a hard push, even for someone who liked driving, and she was awfully glad to be back on familiar territory. Airports and hotels were fine, but she'd long since had her fill of them. Give her plain country living from now on, with shade trees and mockingbirds and home-cooked meals eaten at the kitchen table.

Speaking of which, she'd better see if there was anything in the refrigerator. Except for the snacks she'd munched along the way to keep her awake, she hadn't eaten since breakfast.

The key was still under the curly Boston fern. Val let herself in, wondering how her own houseplants were doing. The poor things were probably lonely without even Ollie for company.

She dropped her bag in the hall and called out a greeting on the off chance that Grace was somewhere in the house. Then she headed for the bathroom upstairs to wash off the day's accumulation of grime before she began foraging for something to eat.

There was no warning. Val stepped out of the bathroom several minutes later, still toweling her face, and he was there.

"Good Lord, what—"

"I see you're back," Charles Reedy observed. In a brown suit, a discreetly striped shirt and a yellow silk tie, with his thin, reddish hair smoothed carefully over his pink scalp, he looked completely out of place amid all the calico and eyelet embroidery and white rag rugs.

"Charles? What are you doing here? Has something happened to Grace?" She'd tried to call just this morning—no, that had been yesterday.

"Grace is fine, just fine. I—we weren't expecting you quite so soon."

Recoiling instinctively, Val resisted the irrational urge to turn and lock herself in the bathroom. Just because the man was a nosy old bore, just because she didn't much care for him, that didn't mean . . .

But he had no business being upstairs in Grace's house. "Charles, what are you doing here? Where *is* Grace?"

"She's aboard the houseboat I've rented for the summer. My girls are home from school, you know. You've never met them, have you?" He smiled, and Val found herself staring at his neat, even teeth. She'd never noticed how very small they were.

"No, I never have," she said faintly. She clutched the damp towel, her fingers digging painfully into its rough folds. Something was wrong, and she didn't know what it was. All she knew was that this man had no business being where he was, looking at her the way he was looking at her.

My God, was he so desperate? She'd been mildly flattered by his interest when Grace had first introduced them. It had lasted about five minutes. After that, the more Grace had tried to bring them together, the more Val had shied away.

"Grace thought you might be coming home. She sent me to pick you up and take you to the party."

Hadn't he just said Grace wasn't expecting her? "What party?" Val challenged. If he thought for one minute that he was going to get her alone on some boat for a spot of moonlight romancing, he was crazy!

Charles and a romantic moonlight sail? The very idea was laughable!

There was something uncomfortable about Charles Reedy. Val had tried to feel sorry for him, but she hadn't even been able to manage that. Her gaze fell to his brown shoes, polished to perfection, as always, against the homey white rag rug. As many times as she'd seen him since she'd first come home, she'd never once seen him without a tie and coat, the tie always perfectly knotted, the coat impeccably cut. On the hottest day, there was never so much as a single bead of perspiration in evidence. The man wasn't human.

Val thought longingly of Cody, of his poor laundry-mangled shirts, his perennially rumpled khakis. *Cody, please, I need you!*

"I really think we should hurry, my dear, before Grace begins to worry," Charles said almost gently.

Quite suddenly, Val knew there was more than a romantic interest under his politely persuasive manner. Far more! A shudder ran through her, and she darted a wary look at him, wondering if he'd seen her sudden fear. The expression in his pale eyes never varied. They were the color of ice, she thought irrelevantly. And just as cold.

Glancing at the open door beyond him, she gauged her chances of slipping past and reaching her car before he could catch up with her. Slim to nil. Schooling her voice to conceal her rising panic, she played for time. "I'm tired, Charles. Why don't you go on back and tell Grace I'll see her later?"

"It's restful out there on the lake this time of evening, Valentine. You can sit back and enjoy the lights from the shore while we cruise around."

"No thanks, Charles. Some other time, perhaps." It wasn't going to work. Val knew it in her bones, knew what was going to happen a split second before Charles dropped a hand into his coat pocket and came up with the ugly chunk of blue steel.

"I'm afraid I'll have to insist, my dear."

So the gloves were off, Val thought, almost with relief. Then anger began to replace the fear that had paralyzed her for a single moment. All this time he'd been playing a game with poor Grace, who prided herself on being such a wonderful judge of character. A well-to-do widower with two teenaged daughters and an orthopedic shoe factory. Grace would be furious.

Valentine was furious! Her purse, her good gray purse—and her apartment! Pushed to the wall, Val revealed a streak of courage that bordered on reckless. "I want my gray purse back, Charles. I paid a small fortune for that bag in London, and I'll never have another one that well made."

"I'll have to admit, the seams were remarkably well stitched. Let's go." He gestured toward the door with the snout of pistol.

Ignoring it, Val cried out, "Charles, you didn't tear it apart!"

"Come along, my dear. I'm sorry about the bag. I do appreciate nice things, but then, nothing lasts forever."

Her mind working furiously, Val allowed herself to be shepherded down the polished, golden oak stairs. Near the bottom, she slowed, gauging her chances of ramming an elbow into Charles's belly and getting through the door before he could recover.

Muscles tensing for action, she felt the nudge of cold steel at the back of her neck. "Don't try anything foolhardy, my dear. Such a lovely neck. Did Scott promise you diamonds and sables to wrap around it, I wonder?''

Val ignored the taunt. When her foot touched the landing, she turned to confront him. "What have you done with my cousin?''

''Your cousin is somewhere where she won't be interfering with my plans.'' His eyes grew evasive, and Val wondered fleetingly if he was lying, or if the truth was too awful to reveal. She felt a film of sweat chill her body.

''Don't look for your lover, either,'' Charles added. At gun point, he hurried her across the wide front porch, across the lawn, and through the camellia hedge. ''As a matter of fact, my dear Mrs. Scott, your lover will probably be quite upset with you. You cost him a very nice car.''

''I don't know what you're talking about,'' Val muttered stubbornly.

''The Porsche. We thought you'd finally decided it was safe to dip into you late husband's, ah, savings.''

''I don't know anything about Albert's business. He never talked about his work except to tell me when we were moving to another place, so why do you think he'd suddenly started confiding in me about—''

About betraying his country, his wife, betraying every shred of integrity he'd ever possessed. It sickened her to think of it, even now, and she directed her rage at the man who stood calmly one step behind her, pointing a small, deadly weapon at her back. ''You *must* know I'm telling the truth,'' she exclaimed, ''so why are you doing this?''

''Let's say my friends and I are almost a hundred percent sure, but there's always the chance that we were mistaken about you. We know, of course, that one of the insurance policies your husband held had lapsed, and another one was invalidated by the, uh, circumstances of his demise."

"Then why—" Val started to turn and felt the gun nudge her back.

"When a penurious widow suddenly starts shopping for customized European-model cars, one does begin to wonder."

"But you know the car wasn't mine!"

"That wasn't very nice of you, Mrs. Scott. I'm afraid you hurt our feelings with your little joke. I only hope Macheris shares your sense of humor."

"What are you going to do with me?"

"That depends on how good your memory is. My friends are a bit concerned about their reputations."

"Stop talking in riddles!"

"Patience, Mrs. Scott," Charles chided, directing her into the double garage that was attached to his house.

There were two vehicles parked inside, one a familiar looking gray van with a contractor's logo on the side and two flat tires, the other a beige mid-priced, mid-sized American-made station wagon. Protective coloration, Val thought in bitter admiration of the man's thoroughness.

"You'll do the driving, Mrs. Scott. We don't really think you're greedy enough to make the same foolish mistake your late husband did. Believe me, if we seriously thought that you had access to the funds Scott appropriated, we would have had our little boat ride long before this."

"But you just said...Cody's car?"

"A joke, my dear Valentine, merely a joke. You aren't the only one who appreciates a joke. Oh, I'll admit that we were annoyed when we discovered that you'd merely borrowed the car from your friend, the ex-army intelligence officer. I allowed my boys to work off some of their excess high spirits by appropriating the car and—"

"But what do you want from me? I don't have any money, so why won't you just leave me alone?" Val cried.

Under Charles's direction, she backed the car out of the garage and then waited. "You were alone with your husband for more than three weeks before he died, Mrs. Scott. Thanks to Meekins, we were unable to place anyone in the room to make sure he never recovered consciousness." He smiled, and his small white teeth were clearly visible in the gloomy interior. Val shuddered. "Switch on the headlights to dim and don't try anything fancy. Take a right on the highway, and then the first left."

Val did as he directed. For the moment, he was holding all the cards.

"We were disappointed, you know," Charles continued. "We really should have been present for any last words, but as you know, only family was permitted at the bedside. Family including cousin Freddie, of course."

Gripping the wheel tightly, Val forced herself to remain calm until she saw a chance to get away.

"For crissake, man, calm down!" Meekins ordered. "You look like hell, you sound worse and before you lay a hand on me, let me warn you—assaulting a federal agent carries a penalty you don't even want to think about."

"Then give me some straight answers, dammit, or I'll find out first hand what the penalty is," Cody snarled.

"Look, we're not getting anywhere like this, so just tell me what you found out and I'll tell you all I've been able to learn from this end."

"Meanwhile what if that son of a bitch finds her before we do?"

"Depends on what answers we come up with between us. Remember, she had enough cash to have bought a one-way ticket anywhere in the country, in which case we'd still be chasing our tails around the flagpole. At least we're ahead of the game there. Thank God you checked out both names with the car rentals."

"For all the good it did us! You and your team couldn't find your—"

"Stow it, Macheris! Just remember, the lady's no fool. If you'd seen her over there when I was first called onto the case, you'd know what we're up against. She's smart, man, and she's twenty-four-karat gold."

"Gold's soft." Cody stopped prowling and flung himself onto the sofa. He'd rented a car at the airport and driven straight through, arriving home to find that Meekins had turned his desk into federal territory.

"She won't break, Macheris," the agent said, the usual hard edge missing from his tone, for once. "I've seen her level an army of reporters from a hospital bed while she was still groggy from having a chunk of iron re-bar dug out of her arm. It's her manner that gets 'em. Treats that flock of jackals as if they were gentlemen, and they fall all over the place trying to protect her from each other. Hell, she was even nice to me."

"Yeah, well Reedy's no reporter. He isn't even a part of the human race! If he finds her before we do—"

"Okay, so let's get down to cases. They were two steps ahead of her from the time she left Cyprus. They had a man on her when she stepped off the plane in Omaha, meanwhile Reedy rented the house next door to her cousin before she even left the hospital. Figured she'd come here at least until she got her second wind. She was pretty banged up, you know."

"How bad was it?" Cody braced himself for the pain that even the mention of her injuries brought.

Meekins shrugged. "Nothing really serious. Concussion, abrasions, a few ribs and the thing with her shoulder. The arm was bad for a while."

Nothing serious! Good God, Cody marveled, was the man totally insensitive? It occurred to him to wonder how he'd ever lasted all those years as a Green Beret.

"Anyhow," Meekins went on, "by the time Val got home, Reedy was all tucked away in the bosom of the family."

"The cousin must be a complete fool," Cody adjudged, bitterness and worry etching deep lines beside his mouth.

"Reedy's good. Don't underestimate him. As for Grace, she's nobody's patsy. Only trouble is, she likes to meddle. Hell, she's even got a woman lined up for me, and I don't mind telling you, I just might—"

"For crissake, Meekins, get on with it! We're wasting time!" Cody snarled, smacking a hard fist into his palm.

"Okay, okay. So maybe Reedy planted the idea of a match between them, hell, I don't know. Anyhow, Grace's been trying to get the two of them together ever since Val got home. It was a natural—lonely widow, lonely widower."

"Congenital meddler," Cody added harshly, seeing the picture all too clearly. They'd been little better, shipping her off to her cousins' place for her own safety without checking the neighborhood first.

"Skip that. I told you the man was good. His setup was perfect, and it worked. He was in a perfect position to pump Grace by pretending a romantic interest. He was right where he could keep tabs on her without being obvious about it, and meanwhile, he was close enough to Lakesboro to direct operations. We have reason to believe he's been using a building contractor's van and a crew of carpenters as cover for the rest of his gang."

"Hell, I don't care if he's using a circus float! *Where is she?*" Cody's face was gray, his eyes glittered like wet agates and a pulse throbbed at his temple. If he lost her—if that bastard so much as touched a hair on her head, he'd...!

"You said she rented the car under her own name. With the make, the license number and the time of rental, it should have been a snap. We took a chance that she was headed this way, figured she'd make it into Georgia, maybe even as far as Atlanta. She spent the night outside Macon."

"Then why the devil don't you know where she is?" Cody demanded.

Meekins's thin lips tightened until his mouth was no more than a knife slash in his expressionless face. "Unfortunately, by the time they'd located her motel, she'd already hit the road again. She threw us off by getting off at Gainesville and going shopping." He shook his head. "Can you figure women?"

Cody's terse stream of profanity was directed more toward himself than toward the operatives who had let her slip away. He'd actually held her in his arms less than forty-eight hours ago! Why hadn't he taken her back to Lauderdale with him? Why the hell had he ever left her?

At Charles's bidding, Val had turned off onto one of the many peninsulas that jutted out into the lake. If she wasn't mistaken, it was one she had visited before, looking for one of Wynn's creations. There were at least a dozen houses, as well as several mobile homes out on the tip.

"Don't do anything foolish, my dear. Don't even think about it. Take this road." With the tip of the gun, he indicated an unpaved road that turned off to the left.

"What's down there?" Val asked, with only the slightest tremor in her voice.

"Nothing," he replied. "Nothing at all," and her stomach lurched sickeningly.

They'd gone less than a few hundred yards when the engine began misbehaving. "I warned you," Charles exclaimed, his voice rising.

Val felt something cold and hard jab into her side. She hardly dared breath. If only he'd forgotten to fill the tank, she thought with the first real glimmer of hope. "I don't know what's wrong—I'm not doing anything."

"It won't do you any good! I—"

The engine shuddered. Something was wrong. "It acts like it's not getting enough gas," Val ventured, careful to keep both hands on the wheel and her face straight ahead. At the first opportunity, she'd have to risk throwing open the door and jumping. It was pitch dark out there. They'd passed no more than a handful of houses since turning off from Sherrill Ford Road, and she wasn't sure she could find any of them in the dark.

The engine coughed again, and Val cut a nervous glance at the tense figure beside her before venturing a look at the gas gauge. It registered a full tank. *Damn!*

"Anyhow, I had the phone in her apartment disconnected, laid in a few groceries and holed up there, figuring she'd head for home if she felt secure enough to use her own name."

Cody strode restlessly across to stare out the window into the dusk, as if expecting to see her come swinging along the sidewalk. "So dammit, where is she? She's had more than enough time to get here!" He still hadn't told Meekins about his own nocturnal visit to Tampa. It had no bearing on the present situation.

The agent had admitted before Cody had headed south with Eric that he'd reserved a suite for Mary Whitmore with the provision that Mr. Whitmore might be checking in later. That, as he'd explained, was just in case they lost control and it became necessary to put a guard on her. Cody had already been working on a plan of his own, one that had nothing to do with security, but he knew damned well he hadn't been followed.

"We've given her about all the time we can afford," Meekins said slowly, checking his watch. He didn't like the shape of the idea that was beginning to form in his mind.

Cody was one step ahead of him, his blood running cold as he imagined her walking into a trap. "Sherrill Ford," he said in a voice devoid of all emotion.

"That's where she went to earth before." Meekins nodded. He was already on his feet, reaching for the harness he wore under the specially constructed sports shirt.

"Then what the hell are we waiting for? We'll take my rental—it's got a full tank!"

"You take it. The van's got more under the hood, and she's fully equipped. Take off, but park a hundred yards south of the house and wait for me."

———————

Chapter Twelve

Cody spotted the car immediately. A silver Escort, it was pulled up in the driveway beside the front porch. No effort had been made to hide it. There was a light showing through the lacy curtains that covered the glass-topped front door, and he coasted to a stop, all thought of waiting a discreet three hundred feet quickly fled.

Five minutes later, he was ready to tear the whole damned county apart. "Don't just stand there, find out what the hell kind of car Reedy drives!" he yelled at the imperturbable agent who had arrived to find him breaking into the garage of the house next door.

"Shut up and let me think."

Val had given up trying to reason with the man. She was furious with herself for not having seen through him, and even more furious with him for having used Grace so outrageously.

Oh, God, what had he done with her poor cousin? She *had* to get away to rescue Grace!

"The gauge must be stuck," she suggested, hoping to deflect his suspicions.

"There's nothing wrong with the gauge!" Charles screeched. "I filled the tank this morning!"

"Then something else is wrong. Maybe you'd better turn back before we get stuck out here in snake country." But Val knew she'd willingly risk snakes and poison ivy and any number of minor hazards, given the choice between those and this cold-blooded creature.

"Shut up!" Reedy ordered, and for the first time since she'd met him, she saw the gleam of sweat on his face.

"Where are you taking me?"

"Try the engine again, and you'd better pray that it runs."

Val didn't know what to pray for except deliverance. She ground the starter, and the engine caught. She expelled a shaky sigh, shifted into drive and negotiated another fifty feet of the rutted, potholed road before it cut out again.

Charles Reedy slammed his fists down on his knees and swore with a fluency that made Cody's efforts pale in comparison. He turned to glare at her, his livid features frightening in the soft glare from the instrument panel. "Get out," he said with deadly softness.

Val swallowed. Suddenly "out" didn't seem all that inviting. "Why?"

"We're walking the rest of the way. It's not far to the end."

"The end?" Her voice sounded like the first tentative notes of a tea kettle. The end of the road? she thought wildly... or the end of *her*?

"I'm taking you to Macheris's car," her captor said silkily, and without the slightest idea of what he was talking about, Val felt the tentacles of her nightmare begin to tighten around her.

They left the station wagon in the middle of the road. Charles pocketed the keys and then nudged her forward. "There's not another soul within miles of here, Valentine, so don't you try anything stupid. I could finish you off right here, you know."

"Then why don't you?" she charged with a recklessness born of despair. *Never to see Cody again, never to know his body melding with hers, never to laugh with him and lust for him as she watched that easygoing stride of his.*

Suddenly, now that it was much too late, Valentine's priorities rearranged themselves into a blindingly simple pattern.

Cody's stride was anything but easygoing as he leaped on to Grace's front porch two hours later. They'd split up. Using the van's mobile phone, Meekins was checking every service station within a radius of twenty miles of Sherrill Ford for a lead on Reedy's vehicle so that they could get out an APB. There wasn't a snowball's chance in hell that it would be registered under his own name.

Meanwhile Cody had doubled back in case they'd returned to her apartment. It was a meager hope, and it had led nowhere. He'd put in a call for Craddock from his own place, only to learn from the dispatcher that Craddock and both deputies had peeled out after a call from Grace Whichard.

Cody had blistered pavement, taking the corner of Doolie Road and Highway 150 on two wheels. He'd never felt more helpless in his life! She could be anywhere in four counties...or beyond, and he was running up and down the highway no closer to finding her than he'd been twelve hours before!

Slowing down only when he reached Sherrill Ford, he cut his lights and coasted to a stop in the shadow of an overhanging tree. From there, except for all the damned greenery in the way, he had a pretty good view of both houses. He opened his door silently and slid out, after first unscrewing the bulbs from the interior lights. Dodging from bush to bush, he approached the front of the Whichard place and then stopped dead in his tracks.

Eyes narrowed, breath hissing softly between his teeth, he took in the jumble of vehicles scattered along the driveway. Bringing up the rear was Meekin's battered old van.

The sound of voices reached his ears before he even got as far as the porch. With the windows open and the front door ajar, he could hear a woman's voice—not Val's—holding forth over a gravelly rumble that sounded like...

Cody crossed the remaining thirty feet like a silvered shadow, moving with a silent swiftness that had once been second nature. Unsheathing a wide, businesslike blade, he took the steps in a single soft-footed leap, flung back the heavy front door and burst into the room. Then he froze.

The hum of voices that had led him across the lawn stopped cold. The only sound was the tinkle of broken glass as it fell to the floor in the foyer behind him.

No one spoke.

Valentine clutched the edges of the petit-point foot-stool she sat on, her eyes never once leaving the wild man who stood panting just inside the room. She was oblivious to the picture she made in her ruined shorts, the rip in her T-shirt baring one bra strap and the better part of a shoulder. Her face, except for the mud and scratches, was milk white, her eyes like twin bruises as they clung to Cody's crouching figure.

"That's genuine beveled glass, young man," Grace announced. "It'll set you back a pretty penny."

"Valentine?" The single sound was choked off, and then he was beside her, sweeping her up off the stool to crush her to him. "Oh, God, Valentine, you're all right!"

Val gave up trying to breathe until the first fierce heat of his embrace was over. Still smothered in his arms, she buried her face in his chest, inhaling the damp, musky scent of this body. *Cody. Oh, Cody—*

There were no words to describe what she was feeling, but evidently, Cody didn't require words. Nor privacy. In the full presence of a fascinated audience, he kissed her until she lost all sense of time and place.

"All right, all right, enough of that foolishness," Grace snorted.

Only then did Cody turn his attention to his surroundings. Craddock was there, notepad jammed in his shirt pocket, one hamlike hand cradling a violet-sprigged china teacup of ridiculously small proportions. The thin, dark-haired woman standing awkwardly beside a mirror-topped pump organ looked as if she'd rather be anywhere else in the world. Meekins was on the horsehair sofa, his bony wrists dangling awkwardly over equally bony knees.

A pudgy woman with short curly gray hair reigned supreme from the most hideous chair Cody had ever seen in his life.

It squeaked protestingly, its elaborate curlicues glistening with lemon oil as Grace began to rock. "Reckon I know who *you* are," she said pointedly. "Fred said you were running up and down the countryside yapping like a dog with a can tied to his tail."

Cody glared at Meekins, who didn't bother to deny the allegation. "Would someone mind telling me—"

"Sit down, sit down. Fred, move over and let 'em have room, will you? Looks like they're not about to turn each other loose short of an earthquake. Don't want 'em trying to settle on my footstool. Valentine, I told you to go wash your face and hands before you started answering Joe's questions. Once that mud sets in your clothes, you'll never get rid of the stains."

Tricia murmured, "I'd better be—"

"No you hadn't. Sit still. Fred, why don't you take Tricia out on the front porch while Joe and I wind this thing up?"

By now Val was thoroughly enjoying herself. At the strangled sound that issued from Cody's throat, she wrapped her arms around his waist and buried her face in his chest to smother her laughter. "It gets better," she promised softly.

The deep rumble of Cody's low voice set off a remarkable series of reactions in Val's body as he said, "If it gets much better than this, I don't think I can stand it."

"I'll stay, if you don't mind," Fred said stiffly. "I appreciate your help, Craddock, but it's a little out of your territory. There'll be a federal marshal by first thing in the morning to clean the scum out of your jail."

"What happened to your clothes?" Cody whispered. His fingers had found the tear in her shirt that had resulted from a wild slide down a steep embankment.

"Don't you care for my new image?" With the release from tension had come a feeling akin to intoxication, and Val felt a giggle arise in her throat.

"Would you two stop all that lollygagging and settle down?" Grace snapped. "Cody, do you want to know how I solved this case or don't you?"

"She's only gone over it three times in the ten minutes we've been here," Fred said dully.

"That's enough out of you, Fred Meekins! If it'd been up to you, we'd all still be playing blindman's buff!"

While Val and Cody settled beside the discomfited agent, Joe Craddock heaved his considerable bulk out of the overstuffed parlor chair. "Well, you folks prob'ly want to get some sleep and I've got a lot of explaining to do to the boys over at the Catawba office. Ain't too often an Iredell County lawman goes riding shotgun on their turf, but when Miss Grace needs help..." He grinned, tipped his hat to two of the women present and jutted an elbow in the direction of the third. "Leaving now, Trish? I'll follow you home, see you get there all right."

With a single guilty look toward Valentine, Tricia made her escape. Cody cringed at the sound of footsteps crunching through the broken glass in the foyer. He had a mess to clear away before the night was over, and more than one apology to make.

"Tricia came by earlier wanting to talk to you about your job, Valentine. I'd just come back from hearing those hoodlums next door talking about deep-sixing some dame and clearing out of these parts, and I figured I might be needing help. I'd have called on Lucy, but she's such an old fussbudget—besides, it'd take her an hour to get her corsets laced and get herself on over here, and I couldn't wait. Trish's been filling in for you at Wynn's, by the way. Think she'd like to make it permanent." Grace's feet thudded rhythmically on the flowered parlor carpet.

Her job was the least of Val's concerns at the moment. After what she'd been through these past few days, and especially these past few hours, she was glad to be breathing. She'd worry about nonessentials later.

"What hoodlums next door?" One arm holding Val close, Cody stared at the attractive middle-aged woman with the red spectacles perched on top of her head.

Meekins sighed impatiently and took control. "Is there any more of that tea, Grace? I could use some." Without waiting for a reply, he turned then to Val and Cody. "Seems Grace here got the wind up when Reedy didn't know about hammer toes."

Grace lifted a felt-slippered foot and smiled smugly. "Pegged him for a phony then and there. I've got one, my father had one and his father before him. Not that I said a word, mind you. Bided my time until I got the goods on him," she declared, convinced in her own mind that she'd been suspicious all along.

Meekins tried again. "Anyhow, as I was saying, Grace went over there late this afternoon to take Reedy a jar of honey—"

"Suzie sells it at the deli, with a chunk of honeycomb in every jar. Richard says it's going to be a good year for sourwood," Grace put in.

Fred was beginning to look slightly apoplectic. "Grace, would you let me tell it? Anyhow, she overheard Reedy's thugs discussing whether to cut their losses and clear out or hang around a few days and see what developed."

"Reedy knew where Val had gone?" Cody demanded.

"No, but my being around was enough to tip him off. I told you the guy was good. He figured as long as I was still here, she couldn't be that far away, so they decided to hang tight."

"So then," Grace explained, "I went back home and tried to call Joe, only my phone was out of order."

Cody lifted a brow, and Meekins nodded. "They were planning ahead. No telling when they'd cut the line."

"Well, as I said before, I wasn't about to go off and let them get away, but I could hardly ask to use Charles's phone."

Val felt as though she were at a tennis match. With her head tucked tightly against Cody's shoulder, she had trouble following the action between the two main players. At this point, all she wanted to do was get away and scrub off some of the dried mud before she turned into a brick. Besides, she'd heard all this before, beginning from the time Grace and Joe had found her slogging along the road. Soon after that, Fred Meekins had roared up in that awful van of his, and from then on it had been a four-ring circus.

"So she—" Meekins started to explain, and Grace shushed him in no uncertain terms.

"So I let the air out of the van's tires, poured the honey in the gas tank of the station wagon and headed for Lakesboro to tell Fred here what I'd discovered, only he was nowhere to be found, so naturally I went to Joe."

"We must have passed each other on the road," Fred said disgustedly. It still rankled that a hick sheriff had been in on the kill and he'd come trailing in like the hind end of a slow dog.

"Anyhow, the rest, as they say, is history," Grace finished smartly. "Fred, you still want more tea? It's getting on for midnight, and tea's got caffeine. You'd better have Postum."

"Dammit, I—"

Grinning from ear to ear, Cody got to his feet, practically dragging Valentine with him. There was a lot he wanted to know, but it wasn't worth sitting through this battle of egos. "You two have a nice evening, hmm? Valentine and I are going home."

"But Val—" Grace began.

"Where am I supposed to sleep?" Meekins interrupted.

Val volunteered an answer. "I won't be needing my room here, Fred. I'm sure Grace wouldn't mind, under the circumstances."

It was long past midnight. Val sat at Cody's kitchen table wearing his pajama top and a towel around her head. By the time she'd removed all the mud she'd collected, she'd been unromantically hungry. Now that she had gorged herself, she was overwhelmingly tired. So much for the grand reunion.

Cody finished his milk and leaned back in his chair, content, for the moment, to feast his eyes. Other appetites would have to wait.

"I still don't know how you managed to get away in the first place, sweetheart, but if you'd rather not talk about it, I understand."

At the concern on his face, Val managed a smile. Perhaps she wasn't so tired, after all. "I screamed. You see, Charles kept poking that awful gun in my back and telling me to keep moving, and I was afraid not to do as he said. But it was all downhill, and I got to thinking that maybe I wouldn't be coming back up the hill again...ever."

Cody felt a knife twist in his gut. He didn't interrupt, though, nor did he reach out to her.

"I figured it was one of the old roads that had been flooded out when the dam was built. People use them for launching boats, and I didn't want to be launched. So I just screamed suddenly and jumped sideways and then scrambled down the bank."

Cody closed his eyes, picturing her blundering around the snake-infested banks of a deep lake in pitch darkness with a cold-blooded killer on her heels. It had been bad enough not knowing. If he'd known what she'd been going through, he'd have lost his mind.

"I could hear Charles cursing up there on the road, but I kept going. There was enough gravel on the road to make it treacherous, and those slick-soled shoes of his were like roller skates."

"You were incredibly lucky."

"Or unlucky," she said quietly. "It depends on how you look at it. Fred told you about Albert, didn't he?" She was drawing cirles in squares again, with the moisture that collected under her glass.

Cody nodded, aching for all she must have gone through before he'd ever met her. She was one hell of a woman. As long as he had a single breath in his body, nothing would ever hurt her again.

"I'm ashamed of that—of having any connection to something so despicable."

"Darling, don't even think that way. You were never a part of that."

"He was my husband for almost eighteen years," she said simply, staring fixedly down at the patterns she'd drawn on the table.

"He used you the same way he used his position. He's gone now, Valentine, and it's ended."

But was it? She'd thought so once before, and she'd been wrong. True, Charles was in custody, and the men who'd worked with him had been rounded up, all but one of them, who'd probably already left the country. "I wonder what ever happened to the money they thought I had taken?"

"Who knows? I have an idea Fred won't close the books just yet, though." Cody covered her hand. Indicating the designs she'd inscribed, he smiled grimly. "Circles in squares. Would you say that's an unconscious bid for security?"

"I remember reading once when I was a child that in Indian lore, a circle within a square was considered a place of wisdom."

"I don't know about wisdom, love, but I've got a king-sized bed that's practically square," Cody said softly, standing and pulling her up with him, "and there's a certain circle I've been meaning to discuss with you." A small gold circle, he added silently, one he intended to have on her finger before many more days had passed.

"More talking?" Val groaned, resting her head on his chest.

"Hey, I thought you liked to talk. In Tampa all you wanted to do was talk," Cody teased. "Now, I can't even get a decent conversation out of you." Laughing, he swept her up in his arms. "No more talking, love. At least not on your part." He carried her and laid her on the bed, which had been turned back earlier.

Val didn't move. It felt so heavenly to be clean and safe and horizontal. She felt the bed give under Cody's weight and smiled, her eyes closed to the light he'd left burning in the next room. A night light. Probably for her sake. Oh, Lord, was there ever a man so gentle, and at the same time, so strong?

"Val? Before you go to sleep, sweetheart, could I tell you something?" Not waiting for her permission, he went on. "I know you have this thing about independence and your job and all that. I know you've got good reason to be leery of getting mixed up with another man. I know I'm no bargain, but—"

Rolling over to one side, Val glared at him. "What do you mean, you're no bargain? Cody, you're the biggest bargain I've ever known in my life! And I'll tell you something more—out there tonight, when I thought I might not ever see you again, the thing I regretted most was that I hadn't told you how much I love you."

"You—" His voice broke, and Val placed a finger over his lips—a finger that he promptly drew into his mouth.

"You listen to me," she said softly, fiercely. "Independence is important to me, of course. I'd like to know that I can take care of myself, but it's not *the* most important thing in my life. I've proved that I can land a job and do it, even if I don't do it all that well. I'm not afraid of the future anymore, Cody. At least not as far as my work is concerned. If I lose my job, I can always come up with something else, something even better. But Cody, if I lost you, no career on earth would be worth having. If I had to choose between you and the most glamorous career in the world, I'd choose you."

She'd done it again. For better or worse, she'd laid it on the line. He hadn't actually offered her a commitment of any sort, but Val was far past the stage of playing it safe. "I don't even know if you love me," she said candidly.

Cody moved closer, so close that she could feel the beat of his heart, the fierce response of his body. "You know. Of course you know, darling. I think we both knew from the first time we ever saw each other."

Holding her as if he'd never let her go again, he caressed her lips with his as his nimble fingers began to unfasten the buttons down her front. "However, if you still need convincing..."

Epilogue

Überstürzen Sie sich nicht. With a small gasp, Val placed a hand on her rounded belly. "That goes for you, too, buster," she murmured just as the phone rang. "Don't be in such a hurry."

"I'll get it," Cody called out. He knew how she hated to be interrupted in the middle of translating, but the junior Macheris wasn't so considerate.

Val dawdled, her concentration broken. Finally closing the folder, she gazed out at the thick blanket of clouds that seemed to scrape the tops of the pines across the lake. Snow? She could count on one hand the number of white Christmases she'd seen in Lakesboro, but this year just might prove to be an exception.

Lost in a daydream, she didn't hear Cody until she felt his hands on her shoulders. Turning her head, she kissed the inside of his wrist. "Business?" she queried.

With the baby due in a few months, Cody did more and more work at home.

"Old business. If you're finished for the day, come lie down and let me make us something to drink."

"Make mine milky. Junior's hyper enough, as it is. You should have felt the last kick." Easing herself from the chair, Val turned off the light in her office. Wynn had designed the house as a wedding gift, including an office overlooking the lake for each of them. The need for a nursery had taken them both by surprise, causing some hasty revisions in the plans.

"She's going to be a ballerina," Cody said indulgently.

"*He*'s going to be a football player," Val corrected, glad they had chosen not to be told in advance.

"If Eric has his way, he'll be working charter boats by the time he's out of diapers."

"Was that Eric on the phone?"

"No, it was cousin Fred. He had several items he thought might be of interest to us, so lie down like a good girl, and I'll give you the news." He draped an afghan over her legs in spite of the efficiency of the large stone fireplace.

A few minutes later he handed her a mug of steaming Ovaltine and settled himself beside her legs. "Remember you were wondering about the money? Well, you can stop wondering. I told you Fred wasn't ready to close the books until the final chapter was written. Seems Charles was the greedy one, only—"

"Charles! Then why did he put us through all that agony?"

"He needed a goat. Or in this case, a herring. As near as they can figure, he and Albert were in it together, only once the deal went down, Charles had Albert eliminated and then covered his own tracks with the gang by taking off after the supposedly missing money."

"You mean me. But how did Fred find out?"

"The guy who got away evidently put out the word, and someone took care of Reedy while he was waiting to go to trial. It was only when they were going through his personal effects that the key was discovered."

"A key? I should have thought they'd have checked out every key in his possession right away." Val stiffened in an involuntary response to a hard kick. Taking Cody's hand, she guided it to the side of her domed belly.

"This one was in his shoe heel. After that, things fell into place. Fred has just been waiting to wind this one up before he retired. Looks like he'll be making his move just about the time our little ballerina makes her debut."

Val knew before she even asked. So that was it. Grace had been making all sorts of puzzling little remarks lately—things like, better late than never, and no fool like an old fool. Come to think of it, she'd even lost a few pounds and taken to using a blond rinse.

"Fred's moving to Lakesboro," she concluded.

"Better than that, to Sherrill Ford."

"But the only house I know of that's for sale is…the brick house next to Grace's?"

"You got it." Cody grinned, his eyes crinkling as they met hers. They'd even joked about the way the older couple had hit it off once they'd got past the crisis and discovered several communal interests. They'd spent hours at the wedding reception arguing James Bond and Mickey Spillane versus reality.

"This baby we made certainly won't lack for family," Val observed. "Big brother Eric, and now cousin Grace and cousin Fred. He's going to be awfully spoiled if we're not careful."

"Tell you what, love, you spoil my little ballerina, and I'll spoil you."

Val lifted her arms in an invitation. "Who's going to spoil you?" she asked as Cody carefully fitted himself alongside her cumbersome body.

"Just go on loving me, sweetheart. That's all I'll ever need."

Take 4 Silhouette
Special Edition novels
FREE

and preview future books in your home for 15 days!

When you take advantage of this offer, you get 4 Silhouette Special Edition® novels FREE and without obligation. Then you'll also have the opportunity to preview 6 brand-new books —delivered right to your door for a FREE 15-day examination period—as soon as they are published.

When you decide to keep them, you pay just $1.95 each ($2.50 each in Canada) *with no shipping, handling, or other charges of any kind!*

Romance *is* alive, well and flourishing in the moving love stories of Silhouette Special Edition novels. They'll awaken your desires, enliven your senses, and leave you tingling all over with excitement... and the first 4 novels are yours to keep. You can cancel at any time.

As an added bonus, you'll also receive a FREE subscription to the Silhouette Books Newsletter as long as you remain a member. Each issue is filled with news on upcoming books, interviews with your favorite authors, even their favorite recipes.

To get your 4 FREE books, fill out and mail the coupon today!

Silhouette Special Edition®

Silhouette Books, 120 Brighton Rd., P.O. Box 5084, Clifton, NJ 07015-5084

Silhouette Special Edition

COMING NEXT MONTH

MISTY MORNINGS, MAGIC NIGHTS—Ada Steward
Recovering from a recent divorce, Carole Stockton had no desire for
another involvement. Then politician Donnelly Wakefield entered her life
and he was determined to be a winning candidate.

SWEET PROMISE—Ginna Gray
At eighteen, Joanna fell in love with Sean Fleming. But he only considered
her a spoiled child. Could she convince him of the promise of a
woman's love?

SUMMER STORM—Patti Beckman
When political cartoonist Leida Adams's sailboat capsized, she couldn't
tell her handsome lifesaver, Senator Grant Hunter, that he was the target
of her biting satire. Would the truth keep their love from smooth sailing?

WHITE LACE AND PROMISES— Debbie Macomber
After high school, Maggie and Glenn drifted apart and suffered their
private heartaches. Years later at their old friends' wedding, they fell in
love. They were determined to bury their pasts and trust their rediscovered
happiness.

SULLIVAN VS. SULLIVAN—Jillian Blake
Kerry and Tip were attorneys on opposite sides of a perilous case. The
situation was getting hotter by the minute. They could agree to a
compromise, but only if the verdict was love.

RAGGED RAINBOWS—Linda Lael Miller
Shay Kendall had grown up overshadowed by her actress mother's faded
Hollywood fame. When exposé writer Mitch Prescott convinced her to
collaborate on her mother's biography, she knew that he would free her
from her haunting past and share her future.

AVAILABLE THIS MONTH:

NOBODY'S FOOL
Renee Roszel

THE SECURITY MAN
Dixie Browning

YESTERDAY'S LIES
Lisa Jackson

AFTER DARK
Elaine Camp

MAGIC SEASON
Anne Lacey

LESSONS LEARNED
Nora Roberts